FLIGHT

ALSO BY NATALIE KELLER REINERT

FLIGHT

A Novel

The Eventing Series
BOOK EIGHT

NATALIE KELLER REINERT

FLATIRON
BOOKS
NEW YORK

FLIGHT. Copyright © 2023, 2025 by Natalie Keller Reinert. All rights reserved. Printed in the United States of America. For information, address Flatiron Books, 120 Broadway, New York, NY 10271.

www.flatironbooks.com

Designed by Gabriel Guma

Library of Congress Cataloging-in-Publication Data

Names: Reinert, Natalie Keller, author.
Title: Flight : a novel / Natalie Keller Reinert.
Description: First Flatiron Books edition. | New York : Flatiron Books, 2025. | Series: The eventing series ; book eight
Identifiers: LCCN 2024055107 | ISBN 9781250387851 (trade paperback) | ISBN 9781250387868 (ebook)
Subjects: LCGFT: Romance fiction. | Sports fiction. | Novels.
Classification: LCC PS3618.E564548 F58 2025 | DDC 813/.6—dc23/eng/20241121
LC record available at https://lccn.loc.gov/2024055107

Our books may be purchased in bulk for promotional, educational, or business use. Please contact your local bookseller or the Macmillan Corporate and Premium Sales Department at 1-800-221-7945, extension 5442, or by email at MacmillanSpecialMarkets@macmillan.com.

Originally self-published in 2023 by Natalie Keller Reinert

First Flatiron Books Edition: 2025

10 9 8 7 6 5 4 3 2 1

FLIGHT

1

MY BAY HORSE'S strides rolled across the soft ground like a peal of thunder shaking the heavens.

Yes, I was feeling poetic on this chilly morning. Who wouldn't? I was on a good horse, speeding over a cross-country course, and even if I wasn't a fan of riding through fine mist on slick ground, I could still appreciate the beauty of the clouds hugging the nearby folds of the Catoctin Mountains, and the shock of color from autumn leaves still clinging to their branches.

Beautiful, but not comfortable. "Easy, Flyer," I warned, as my horse fought for free rein. "Once we get down this slope—there we go. Give us some speed, little boy."

I tipped my weight gently onto my hands, settling the reins over his neck and the top strap of the breastplate. Flyer correctly read my shift as permission to drive harder with his forelegs, making up some precious time without tiring out the big engine in his hindquarters, and his stride lengthened accordingly. This little Thoroughbred had some serious speed locked away.

Maryland's green hills and autumn-gold trees whipped past us in a blur. I felt like I was piloting a plane, ready for takeoff. All that was left now was for the wind to slip beneath Flyer's wings and lift him inch by inch, nose to tail, until we were free, until we took flight.

I contemplated a whoop of happiness, considered the way the Maryland competitors would likely take this and the possibility that Flyer would get a little too excited and buck, and kept my mouth shut.

We were about halfway along the longest, most open gallop on the course when the cold air driving against my face took on a new texture, fog droplets soaking into my skin, and then the rain began again. *Ugh, Maryland. Why are you like this?*

Flyer's ears flicked back and forth, but he never slowed his stride. He was committed, even if I was annoyed.

As the mountains ahead slowly disappeared beneath a veil of gray, I stood in the stirrups and leaned back gently on the reins, bringing the horse's balance back to his hindquarters. The next jumping complex loomed in front of us: Catoctin's Conundrum. A cute name on the cross-country map, in real life it was a series of banks, logs, and of course one of those infernal skinny hedges to gallop out on. This one would take focus. Even at Training level, the course at Catoctin Green was meant for advanced, experienced horses.

Fortunately, I was riding Flyer. He'd been bouncing around Training level competition for the past three months, and we'd been schooling Prelim and above. I had total faith in this little guy. I'd wanted a comeback horse, a summer project to reorient me in the saddle after my first challenging spring of motherhood. Frequent Flyer had been that horse, and then some.

As the first bank opened beneath his hooves, I leaned back, offering balance with my body and arms. He hopped down the bank, ears pricked against the rain as he looked for the next obstacle. He spotted it and quickened his step: a ditch two strides away, which he hopped like a bullfrog before charging back up the slope toward flat ground, the studs of his shoes clawing into the slick turf.

Thank goodness we were only the fourth ones on course; this hillside would be a skating rink by the last horse of the day.

The thought was fleeting. I was already rising in my stirrups to help him over the log atop the hill. The fence was airy, without much evidence of what waited on the other side, and Flyer seemed to waver in midair, his ears flicking anxiously—*Where to next?*

I was the one who had walked the course, so it was my job to know ahead of time where to point my horse. But I'd been distracted by the slippery hillside and forgot to find my line ahead of time. "Sorry, buddy," I said, opening my right hand and looking directly at the next fence, trusting the shift in my weight to turn his mid-flight trajectory. *This way.*

The cue was enough. He cleverly landed on his right lead and skipped across the even ground, his entire being focused on the hanging log between two ancient trees. Over the narrow fence, down a slight slope pebbled by gravel—we were in the woods now, trees dank and dripping—and splashing through a shallow creek. Flyer did it all with his ears pricked.

I sent him charging up the final slope on the course, toward a gate that hung at the top, gray sky swirling through its bars. Like the fence before the forest, this jump was airy; on the best of days it would have popped against sunlight, but today it was wreathed in ghostly fog.

Flyer locked his ears on the gate and scrambled up the graveled path. Now that we were out of the trees, the rain began to fall harder and water was running down the slope, rivulets starting to threaten the footing. He tripped once, his nose coming dangerously close to the ground. I hung back, breathless, leg on, waiting.

He jumped out and over the gate, triumphantly snorting as his forelegs touched solid ground again, and we galloped through the open field, nothing between us and the finish line now but a simple fruit stand and a downpour that seemed to pack the punch of a tropical storm.

"Good *boy*," I told him, running my hand down his neck. "Good, good, good boy!"

Flyer put his head down and ran as hard as his little legs could take him.

The fruit stand rose in front of us and he jumped it in stride. I hung atop him like a steeplechaser, reins wide open, legs out in front. We were making time now. If we could get through this course without time penalties, we'd be sitting pretty, because almost no one going after us would be able to navigate the muddying course without taking it very easy.

We flashed past a few hardy fans and volunteers in rain slickers and drenched ball caps, then passed through the timer's electronic eyes. As Flyer's strides slowed, I leaned down and wrapped my arms around his neck. "Such an amazing horse," I whispered. "Oh, buddy. Oh, boy. I'm so proud of you."

Along with my deep pride in Flyer's performance was another emotion that bubbled up with every cross-country course I completed: *relief.* A sense that I was back, competing successfully again after I'd been sidelined last winter. For a while in spring, I'd struggled with riding, drawn back to my little son even though he cooed contentedly in his nanny's arms—or maybe *because* he'd been so happy with Pete's cousin, Gemma, the moment she stepped off the plane from England and joined us at Briar Hill Farm.

But I had an incredible support system: friends, husband, horses, mentor. I found Flyer and worked on the bad habits that had held him back, getting help from Kit, Pete, and Grace along the way. Gemma and the co-op kids did an incredible job keeping Jack within my line of sight until I progressed to the point of leaving him with her at home. Lindsay and Maddox became working students at Briar Hill Farm and helped balance the hard work of running an equestrian facility while I trained horses and taught riding lessons. Lacey kept the co-op in apple-pie order so that I could work between two farms without stressing about horse management. Everyone worked together to get me competitive again, and now here I was, exactly where I belonged. On an off-track Thoroughbred who had just flown through a cross-country course and was looking around eagerly for the next fence.

"You're a star, buddy," I told him.

Flyer was hot, his sweat burning against my cheek. He'd cool out quickly in this weather; in Florida, even in early October, we'd need cold water and lots of it. Here in Maryland, it just fell out of the sky.

Convenient? Kind of, although I wasn't willing to give Maryland too much credit. If I felt like I was back where I belonged competition-wise, there was one important caveat: I was in the wrong state. Pete had us competing in Maryland, and boy was I ready to go home to warmth and sunshine.

I thought Flyer was, too. He shook his head as the rain pelted down harder, tugging on the reins. I wanted to let him canter us back to the stables, but that would be frowned upon. I ran a hand along his neck as he jigged, and tried to speak soothingly. "Okay, buddy, we'll get you out of the rain in a minute."

"Jules!" Pete's voice cut through the rain pounding on my helmet. I looked up and saw him running toward us, his raincoat open despite the downpour. "Over here!"

The five-gallon grooming bucket bounced against his side, packed with everything we might need to use on a hot horse and rider after a strenuous gallop. There was a wrench to take studs out of horseshoes, water, sports drinks, electrolyte paste—for the horse, not for the rider, although on some summer days I'd considered taking a dose of the stuff myself—scissors to cut loose bandages or broken straps, and a dozen other little things.

But in this weather, we didn't need any of them, not even the wrench—I'd leave Flyer's studs in until we walked back to the barn. They'd be so tangled with wet grass and mud that I wouldn't want to try to wrestle them free while he was still high-spirited and exhilarated from his run. The paste was probably unnecessary, too. I'd guess neither of us were dehydrated. Instead, we were soaked to the skin and, actually, I was starting to feel a little chilly.

"Did you bring a cooler?" I called, jumping down from the saddle. I kept Flyer moving next to me, making sure his muscles didn't have a chance to stiffen. "I don't want him to go from hot to freezing."

"Vane's bringing it," Pete said, catching up with us. Kit's groom was helping us out; our travel budget hadn't extended to bringing a groom of our own. He gave my gloved hand a quick squeeze. Water trickled down my wrist. "How did he do on the Conundrum? I heard the caller say you were clear through it, but I couldn't see. The fog came up just then."

"He was incredible," I gushed. "Oh my God, Pete, he was amazing. This horse is a star." I gave Flyer another pat. He snorted and danced sideways.

Pete's smile was knowing. "You say that about all your horses. Why are they all stars, hmm?"

"Because I only choose the good ones," I told him archly. "And, oh, why do all of Jules Thornton-Morrison's horses win their divisions? I'll tell you why. Because I am an *amazing* horsewoman."

Pete shook his head, his gaze amused as he took Flyer's reins from me, freeing me up to wrangle off my soaking gloves. "Your confidence after a good run on course is even more terrifying than your usual confidence," he said. "I like this version of you, though."

"And what version is that?"

"All ambition."

I grinned, taking the water bottle from Pete's grooming bucket. "But where's Jack? I wanted him to see his mother come through the finish flags."

"Gemma took him back to the motel," Pete said. "She said he was cold."

"More like *she* was cold." I sniffed. "You know, when you said your English cousin wanted to be our nanny, I think you were just fulfilling her lifelong dream to move to Florida."

"I'm a dream-maker," Pete replied. "A genie. Look how happy you are, dear wife. A successful trainer, a great big boy ten months of age, and a fall season in Maryland running up to the Chesapeake Three-Day Event. Riding one of *my* horses while you're at it. I have made all your dreams come—"

Flyer spooked at a ghost only he could see and jumped sideways into Pete, cutting off his speech.

He was a good horse. I'd give him an extra carrot for that, once we were back in the barns. *All* the carrots. This horse had been so good, and since he was the last of my rides at Catoctin Green Horse Trials for this weekend, this ride could be the cherry on top of some pretty solid runs. First thing this morning, before the rain set in, I'd done an Intermediate run on Mickey that felt like poetry, and I took Rogue over the Preliminary course—which he loved, naturally. Between the three of them, I'd gotten over my pregnancy and my postpartum blues, and now I was taking my comeback season on the road. I felt another swell of confidence that transcended the rain and the cold and the feeling of displacement I'd had ever since we arrived in Maryland two weeks ago.

"Rogue is my horse now," I reminded Pete. "You said I could have him."

Pete made a sound suspiciously like a snort. "You *took* him, is what I remember happening. Didn't you say something like 'I'm taking him and there's nothing you can do about it'?"

"I don't remember it that way."

The months before I'd started competing again were oddly hazy. I remembered Jack when he was tiny, and quiet days in the house with Marcus always underfoot, but until I really started riding again, my memories were hard to grasp. A few of the co-op moms said their first six months of motherhood were much the same. It was as if there was nothing going on in my brain but baby, baby, baby, and then the swim back out of that deep pool was a return to myself, horse by horse and ride by ride.

But now I knew exactly who I was again. I looked over at Flyer, his head bobbing with every stride, his ears pricked as we approached the long white rows of temporary stabling. I was Jack's mom, and Pete's wife, and I was Jules Thornton-Morrison, the queen of Florida eventing, here to swipe all of Maryland's pretty ribbons and take them back to Briar Hill Farm.

Four more weeks, and we could go home.

2

I LOOKED FLYER over as Vane walked him up and down the shed row of the event grounds' comfortable show stabling. His small bay frame was completely covered up with a fleece cooler, but I could see he walked as evenly now as he had on the way to the starting box this afternoon, his head traveling smoothly and his eyes bright as he watched the event beyond the stable eaves. Incredibly, they were continuing with the Training level division. Pete said Maryland eventers were used to fall rains and slick courses.

"But they'd die in our summer heat," he teased when I made a face. "That's why they don't come to Florida until winter."

"This clay ground is terrible, though," I argued, just for the sake of arguing. "And Joan said it goes hard as rock in the summer." Joan owned the farm where we'd rented space for our six-week season.

"They're used to it," Pete said again, refusing to take the bait, and went off to find some hot coffee.

Vane stopped Flyer and showed him a bucket of water sitting in the shed row. "You want it?" she asked him. "Go on, take a big old drink."

Flyer took a short, polite sip before tugging at his lead, asking to walk again.

"How is that horse not tired?" I shook my head.

Vane laughed and let him drag her away. "I only have half an hour until I need to get back to Kit," she called over her shoulder to me. "He should be ready to go in before then, though."

"Just let me check him before you put him away," I reminded her, aware it was an unnecessary request. Vane had been grooming for Kit for several years and now they were a couple, as well, so she was all too aware that every upper-level event rider was a micro-managing paranoid mess, both at home and on the road.

I wanted to check my horses constantly, after turnout and before bed and the moment I woke up and during random episodes of sitcoms I wasn't actually watching. I was so afraid of injuries and bad steps and rough arguments in the pasture that I wanted to roll them up in bubble wrap. But they were horses, so I had to let them go outside together and roll in the dirt and kick out and bite and make questionable decisions, all the time, and content myself with watching them closely, to the point of paranoia.

It was a good life, really.

"She's such a great helper," Pete observed, slipping onto the tack trunk next to me. He'd shed his wet raincoat and pulled on a sweatshirt against the autumn chill. It was as cold on this October day in Maryland as it would be in January in Florida. Thank goodness we'd be home by then. He handed me a hot coffee in a thin paper cup. "Nice of Kit to share her."

"Well, Kit always feels like she owes us," I reminded him, wrapping my shirt sleeve over my fingers to protect against the cup. Kit didn't owe us anything, really, but she just had that kind of personality—she worried a lot, about people as well as horses.

And she had plenty to worry about; her first big three-day event in over a year loomed just four weeks away. Like us, she'd come to Maryland to prep for Chesapeake Three-Day Event on the last weekend in October. We were riding our horses in different divisions, but our goals remained the same: get around one of the toughest courses on the North American eventing calendar and look good doing it.

Kit was a friend, a client, and an employee, which probably made our relationship complicated for her. We'd become friends in the summer running up to the Central Park Arena Eventing show, which had been a rough year for all three of us for different reasons. Since then, she'd begun teaching the younger kids at Alachua Eventing Co-op, under my direction, and she kept her competition horses at Briar Hill Farm. It helped us to have someone share the expenses of maintaining a barn, paddocks, arena, and jumps. The truth was that those expenses were somehow both infinite and ever-expanding, like a universe, and every dollar we threw at them was but a drop in the bucket.

That was another reason why we were in Maryland: money. Pete had snagged a new owner, and her horses were here in Maryland. No matter what I said about wanting to own my own horses, there was no way forward in eventing without owners and syndicates to help with the bills. At this point the only way I could afford a new horse was if it was free (or close to free, like Flyer had been), and even then I'd have to get creative to cover its bills.

I could have charged Kit more for stalls and turnout space, and that would have helped us stretch the budget. But Kit's friendship was worth more to us than money.

"Kit doesn't owe us anything," Pete said, echoing my thoughts.

"I know she doesn't," I agreed, "but if lending us her groom makes her feel better about getting a break on her horses' board, I won't say no. And Vane is used to grooming on the road like this." Kit and Vane were no strangers to traveling the East Coast on a wider eventing circuit than the Florida and Georgia competitions Pete and I stuck to.

"If we're going on the road more often," Pete said, "we should consider a second groom for the travel. We've got Lindsay and Maddox helping with the horses who stay home, and if the co-op can spare you for six weeks like this, they can spare you for a few weeks in spring, too."

"Spring?"

"Kentucky," Pete said.

"What about it?" I replied warily. "Neither of us will be ready for the four-star at Kentucky." The Kentucky Three-Day Event was held at the end of April every year, and while everyone wanted to compete there, that course was a huge ask of any horse. I wasn't going to make it Mickey's four-star debut even if he competed at Advanced events all through winter. Pete was getting ahead of himself. That was usually my job.

"Kit will be going," he said.

"So go with Kit." I toyed with the zipper of my paddock boot, crossed over my knee. I didn't want to admit how homesick I was. We'd lived at the new farm for less than a year, but I was already so attached to it—our little cottage on the hilltop, the new barn we'd built over the summer and the paddocks stretching over the slopes in front of it, shaded by the protective boughs of the live oaks. This new version of Briar Hill Farm was our personal paradise, no clients allowed (Lindsay, Maddox, and Kit didn't count), and I loved my farm so much it was absurd. I could get sentimental thinking about our brief time there, playing back mental images of Jack playing with brushes in the barn aisle while Gemma watched him and I tacked up a horse to ride in the arena nearby. Trail rides through the forest to the jewel-like spring nestled beneath the trees. Sunset pinks and purples lighting up the pale boards of new fencing, horses grazing in a glow of summer light. Briar Hill Farm was heaven on earth. Why should I ever leave for more than a weekend?

Pete was looking at me with mild concern.

I huffed a drawn-out sigh, taking refuge in being difficult. "Anyway, do you really want to travel constantly? This has been a tough trip already and we have *four* more weeks until we can go home. I wish we could just pick up those horses on Monday and go back to Florida."

"No, I don't want to travel constantly," Pete said, his voice going soft in that way I knew was meant to gentle me. If anyone else tried it, I'd have popped like a balloon, but I allowed Pete to, even when I considered it a lost cause. Sometimes, he even succeeded. "But you know we've reached the point where we need to leave Florida once in a while. The new horses were just a good excuse to make this trip."

I sighed. "I know, I know. We need new courses, new terrain." We couldn't exactly ignore chances to compete at the top of the sport just because some of the events had the nerve to take place outside of Florida. Variety was part of training for upper-level eventing—variety in footing, topography, and even course design styles. Our friend Haley Marsh had competed all over the US and Europe, and she could look at a jump complex and tell us who designed it in one guess. We had to get out there.

It was a sad truth, but world domination wasn't easy. I knew, because I'd been on the cusp of it two years ago. On the way to the World Equestrian Games, just like Kit. But my horse had to retire, and my body felt the need to get pregnant, and suddenly my whole life was different. Now, on the other side of those huge changes, I had to think about the future, right when my new-mom brain wanted to settle down and enjoy the present. If Pete hadn't finalized a deal with this new owner that involved competing her horses one last time in Maryland, before taking them back with us to Florida, I wouldn't be here. And I should be thankful to Pete, because a big finish at Chesapeake Three-Day Event would be the perfect cap to my comeback season.

As a rider looking forward to my next big year, and the decades to come, every season was important. I needed people to like me. I needed new owners, new students, and new enthusiasts willing to chip in for coffee or gas money now and then.

We always needed more, more, more.

Maybe it wouldn't have been so difficult giving up fall at Briar Hill Farm if we'd just been slightly more comfortable here in Maryland. But living in close quarters was taking its toll, too. While Pete and I had survived cohabitating in a horse trailer and somehow not gone completely crazy, it was awfully hard living in a motel room with Jack and Gemma. Being on the road with a baby was a challenge, anyway, and that was before the issue of space came up. Jack was delighted by change at first, then rapidly reverted to wanting the comforts of home. And even bringing along Marcus, our beagle who worshipped Jack like a tiny god, plus Jack's sizable collection of plushies, wasn't always enough to convince the baby that motel rooms were good places to sleep.

I really wanted to stick to Florida for now. My own space, my own bed, and my own barn—was that so much to ask for?

At least until Jack was older.

Much older.

A pair of riders walked along the stable aisle, hunched under raincoats. "Florida," one said to the other. "*Please.*"

I gave Pete a significant look.

He patted my knee. "After Chesapeake."

"Even the Marylanders don't like Maryland," I said, petulant. "I'll bet those new horses are just desperate to get on the trailer and head south. They've probably been talking about their new daddy for weeks."

"Please don't call me their 'new daddy,'" Pete said. "That's so weird."

"The barn moms call me Mickey's 'mom,'" I mused. "And they call each other that, too. Leah is Ares's mom. Why can't we do that with dads?"

"Now you're just changing the subject."

"Do you want to keep arguing about Maryland? Because I can argue all day."

Vane walked Flyer past on another lap. The day was slipping by.

"No," Pete said. "But if it makes you warmer, go for it."

I fell silent. Because the truth was, I *had* forgotten I was cold, and now I was cozy from the fleece cooler draped over my shoulders and the hot coffee cup in my hands.

"I'm going to call Lacey," I decided.

Lacey, Lindsay, and Maddox were running the farms we'd left behind. I had Lindsay and Maddox staying at Briar Hill Farm to make sure all the horses there were taken care of and exercising a few days a week, then teaching some of the lessons at the co-op in the afternoons. Lacey continued to preside over the co-op with the management style of an empress, and she taught a few lessons, as well. Alex pitched in on weekends, and Haley Marsh was giving a weekly jump school to keep everyone fresh until we returned. No one was competing while we were gone, but the co-op parents felt like they would be compensated if their trainers put in a good showing at Chesapeake. A win for us was a win for all of them.

And of course we'd promised to hit the Florida circuit hard the minute we got back in November.

Lacey answered her phone on the first ring. "How did you know I was going to call you?"

I glanced at Pete. With the phone on speaker, he'd heard that, too. "Um, is everything okay?"

"Delightful," Lacey said drily. "The kids have all gone on a group ride with Alex. They're in the gelding pasture now. About half of them are still mounted. The rest are walking home."

"*What?*"

"I have to go catch some of these horses in a second. So, what's up?" Lacey tipped up her voice in a teenage girl parody. "Having fun in Maryland?"

"No, and is anyone hurt?"

"They're walking up the hill, sound as a dollar," Lacey said. "I think this is going on the fall board as 'dumped off' for all of them."

The fall board was a recent addition to the boarders' tack room, where the kids reigned in messy chaos. Someone had the bright idea to put up a whiteboard to tally everyone's tumbles from the saddle. There were categories of falling off—bucked off, dumped off (this meant poor riding), and slipped off (for bareback riding). The kids had a complicated measuring system for who won the fall board prize every month, and the prize was riding bareback while everyone cleaned the winner's tack (and hoped the winner slipped off).

"I think that fall board was a bad idea," I said.

"Alex is probably to blame for this one," Lacey said. "She had them all hike up their stirrups like jockeys before they went out."

"Lacey! You have to stop her from doing things like that!"

"I guarantee she doesn't do this again," Lacey said. "Okay, the first horses are arriving at the gate. I'll text you after dinner. Bye!"

I looked at Pete.

He shrugged back at me. "You going to call Alex?"

"Later," I said. "When she has a half hour free for me to yell at her."

"You know this was just as likely to happen while you were

there, right? All you have to do is turn your back for one minute and wham, pasture full of kids pretending to be jockeys. That's what growing up with horses is *for*."

"I know," I said. "But I'd like to yell at them in person."

Pete rubbed my back and smiled at me. His eyes crinkled at the corners when he smiled. They always had, but the years out in the sun were making the lines deeper. I liked them.

"You're handsome," I said, tipping my head onto his shoulder. "Did anyone ever tell you that?"

"Loads of people," Pete said comfortably. "Thousands, I think."

"Arrogant bastard," I murmured, still snuggled up against him. He squeezed my arm.

Vane walked back around with Flyer and halted the horse in front of us. Flyer reached out with his nose and left a moist splotch on my knee.

"Thank you, dear," I told him.

"He's all done," Vane announced. "Are you two having a moment?"

"Yes," I said. "We can't be disturbed."

Pete laughed, letting go of me. "Go feel your horse and give Vane permission to get back to her own responsibilities. I'm going to head over to the arena and see if the show jumping course is ready to walk."

"Fine." I hopped down from the tack trunk and ran my hand down Flyer's neck, then reached inside his cooler and pressed the back of my hand against his chest. Nice and even temperature, just like Vane said. "He can go back to his stall. Thanks, Vane."

"No problem, boss." Vane unbuckled the cooler and whisked it off, leaving me with an armful of damp fabric. "Let me go get Kit's last horse ready for Novice and I'll see you tomorrow morning for the show jumping, okay?"

"Sounds good."

I watched Vane head down the shed row, then turned to Flyer. "Do you like her?"

He snorted.

"Better than *me*?"

Flyer rubbed his face against my shoulder.

"That's what I thought," I said.

I put Flyer away, made sure he put his nose directly into his hay, and snapped his stall guard into place. I was just turning away when I saw an older man with a white head of hair walking up the shed row. He was oddly familiar, and his gaze seemed fixed on me.

"Jules Thornton-Morrison?" he called in a reedy voice.

With a start, I recognized him. This was Sandy Sullivan, an eventing old-timer and a contemporary of Pete's grandfather. I'd seen photos of him in magazines and books, younger and spryer and with considerably more hair. I assumed he knew Pete, but we'd never met.

What could he possibly want with me?

3

I HAD TO fight an unfamiliar urge to duck under Flyer's stall guard and hide in the horse's stall. Normally, I wasn't a person who hid from strangers—especially not someone like Sandy Sullivan.

But something about this situation didn't feel right. Maybe it was just that Sandy was a representation of eventing's old guard, and here in Maryland I felt like *everyone,* even the young riders, were part of some bougie, fox-hunting, land-owning-since-the-Revolution scene that had no room for a suburban girl from southwest Florida who started her career on cheap auction horses and racetrack rejects.

Again, I had very little evidence for this claim; I was just feeling left out. I hardly saw anyone I knew at events here, whereas I couldn't go anywhere horsey in Florida (or anywhere at all in Ocala) without seeing someone I knew. I didn't feel like I had the right clothes, either, just layering everything I had, one on top of the other, while my competitors matched in stylish, aerodynamic windbreakers. Besides, the farms here seemed so old and classy and traditional, with their stone farmhouses and willow-hung creeks. Maryland was an entirely different planet from Florida.

But I wasn't entirely unknown at events; there were plenty of riders here who were finishing up the season with Chesapeake before heading to Florida. Even if Sandy Sullivan didn't fly south for the winter, if he knew who I was, that had to be a good thing. It meant someone else had pointed him in my direction. Maybe he had a horse for me to ride, or an owner he wanted to set me up with.

Taking a deep breath, I squared my shoulders and waited for him to reach my set of stalls. The guy was still a wizard in the saddle despite his advanced years, but the long walk down the shed row seemed to take him forever. He actually looked a little winded as he drew near.

"Mr. Sullivan," I said, tugging free a director's chair that was stowed behind the tack trunk and popping it open for him.

"Sandy," he corrected me. "Please call me Sandy."

"Sure," I said. "Sandy. I'm Jules. It's nice to meet you."

He sank into the canvas chair and gave a little sigh. "I should have ridden over."

"Always more convenient," I joked feebly. "Did you have a good cross-country run?"

He was probably going to beat me in the Prelim division, now that I thought about it. Beaten by a man who was, what, eighty years old? What a great sport.

He nodded. "Very good, thanks. I hunted this horse all last fall, and it's really showing now that we're hitting the bigger courses."

I imagined him going out fox-hunting and wondered if everyone around him formed a sort of protective cavalry to make sure he had the best ride possible. "I've never hunted," I admitted, knowing that he'd probably think less of me for this omission; so many top event riders learned their cross-country skills by following the hounds. "It's not a huge deal in Florida, I guess."

"What a shame. You should stay through November and join my club. That little bay horse of yours would love it."

I glanced back at Flyer, munching hay with his head over the stall guard and inquisitive ears trained on the two humans in his shed row. "You know, he loves to gallop, and he never questions any jump. I bet he *would* love it."

"Think about it and let me know." Sandy Sullivan sighed heavily, as if the idea reminded him of something unpleasant. It was an odd way to follow up on an invitation. "I was hoping to speak with you about your husband," he said.

I raised my eyebrows. How delightful. Someone wanted to talk about my husband.

What else was new?

Pete had been extremely successful over the past few years at a variety of things—really, whatever he put his hand to. Show jumping? No problem. Writing a dressage manual? Easy-peasy. Transitioning to fatherhood without blinking an eye? Oh, you'd better believe it. And how about managing a farm while also competing? Well . . .

Okay, before we left, I noticed he was starting to struggle a little with the daily grind, which I sometimes suspected had been part of his cheerful acquiescence when Hannah Grayer, his new owner, asked him to come to Maryland and compete her horses here. I would have refused, planting in my heels and insisting the horses would be happiest if they were shipped directly to me in Florida, but Pete didn't even kick up the slightest resistance. It was like he *wanted* to leave home for the season. He came up with the idea to stay for six weeks and compete so quickly I had to wonder if he'd been cooking it up for a while.

So maybe Pete was floundering a little with time management. He was winning at everything else in life.

Sandy Sullivan cocked his head, waiting for my answer.

"Sure," I said, pretending I wasn't annoyed at all. "Let's talk about my husband."

The persistent rain faded to drizzle and then blew away altogether by the time we fed for the evening, and a yellow-gold sunset was lighting up the treetops even as the dark clouds still tumbled over themselves to the east. Catoctin Green Farm was situated in the foothills of a long, low roll of mountains to the west, and on a clear evening, those mountains were silhouetted in black against a rich amber afterglow as the sun slipped below the hidden horizon. Some people saw this kind of thing every day, but for a Floridian like me, the sight was spellbinding.

Almost enough to make me like Maryland.

I came back into the barn just as Pete was coming out of Flyer's stall, brushing hay off his sweater. He was dressed in navy wool and gray breeches. With his fox-colored hair, he looked like an Irish groom after a particularly chilly day of hunting. It reminded me of Sandy Sullivan and the odd conversation we'd had. I needed to talk to Pete about it, but he had that distracted look he got when he was tired and trying to finish up the evening chores without forgetting anything.

He glanced up as I walked over. "Where've you been?"

"I took the hose back to the stand and got distracted. You missed the best sunset since we got here."

"Thanks for letting me know," Pete said shortly. He was tightening the knot on Barsuk's hay net. The gray horse grabbed hold of the hay net and tugged it from Pete's grip, his iron-colored mane tossing as he twisted his neck to yank the net into his stall. "Fine, dummy," Pete told him. "Be difficult. But at least let me see if you're warm enough."

Like our other horses, Barsuk was wearing a navy-blue sheet. Pete slipped a hand beneath the chest straps to check the horse's temperature. "They should be good in sheets tonight, I guess." He sounded uncertain. We were always playing a guessing game with getting the temperatures right. When would our horses be too cold, or too warm?

I thought we were in the sweet spot for horse comfort tonight. "It's going to be in the fifties. They'll be fine. You know, you can walk outside and see a sunset once in a while. The hay nets could wait one minute."

"*You're* the one who is always so cold," Pete countered. "I thought you'd want to be done and out of here as quickly as possible."

He was tired; I was tired. If I kept talking, we'd end up arguing again. I went into the tack room to straighten up for the night, slipping dust covers over the saddles we'd used today. While I worked, my hands busy at familiar tasks, my brain took a moment to run through Sandy Sullivan's odd message once more.

His purpose in visiting me, he'd explained, was to be a friend, not an enemy. "But I know how things might look if I said this to Pete face-to-face. I was friends with his grandfather, knew Pete as a boy, and I want nothing but the best for him, you understand? I just don't know that he'd see it that way. This whole business he's got himself into is complicated, though. So I thought you'd be best to pass the message along."

I'd stared at Sandy blankly. I wasn't good at puzzles, and I couldn't keep up with people who kept their true purpose hidden under layers of double-speak. Horses were straightforward and said what they meant, and horses were what I understood.

Basically, the closer a person was to being a horse, the better the chance they stood with me.

"The message?" I asked after a moment. "Are you asking me to say hello to him or something?"

"I'm talking about Hannah Grayer," Sandy said, looking a bit exasperated for having to spell things out.

"Pete's new owner?" I was instantly on high alert. It would not surprise me one bit if Pete's new owner was trouble, because, honestly, it was the horse business. Hannah was nice enough on the surface, and when she reached out to Pete, I'd been happy for him. Only the tiniest bit jealous; a very *normal* amount of jealous.

Anyway, her reasoning for offering Pete the ride was sound; she was moving to Florida herself in January, and she wanted to keep enjoying days out in horse country, watching her horses compete. She'd been looking for a Florida-based rider and Pete's style and philosophy checked her boxes. She was especially fond of his recently published dressage manual, which led her to contact Pete in the first place. And as they'd talked through her desire to see her horses compete in Florida once she retired there this winter, everything about the new partnership seemed great. But once she'd asked Pete to come to Maryland for the horses' final fall season, I'd been more guarded. It seemed like one of those innocent little requests that requires a lot of the rider, nothing of the owner, and sets high expectations from the very beginning of the relationship.

And here was Sandy saying there was an issue? Well, color me not surprised.

"Okay," I said. "What's wrong with Hannah Grayer?"

"Hannah is moving the horses to Pete's string against Mimi's wishes."

"Mimi?"

"Pulaski," Sandy said. "Their former rider."

"But their former rider is retiring," I said. "And why does she have a problem with Pete?"

"Mimi would have a problem with anyone. She doesn't want to retire."

"But she is . . . right?" Was I missing something?

"Well, she broke her collarbone," Sandy said. "For the third time. Poor Mimi. But she's not dead yet. And she told me she'd drop in the traces. So, you see, no one expects this retirement to stick. She's furious that the horses are going to Florida. She wants them back after her collarbone heals up and she's cleared to ride again. Cleared by her wife," Sandy clarified, "not a doctor. Because no doctor would ever clear her for this. But she thinks she can talk Diane around in a few months. And if the horses are still in Maryland, she won't have such a hard time convincing Hannah to give them back to her."

I sighed. This was the thing with horses and horse people. Nothing was ever simple. "Maybe you could tell me what you want Pete to know," I suggested, "because I'm not sure how this affects him."

The horses were going to Florida. Everything was signed and moving forward, whether Mimi liked it or not.

"Pete should know that Mimi wants them to go to Chesapeake," Sandy said. "She got them both ready. They just need a qualifying ride at Pin Oak, and they'd be in."

I blinked at him. Pete was supposed to ride the horses at Pin Oak Horse Trials. It was to be their first outing together, and the one Hannah wanted to see them run around before they went to Florida. The event was coming up in two weeks, and it would be our horses' last big outing before Chesapeake, two weeks later.

"The two-star event," Sandy added. "Preliminary level."

I shook my head. "Pete's not taking two horses he just got on for the first time to a three-day event. Honestly, it's bad enough he's taking them to Pin Oak with just two weeks. At the two-star level, that's asking too much. They need to get to know each other for longer than a month."

"You know that," Sandy said, "and I know that. And Mimi knows that. Hannah might not. And Hannah's the one who needs convincing, in Mimi's opinion."

"You're saying Mimi wants him to fail out there on course," I said, shocked. "I don't believe you. No one would put their horses in danger like that, let alone another rider."

"Mimi's hoping for a retirement on course," Sandy said. He shrugged. "I'm just telling you. She's hoping to convince Hannah that it would be fun to see her horses go around Chesapeake before they leave Maryland. A final hurrah. She thinks Hannah will really like the idea."

"What is with this state?" I burst out. "You didn't invent eventing, you know. It happens in other places. We jump horses over logs in Florida, just like you guys do here."

Better, even.

Sandy regarded me with a mild expression. "Maryland inspires a certain loyalty in its residents," he said finally.

I shook my head. "It's not happening, even if Mimi convinces Hannah it's the best idea ever. Pete wouldn't even dream of taking a horse he just got—"

"Mimi and Hannah are old friends," Sandy said. "She's very confident she can twist Hannah to her way of thinking. I have asked her to reconsider, but Mimi's very determined. I don't think she's handling things well."

"Obviously not." I wanted to find Mimi and shake some sense into her. But I had no idea who she was. I'd never even heard of her, and now I wished that was still true, because this whole situation sounded like some silly idea one of my barn kids would come up with.

"Why are you telling me?" I asked, suddenly suspicious. "Who is Mimi to you, anyway?"

Sandy sighed. "She's an old, dear friend," he said, "which makes this whole thing very uncomfortable for me."

"Can't you talk some sense into her?"

"Mimi is very hard-headed when she gets her mind set on something," Sandy said. "I'm sure you've known someone like that."

I had, actually.

Sandy had excused himself after that, and shuffled off, leaving me to sit and stew until Vane called me to come and watch Kit's cross-country run. I'd thrown on a fresh raincoat and gone with her to cheer on Kit's Novice horse, who performed like a champion despite the rain. And I put Mimi and the Chesapeake Three-Day Event and those horses of Hannah's out of my mind—until now.

I decided I was more annoyed than anything. Pete wasn't going to take the horses to the three-day event and that was that. The annoying part was that I had to relate the conversation at all. But I had to, or Hannah would blindside him. Assuming Sandy was right, and Mimi really was talking her into it.

What kind of person would put horses into this situation, though—horses she supposedly wanted back in her barn? Mimi must not be thinking clearly.

Maybe she was so overwhelmed with love and rage for the life she was losing, she couldn't make good decisions anymore. I could understand a little of that.

"Jules?" Pete poked his head into the tack room. "Are you ready to head out?"

I was so ready. On cross-country days I barely ate anything, and I'd had three runs today—enough to leave me starving by six o'clock. "Definitely, but where are the kids?" I asked.

"Gemma never came back from the motel," Pete said. "I suppose Jack's still napping."

"In the evening? But now he won't sleep all night."

"How is that different from usual? At least he'll be in a good mood while he keeps us up all night."

Well, there was nothing to do about it now.

"Back to the motel, my lady?" Pete asked.

I winced at the thought. "Do you think they're asleep? We could go get dinner and bring some back for Gemma . . ."

Pete nodded, and I could see the relief in his eyes. He didn't want to go back yet, either. "Let's do that. Give her some time off from us."

We both knew she probably needed some time off from Jack, too. But that wasn't happening until the weekend was over. Then it would be up to us to amuse the baby while our hardworking nanny got a break.

Keeping Gemma happy was as important as keeping our horses sound, and our clients from making us crazy. I thought about Hannah and Mimi and the horses we hadn't even met yet.

Oh, horse business, I thought. *Never stop being weird.*

"Okay," I said aloud. "Food. Now."

And once there was food inside me, I'd tell Pete about Sandy Sullivan.

4

THE WEATHER WAS cool enough to leave a dog in the truck, snoring contentedly, and so that's what we did with Marcus. My old beagle slept more than ever these days, and he didn't stir as we went into Applebee's without him.

The hostess tried not to stare at our muddy horse clothes, but mostly failed. I remembered I'd taken off my bra when I stripped out of my wet riding clothes, and folded my arms across my chest; the girls had gotten much larger after Jack and, so far, they'd stayed that way. I was still hoping for a miraculous shrinking event.

"You can sit us in a dark corner," Pete assured the hostess. "It's fine. We know we're messes, and we promise not to shed horsehair on your carpets."

The hostess, who looked about sixteen, laughed a little anxiously before leading us into the darkest corner she could find.

I slid into the booth and wearily asked for an iced tea.

"Lemon?" the hostess asked.

I stared at her. Suddenly, the exhaustion of this cold, wet weekend of competing was all I could think about. Sometimes it just takes one innocent question to push you over the edge.

"She'd like lemon," Pete assured the girl. "And so would I."

The hostess ran for the kitchen, thrilled to get away from us.

"Someone needs a nap," Pete said with a smile.

"For a hundred years." I yawned. "Maybe once we get back home."

"Were you talking to someone while I was checking out the show jumping courses earlier?"

I raised my eyebrows at the jump in topic. "Yeah, actually," I admitted. "Sandy Sullivan, if you can believe it."

"No way! I saw he was competing here. He knew my grandfather."

"That's what he said."

"Is that what he wanted to talk about?"

I shrugged. "I think he would have liked to, if you'd been there. But no, he wanted to talk about Hannah and Mimi, actually."

"Hannah and—our Hannah and Mimi?"

"Yes. Apparently Mimi is plotting to get you in over your head with the horses at Chesapeake and retire them on course."

Pete blinked. "But . . . why?"

"Because she wants the horses back. She doesn't want to retire."

Pete still wasn't making the connection. I tried to make my brain come up with some context for him. "Mimi doesn't want the horses to go to Florida with us. She thinks she can make a miracle comeback from her third collarbone fracture. So she has decided that if you have clear rounds at Pin Oak, you should take over her entries for Chesapeake's two-star division and compete them there. Where you'll embarrass yourself because you don't know those horses and that's a huge course. Then magic happens for Mimi and she keeps the horses and Hannah pretends she never met us. Make sense?"

"No," Pete said.

"No," I agreed. "It really doesn't. I think she's desperate for any chance at keeping the horses."

"The horses, or her career?"

"Does it matter?"

"Would it matter to you?"

I considered this. "I guess it depends on the horses," I decided. "If those two horses are her Mickey and Dynamo, I'd do much worse to keep them in my barn."

He leaned back in the booth and looked at the wall above my head. "I really don't think Hannah will want the horses to run at Chesapeake. That's not what we agreed on."

"Sandy says Mimi's going to push for it. And he said no one can convince her otherwise. Apparently he and Mimi are old friends, but that doesn't count for anything." I got it. No old friend could have convinced me that some harebrained scheme wouldn't bring my horses back to me.

Pete rubbed his face. "Well, if it comes up, I'll have to explain to Hannah why it's a bad idea."

"And you think she'll understand that?"

"It's my job to make sure she does."

The iced teas arrived, and Pete thanked the server. "Could you bring us both the chicken Caesar salad and—" He glanced at me and I nodded. "—an order of mozzarella sticks?"

"You're a good husband," I told him. I'd developed a thing for mozzarella sticks while I was pregnant and they were my go-to comfort food now. "But back to this horse madness. You know how owners get. If Mimi already had her revved up about competing them at Chesapeake, nothing you say will change her mind."

"I'm the decision-maker here. Hannah needs to understand that right away."

He was right, but owners could have this silly idea that *they* had some power in the relationship, and some were tough to convince otherwise. And it only got harder at the upper levels. As the fences got bigger and the course questions got more complicated, so too rose the danger level for a horse-and-rider team who didn't know and trust each other implicitly. A few weeks wasn't enough time to build that bond. Especially when Mimi hadn't been winning consistently with these horses. They were not cross-country machines. They were developing horses who sometimes had questions, and they needed to trust their rider to always steer them in the right direction.

Pete barely knew Hannah beyond a few phone calls—what if she didn't buy into Pete's reasoning when Mimi had her believing those horses could do anything?

"I'm just worried it won't be straightforward, that's all," I told him.

"Oh, she'll be fine," he said. "We've had worse owners."

That was definitely true. And we would probably have worse owners in the future, too. As infinitely deep as the money pit of running a farm was the pool of terrible people who wanted to own horses.

There were nice people, too. *Lots* of them. I just got to mainly experience the very difficult ones. Lucky me. And, apparently, I had a tendency to paint everyone with the same brush.

(Pete's words, not mine.)

The mozzarella sticks arrived, and I fell upon them like a starving animal.

"So, you're not worried about this Mimi/Hannah thing?" I asked, two mozzarella sticks and an entire personality shift later. I felt calmer now. At peace. Full of cheese. The way the universe intended me to be all along. "You think you can handle it?"

Pete shrugged, waving a mozzarella stick of his own. "I think I can handle it. And I hope I run into Sandy myself, because I'd like to get his take, but it was kind of him to give us a heads-up. I guess he must have been thinking of my grandfather and decided to look out for me. But for now, I'm going to focus on getting through this weekend, winning my division, and surviving your wrath when I get a blue ribbon and you don't. *Much* scarier than telling an owner why I won't event her horse where she wants."

"I've got Mickey sitting in sixth right now," I reminded him. "I could still win the Intermediate." He'd run a clean course this morning, not showing any concern at the size of the Intermediate level fences or the length of the course. With no time or jumping penalties going into the show jumping, we were poised to pounce on a good placing, as long as we didn't make any mistakes in the arena—and as long as someone else did.

"You need the five horses ahead of you to have a rail, a time fault, or a refusal." Pete shrugged, wisely avoiding my icy gaze. He said, "It could happen, but I don't like the odds."

I shifted in the booth, annoyed. I knew winning every time out was not an option—that simply wasn't how eventing worked, there were too many variables—but I had come all the way to Maryland with my three horses, and I wanted some rosettes to show for it.

Of course, there were good reasons we weren't number one in every division. Each horse had their own excuses. For Rogue, it was fitness, always fitness . . . and this time, the dressage needed work, too. Maybe I had a lot to learn about rolling Appalachian foothills and clay footing, but a silly spook in the dressage had thrown off the entire second half of his test. Poor Rogue was sitting so low in Preliminary, we'd have to knock everyone else out in a sudden-death jousting match before we had a shot at a ribbon. As for Flyer, he was still working on the Training level dressage test, and we'd had time penalties on the cross-country. He was sitting in fourth.

Not bad at all, really.

And as for Mickey . . .

Well, even I could admit Mickey should have placed better than sixth going into the final phase.

Maybe I needed a new dressage coach?

But no, the current coach was sitting across from me right now, and he was leaving me the last mozzarella stick.

My best shot at a first place, I thought, would be Flyer. Horses running at Training level were more likely to have show jumping faults, and fourth was an excellent place to be sitting, stalking the top three. He deserved this win. My newest horse was a brave little jumper, and he was taking to Training like a duck to water.

Honestly, he could probably move up after just one or two more outings.

Maybe we'd do a Modified division in December, I thought, and another in January, and then in February we could—

Suddenly, my thoughts were scattered to the winds as a jovial voice cried, "Pete! Jules! You're here!"

I scowled at Pete before I could stop myself; then plastered on a welcoming smile as I looked up, not sure what to expect. Whoever had found us was *way* too enthusiastic for seven o'clock in the evening after a wet cross-country day.

Clearly, it wasn't a fellow competitor. Even Kit and Vane had gone somewhere else for dinner to avoid talking to us.

Hannah Grayer smiled down at us, her silver-threaded brown curls bobbing around her face as she looked between us with clear satisfaction. Now, here was a woman who had no idea how tired we were. She owned horses to watch them, not to ride them.

And now she was sliding into the booth next to me, her ringed fingers squeezing my thigh with friendly abandon. "Look at you two," she announced. "My *team*!"

I glanced at her, surprised. Pete was the one taking on Hannah's horses, not me. As far as I was concerned, she only paid for *his* time and attention. Before I could say anything stupid, though, I felt Pete's boot gently placed atop my foot.

So, I gave her a taut smile instead.

"I have great news," Hannah went on, her attention focused on Pete now. "I worked it all out with Mimi. She had the horses almost qualified for the two-star event at Chesapeake, so you can take them after you qualify at Pin Oak!"

Well, that didn't take long.

Pete's foot pressed down on mine. I was the one who should be stomping on him! This was exactly what I just told him was going to happen, and he was so sure it wouldn't be a big deal. Well, go for it, Pete. Explain away.

Hannah glanced at me as I shifted to get my foot free of Pete's boot. "Are you okay, dear?"

"Fine," I managed. "Quite an announcement, that's all!"

Pete's voice creaked a little as he repeated, "Chesapeake Three-Day Event?"

As if Hannah might be talking about a Chesapeake horse show we didn't know about.

"Well, yes!" Hannah was delighted. "They're fit and ready. You won't have to do a thing but get to know them over the next month. And if you take them to Pin Oak in two weeks, you'll meet the minimum eligibility requirement for the short format. I had Mimi explain it all to me. And she said you'd know how it works."

I surveyed Hannah as I bit into the last mozzarella stick. She was so happy. She was thrilled, ecstatic even, to make Pete's dreams come true with two ready-made two-star horses. She had no idea she was proposing something potentially dangerous for both Pete and her beloved horses.

"That's quite impressive," Pete finally said. "Getting them qualified, I mean. But I'm not sure—I mean, did Mimi really think it was a good idea—" He was stumbling already. Oh, Pete.

"Mimi knows you can handle it," Hannah said brightly. "Oh, good. There she is. Mimi! Mimi, we're over here!"

Pete looked past Hannah with an expression that suggested his will to live was drying up and blowing away.

And who could blame him? I looked mournfully at my empty plate. There wasn't enough fried cheese in this entire town to make up for this suddenly social dinner. Didn't anyone care that we just wanted to eat, drive back to the motel, and *sleep*? Or failing that, cuddle with Jack for a few hours?

I fastened a fresh smile on my face as a woman wearing a neck collar walked across the dining room. Walked? It would be more accurate to say "hobbled"—because poor Mimi Pulaski was not passing the vet anytime soon. She looked like she'd fallen off a million horses in her career and every one of them had trodden on her somewhere tender. With their studs in.

Mimi slid into the booth next to Pete with slow, careful movements. "This is awkward," she told him, smiling. She had a chipped front tooth, too. "I can't turn my head that far right now, but Pete, good to meet you in person."

Mimi's eyes slid over me, narrowed slightly, and moved on to Hannah. She didn't greet me.

"Well, boss," she said to Hannah, "the passing of the torch is upon us."

"It's a good move for them, but I'll miss you, Mimi."

How nice. We were here for the goodbye ceremony. Not at all

awkward. I felt like this could have been done in private, or at least at another booth, but what did I know?

"I can't believe I'm not being dragged out in a body bag, to be honest," Mimi said. "I never thought I'd quit competing while I still had breath in my lungs. Not sure how I'm going to live without it."

It sounded as if she was actually resigned to retiring. Maybe Sandy had that part wrong. I lifted my eyebrows at Pete. He widened his eyes in reply.

"Oh, Mimi." Hannah laughed, somehow missing the gravity of it all—or maybe choosing to overlook it. "Sure, maybe eventing isn't an option anymore, but you're going to be riding again in no time. You can still do dressage, and trail ride."

Mimi gave her a grim smile. "Sure, I can still do that."

The battered rider glanced at me again, didn't seem to care for what she saw, and then shifted her entire body so that she could face Pete. I stiffened. Pete looked as if he'd like to slide away to safety, but the wall was already at his shoulder. The only way out would be to slither under the table. I remembered doing that as a child and closed my eyes for a moment to recall the feeling. I could almost hear my mother yelling at me to *Stop that, Jules!*

"Are you ready to take the boys?" Mimi asked Pete. "My working student has been riding them, but they need a pro on their backs before Pin Oak. Certainly if you're going to be taking them in the two-star, you'd better start immediately."

"About that," Pete began.

"I think Hannah said you're coming Monday, is that right?" Mimi went on, as though he hadn't said anything.

"Of course, Monday, whenever you can accommodate us," Pete agreed.

"I have all day," Mimi said. "Retirement opens up your schedule."

Our server appeared with our salads. She cast a confused look at the additional two women at our table. "They're going to get their own table," I told her. "Just stopped by to say hello, that's all."

Mimi looked at me then, her gaze cold enough to raise goose bumps on my arms. I picked up my fork and prepared to dig in, too hungry to be polite. I hadn't asked these women to eat dinner with me.

"Hannah," Mimi said coolly, still watching me with those icy gray eyes. "I think we should leave these two to their dinner. They've had a long day."

"Oh, of course," Hannah agreed, suddenly all hustle and bustle. "Let's get out of their hair—have a nice night, Pete, Jules! Can't wait to see you get started with the boys!"

They slid out of the booth and Pete waited until they were occupied with the hostess before he dropped his face into his hands.

I was too hungry to stop eating for very long, but I did manage to mumble, "We've got a big problem," around a mouthful of chicken, and Pete nodded.

5

"INTERESTING," LACEY SAID, in a voice that suggested maybe it wasn't.

I couldn't always read her expression when we were sharing a video call in very dark spaces—I was hiding in a stall, and she was in her barn office with the lights turned off for some reason—but I had thought she would be more intrigued by my story of last night's uncomfortable dinner conversation. "I guess Mimi isn't loving this move for her horses, huh?"

"That's all you've got? Because I think that woman wants to kill us both. She gave me a look that honestly should have turned me to stone."

I could hear voices coming from the tack stall a few doors down, so I wasn't as alone as I'd hoped. Pete was getting ready to ride his show jumping round, and Vane had come over to help him tack up. As for me, I was supposed to be double-checking my course for Mickey's round, but the moment I was alone, I'd called Lacey instead.

Someone else needed to know about the levels of crazy we were reaching here in Maryland.

I looked both ways before slipping out of the empty stall and walking away from the barn. When I was a few dozen feet away, I went on with my story. "She seriously didn't speak to me directly all night. And they both came back after dinner to talk to us again."

"What did you have for dinner?"

I sighed. "Salad."

"I had a bacon cheeseburger."

"Of course you did," I retorted crisply. "My growing girl."

"Oh, shut up." Lacey laughed. "Are you doing that thing where you swear if you have a burger, your breeches are too tight to zip?"

"Yes, and I hate it."

"Getting old sucks, is what I hear."

"Getting old, having a kid, both of those things." Lacey and I were about the same age, but I didn't see kids in her future. Aside from watching over the rugrats at Alachua, she didn't seem to have any interest in children. Or dating, for that matter.

"Why are you in the dark?" I asked.

"Oh," Lacey said, glancing around as if she hadn't noticed. "I'm hiding."

"From who? From the kids?"

"From Alex. She's been constantly underfoot while you've been gone, Jules. Something about not having anything to do because all the babies are off right now. Is that horse racing speak?"

"She starts the yearlings under saddle in September and then gives them a few weeks off," I remembered. "What is she doing at the farm, besides teaching the kids to be jockeys?"

"Asking me to go to lunch with her, asking me to trail ride with her, making up nicknames for the horses that she wants all the kids to use. She's calling Tiger 'Snapper,' and I told her that makes no sense because a tiger bites already—"

"I'm sorry that Alex wants to be your friend," I said. "I hope it gets better for you soon."

"Fine, let's talk about your tight breeches again."

"I think we're off that subject. I'm still trying to figure out what to do about the crazy up here, so the Florida crazy is all yours."

Lacey sighed. "Okay, tell me more."

The sun came out from behind the clouds and blinded me; I closed my eyes against the yellow glare. I didn't like the sunlight up here. It was too slanted for so early in the year. Living in a new latitude was having a jetlag effect on me, like I'd accidentally skipped ahead several months. "So anyway, of the two of them, Mimi is the more dangerous. And she clearly has it in for me. She looked at me like she was the villain in a Bond movie."

"And you're James Bond?"

"Obviously."

"Which villain is she, again?"

"I'm not getting that specific." I had never seen an entire James Bond movie.

"Well, maybe she's in love with Pete," Lacey suggested. "Or, she has a death-ray that she's planning to unveil at Chesapeake and she's afraid you're going to get in her way. I'd say it's one of those two things, definitely."

"So, I'm going with the death-ray." I sighed. "Why would she be in love with Pete?"

"Jules, really? Half of eventing is in love with Pete and the other half is in denial about it."

"Which one are you?"

"The exception that proves the rule," Lacey said archly.

Dammit, she was always too smart for me.

I looked back at the shed row. My husband was adjusting tack on Barsuk, the dapple-gray gelding who was more gray than dapple these days. Pete was lean and muscled, dapper in his boots and breeches and dark coat. These days, I mostly knew him as the tired father of our child and exhausted partner in our business, but there was no denying Pete was still a bit of an eventing heartthrob.

Maybe more than a bit.

"Okay," I conceded. "She *could* be in love with Pete. But I don't think the age difference is going to work out."

The PA system coughed itself awake, and a woman's authoritative voice ordered the upcoming riders to the show jumping arena. She didn't sound like she would appreciate it if anyone slowed down operations today. "I need to walk over to the warm-up with Pete," I told Lacey. "What should I do if Mimi shows up?"

"You could stab her with a hoof pick," Lacey said thoughtfully. "But I don't know if you have the guts. Push her into the water complex?"

"Be serious." Behind me, hoofbeats thudded on the clay as Pete led Barsuk out of the barn. "I'm actually a little freaked out here. Like giving up those horses has her going off the deep end. She looked at me like a crazy person, I'm telling you."

"You would know."

"If you could stop making comebacks for one second and just help me—"

"Jules?" Pete called. "Are you ready?"

"Ready," I called back, waving to him. "Walking over with you!"

"Just remember you're Jules Thornton," Lacey said. "That should be armor enough. No one can scare you, because you're the scariest woman in the business."

"I used to think so," I replied. "But now, I'm not so sure."

"Damn." Lacey whistled. "Now you've got *me* scared of her, too."

Barsuk went around the jumping warm-up with his head high and his tail flagged, obviously feeling way too good after his cross-country run the day before. I shook my head, grinning to myself, as I watched Pete take him around the arena murmuring *Whoa, whoa, whoa* all the while. This horse was finally in his element, in love with the speed and complicated jumping complexes found at the upper levels. Our lives had been far from simple over the past few years, and that had affected how quickly we could move our horses up, but Barsuk was finally at the top, where he belonged.

And Mickey was very close behind him, even if this weekend's outing showed we still had some room for improvement. I checked the time on my phone, aware I needed to hustle back to the barn and get Mickey tacked up the moment Pete was finished with his round. The moment the last Advanced rider went through the timers, the jump crew would race out to reset the course for Intermediate.

I stood at the gate, waiting, as the steward called Pete's name on deck. I had a cloth out, ready to wipe any smudges off his boots, and the foam off Barsuk's mouth.

"Now, buddy, you gotta look cute for the camera," I told the horse as he fussed and pulled away from me.

"I have a good feeling about this round," Pete said. He was looking over the course, watching the horse in the arena knock a rail. *Clunk*, the rail hit the ground. *Sigh*, the crowd commiserated. "Now more than ever."

I folded the cloth over so that Barsuk's spit was on the inside and used the dry part on Pete's boots, buffing the toe caps to bring out their shine. "So do I," I told him, "but you guys look like you're ready, so I won't say anything else."

"Actually, I have a good feeling about everything," Pete continued. "About Maryland, about Hannah's horses, about today. I just have a really good feeling."

I looked up at him. His face was glowing. He looked healthy, happy, in control.

I wondered what he knew that I didn't. Or maybe it was just the exhilaration of the moment, of a fit horse who loved his job and a course that looked inviting instead of tough, and an air temperature that could only be described as ambient.

"Pete, you're up!" The ring steward pointed to him, then the in-gate, just in case there was any confusion. The prior horse in the arena was just clearing the last fence. There was a telltale thud as another rail hit the ground, and another sigh from the audience. A teenager who'd been leaning against the arena fence ran past the circling horse and popped the rail back into place.

"Go win this division," I told Pete, and patted his boot.

It turned out that Pete's good feeling was justified, at least in the jumping arena.

Barsuk came in clear and under the time, finishing on the same score they'd trotted in on, and up one spot overall, thanks to the horse before him and those eight faults. Not a blue ribbon today, but at least he was taking home a rosette. It was always better to be near the top of the board rather than somewhere down in the also-finished.

As soon as the round was pronounced clear, I begged a ride back to the barns on a golf cart driven by a pigtailed Pony Clubber in jodhpurs. She couldn't have been older than twelve, but driver's licenses weren't checked at these things and most trainers had assistants well below the legal age for, well, anything.

"You're Jules Thornton," the kid gasped as I flagged her down.

"Yeah, I sure am. Got room for me?"

Starstruck, she shoved halters and buckets off the passenger seat. "Where are we going?"

"Barn three, and put the pedal down," I told her as I slid into the seat like a gangster making my getaway. "I'm flying without a full-time groom this weekend and it's not pretty."

"You got it," she said, and nearly drove us into the side of a food truck parked near the ring. She swerved to avoid it and we lost a halter. "It's an old one anyway," she panted, nearly hyperventilating.

"You're a good driver," I lied as she dropped me in front of my stalls, running over several sponges I'd left out to dry in the sun. "Thanks for the ride."

"I could help you groom," she offered tentatively. "I'm a C2 in Pony Club, so, you know, I've got a lot of experience—"

"Maybe next year." I hopped free of the cart before she could crash it into one of the trucks parked nearby and hotfooted it into the barn.

To my surprise and delight, Vane already had Mickey booted and saddled.

"You took long enough," she told me as I hustled into the tack stall to tug on my own boots. "I had a feeling you'd need help, so I told Kit I was coming down here to get him together, but you should have called me."

"Sorry, I thought I had it under control. I'm moving as fast as I can," I promised. "Hey, have you seen Gemma and Jack? And—" I looked around the tack stall for any sign of a snoozing beagle. We'd left him here snoring, lead fastened to a tack trunk so he couldn't come looking for us if he woke up. "Where's Marcus?"

"Gemma took him for a walk," Vane assured me, fastening up Mickey's noseband. "They're going to be at the ring for your round. Gemma wants to make sure Jack sees Mummy win. Her words," Vane added, and I suspected she was just barely managing to restrain an eye roll.

Vane better hope Kit never wants kids, I thought, lacing my spur strap closed. But I had a feeling she would. Kit's soft and kind teaching style had made her a favorite at Alachua Eventing Co-op, especially with the younger kids. She was a natural with children—and with Vane, who worshipped her and would give her anything she wanted.

Even a house full of kids and a barn full of white ponies.

"I'll make sure I win for Jack," I told Vane, mostly to annoy her.

Vane handed me my horse's reins. "You gotta get over there and jump all the jumps first, big shot."

I grinned. "Are you saying I have a chance?"

"Just barely," Vane said. "You're no Kit, but you do okay."

"Fair enough."

"Let's get you in the saddle so I can go do my actual work." In thirty seconds, she had me legged up, my boots wiped clean, and my jumping bat in hand. "See ya," she told me, and took off without looking back.

Once I was settled in the saddle, my brain went into its normal, all-systems-go state. It was hard to be anxious when I was riding this horse. I ran a hand along Mickey's gleaming neck. Vane had found time to give him a quick spray with coat polish, and his gray curves had a silver sparkle in the sunlight. She was a damn fine groom.

"Maybe I should steal her from Kit," I muttered, and then I had to laugh. Vane would push me off a cliff and steal my dog before she'd abandon Kit.

Mickey tugged at the reins and plunged forward, jigging his way toward the arena. His nostrils fluttered with a snort every time he bobbed his head, and his ears were pricked on the action in the distance. I sat in the middle of the saddle, my seat bones heavy to keep his attention on me, my stirrups slightly forward of my knees in case he did a funny spook or bolt.

Racing-fit event horses could be capable of just about anything, and this version of Mickey felt like a firecracker with a lit fuse.

Not a problem. I was going to use all that energy in the jumping ring.

"Bounce your way to the arena," I told him, easing the reins a little and giving him the room he wanted to trit-trot like a parade pony all the way to the warm-up.

The jump crew were already dropping the poles and adjusting the distances for Intermediate when I arrived at the arenas. Pete walked over to meet me at the warm-up ring, his bright-eyed horse skipping along beside him. He'd loosened Barsuk's girth and noseband; the yellow rosette for third place was tucked into his browband.

"I can warm you up," he offered. "Barsuk can walk around with me."

"That would be great, because this guy is hot and—" I was interrupted by a familiar voice.

"Pete, a word!"

I looked past Barsuk and saw Mimi Pulaski walking up to us, her brown leather boots dark with morning dew.

Pete and I exchanged glances. I shook my head slightly—*Be careful*—then nudged Mickey into a walk. We had to warm up for this course, whether Pete could give us pointers or not.

We went twice around the ring, hugging the rail to stay out of the way, then I let Mickey break into a trot. He was fresh as a daisy, tugging at the reins and looking around at the other horses in the ring with undisguised interest, as if he thought they'd all make great new friends.

I rode him absently, chewing at my tongue, wondering what on earth Mimi could want in the middle of another rider's warm-up. I thought it was pretty clear Pete was planning to help me. Was she always this rude, or was I getting special treatment because she didn't like me? And why didn't she like me, anyway? I wasn't the one who told her to retire from competition. I wasn't even the one who was taking over her horses.

My mind was entirely consumed by Pete and Mimi—right up until the point when poor Mickey, raring to go and desperate for my attention, put down his head and crow-hopped like a bronco.

His big, athletic bounce wasn't designed to get me off, but it still pulled me right back to the present. Luckily, I had my heel in front of me, and that defensive seat saved me from getting my white breeches dirty—just barely.

I heard some titters from my fellow riders as I got Mickey back into stride and brought him down to a trot. Even my supposed friends back in Florida liked to see Jules Thornton-Morrison get her overly confident ass handed to her, so it was no surprise the Maryland riders thought it was funny that my big horse nearly bucked me off.

Well, there was a price to pay for all this God-given talent, I supposed.

"You're a brat," I told Mickey, who ducked his head and snorted, pleased as punch to have gotten in a buck before the biggest class of his career. Pulling one over on Mother was his favorite trick. "Focus up, now," I said, as much to myself as to my horse. I had to get Mimi out of my head.

So, naturally, I looked over at Pete and Mimi again. She was still talking his ear off.

As I stared across the arena at the two of them, Mimi slowly turned her head, letting her gaze find mine. Her eyes held me for a moment, cold and gray as yesterday's storm clouds. And then, I'd swear on a stack of old *Chronicles,* she smirked.

I felt a prickle of unease at the back of my neck. She smirked like she knew something I didn't, like she had plans for me and I wasn't going to like them. She smirked like I had a nemesis in this sport and dammit, wasn't I too old to have a nemesis? Especially a retired rider from another state? Mickey flicked his tail so hard it smacked my boot, desperate to get my attention back on him again.

Somehow, we pulled it together. Well, somehow I got myself back in control and Mickey put in his usual performance. We danced through the jumps, making the big fences look easy. And as we cantered away from the final obstacle, a smattering of applause from the small crowd gathered by the arena was all I needed to hear. We'd gone clear.

"Danger Mouse and Jules Thornton-Morrison finish on their dressage score for a flawless weekend," the announcer said with a little extra panache—undeserved really, since our dressage score had been abysmal. I glanced at the sound booth as Mickey dropped down to a canter; the woman behind the mic gave me a little wave. *A fan,* I thought.

She went on, "They'll round out the top three with a third-place finish overall. Congratulations!"

Not a win, but top three wasn't bad. "We'll take it, won't we, boy?" I asked Mickey, clapping his neck. "That's my little jumping machine!"

Mickey flicked his ears back and forth, enjoying the applause even if it was sparse. Ex-racehorses never got over their love of a crowd, even if they sometimes had funny ways of showing it. Lucky for me, Mickey didn't express his appreciation with leaps and bucks. He reserved that nonsense for when I wasn't keeping my mind on the job.

I waved back to the announcer and jogged Mickey to the in-gate. As we exited the arena, I saw Hannah Grayer, with grandchildren climbing all over her and a spotted Great Dane on a leash, waving energetically from the top of the small grandstand. I gave her a wave as well, pleased that at least Pete's new owner was a fan.

"Third place from sixth," someone was saying. "How does that even happen?"

"The riders ahead of her had rails down," a more experienced eventer replied. "It's the only way to move up on the last day."

"Other people's bad luck," the first person said, sounding skeptical.

"Other people's bad *riding*," the experienced person corrected. "Or bad luck. It's all the same thing on the score sheet."

See? Some people got it.

6

IT WAS A relief to load up the horses and head back to the private farm where we were staying during our Maryland trip. Catoctin Green was a lovely property, but I was tired of being surrounded by hundreds of other people and their horses. Constant whinnies, the thuds of nervous horses kicking walls or stomping in trailers, radios blaring discordantly as grooms mucked out in the morning and evening, children screeching, dogs barking—it got to be a lot over the course of a weekend. Luckily, Hannah had a friend with a beautiful farm and an empty barn, and she'd arranged for us to rent stabling and turnout at a price I'd have considered rock-bottom if we were down in the bustling Ocala market.

I felt my shoulders relax as Pete turned in at the farm lane, marked by a white wooden sign that rocked on its hinges: CREEKSIDE FARM—JOAN PATTERSON. This was a calm place.

We drove past Joan's lovely restored stone farmhouse and a collection of equally charming old farm buildings before reaching the equestrian facilities: two center-aisle barns, their windows shut up tight against the cold wind; an arena with a gravel footing Joan called "stone dust" that was entirely foreign to me, but was apparently common in the north; and rolling pastures that still radiated a summery green glow despite the change of seasons.

A round pond next to the arena was scattered with brown ducks and a few gray geese, their feathers ruffled. In Florida, that pond would have been perfectly round because it was a sinkhole filled in with spring water, but in Maryland, Joan told me, ponds were round because they were dug that way. In fact, she went on, there were no natural lakes in Maryland—just farm ponds and reservoirs.

This fact alone made me suspicious of the state.

A few miles west of the farm, the browning folds of the Catoctin Mountains rose over the foothills, a few brightly colored trees still shining beneath the morning sun. I had to admit I liked those mountains. They weren't tall and rocky like mountains out west; these were mellow and smooth, all their crags and sharp edges worn away over the millennia. As a person with many sharp edges of my own, I found it somewhat calming to think there might be a time, somewhere far in the future, in which I would be a relaxed, comfortable version of myself.

We turned out our horses for the night as dusk settled around the farm. There was frost in the forecast, something I was not looking forward to, but the horses all loved the cold air. Steam rose from their nostrils as they pawed the ground, looking for good places to roll.

"Please do not rip your good blankets," I called.

Legs waved in the air, along with a lot of energetic snorting and grunting. I winced at the expensive new rugs being ground into the dirt. We didn't blanket more than a dozen or so times during the Florida winter season, so blanket repairs weren't built into my annual budget. These rugs needed to last at least a few years.

"Please stop," I called lamely, knowing there was nothing on earth I could say to make them quit rolling. They were going to look like little ragged hobo-ponies back in Florida. So embarrassing.

"They're ignoring you," Pete observed, extremely helpful as ever. He was perched on the wheel well of the horse trailer, a little too far away for me to smack him. "They think they've done enough behaving this weekend."

The horses got up one by one and shook, clumps of clay tumbling from their blankets. This clay dried rock-hard; the rugs would be stiff as boards in the morning.

Oh, well. This was life with horses: messy, chaotic, weirdly fulfilling. They looked so *happy* with their manes matted with red clay and their blankets smeared and crooked.

"Pete, I think we've all behaved enough for a while." I tugged my hair loose from its ponytail. "I'm worn out with not knowing anyone and feeling like I have to be on my best behavior all the time."

"I hadn't noticed."

"You didn't notice I didn't publicly attack Mimi for talking your ear off while I was supposed to be getting a nice helpful warm-up from you? I'm disappointed, Pete. She must have been fascinating."

"Well, I did notice," he admitted, abandoning his seat on the trailer and walking over to join me. He leaned against the fence, propping one boot on the lowest rail. This was, scientifically, the most comfortable position in the entire world. "And she had a lot to say about nothing much, so I think it was just her nerves pouring out, or something."

I snorted. "It's a weird way of showing her nerves. She kept glaring at me like I insulted her mother."

"*Did* you?"

"Come on, Mimi's ancient. There's no way I'd have known her

mother to insult her. Anyway, I'm being serious. Everyone in Maryland seems to think I'm a grenade about to go off. At least back in Florida everyone knows who I am. Whether they like me or not, I'm established."

"You could be established here, with time. Don't you want to be a Delmarva equestrienne? Like Jackie O?"

"Or Elaine Benes? If this was a fact-finding mission to see if you can move me up here, forget it. I am Florida Woman."

Pete gave me a little tickle in the ribs, and I elbowed him back, not nearly as gently. He grunted. "Easy, woman. I have to pick up new horses tomorrow and ride them in front of their former trainer. I can't be bruised for that."

"I'll save the beating up for later, then," I reassured him. "So, are you freaked out about riding in front of Mimi?"

"A little," he admitted. "After talking to her today, I can definitively say that the vibes are . . . off."

"See? It's not just me."

"Oh, no. It's not just you. I mean, I don't think she has it in for you in particular—she's just weird, period. And she's not really happy with me or Hannah. She's saying that she's glad the horses are coming to me, but she'd definitely prefer Hannah let her keep the horses."

"But that's not realistic of her, not when we're mid-season," I argued. "Even if she changed her mind about retiring, she can't ride them right now." *She can barely walk,* I thought, but dismissed that because walking and riding were not at all the same thing. Look at the way Sandy Sullivan hobbled around, and he was still bringing home ribbons and hunting all winter.

Thinking of Sandy Sullivan made me annoyed with him all over again. But at the same time, five minutes of warning was at least something.

Pete was stuck on Mimi. "She's still saying that she's retired. She keeps repeating that her doctors are telling her not to risk another fracture and the only way she can guarantee that is to stay out of the saddle. But honestly . . . you know horse people. She probably has some idea that she's going to heal up better than her doctors are telling her, and then she can get right back out there and ride better than ever."

"When it's usually the other way around." Stuff never healed the way we wanted. Not on horses, not on humans. "She's in denial."

"True." Pete nodded, then shrugged. "I don't know why she had to talk my ear off at the event when we're going to see her tomorrow, but hopefully once we have the horses, that's the end of our dealings with her."

I doubted it. Mimi struck me as one of those difficult people who would keep making up reasons to stick her nose in our business. Until she found something else to occupy her, she and Hannah's horses would be a package deal. "And what are you going to do about the three-day event?" I asked him.

"I'll deal with the three-day," Pete said.

I didn't know what that meant, but he sounded done with the topic.

Together, we watched the horses nose around in the dusk. They were almost disappearing into the darkness now, shadows that would become invisible as the sky overhead slipped from navy to ebony. Lights gleamed along the lowest slopes of the mountains just beyond the farm, and a few shone out from among the trees higher up. The nights here might be cold, but the sunsets and dusks were undeniably picturesque.

"Would *you* ever retire?" Pete asked suddenly. "Let's say you were sixty-odd years old, and you just broke your collarbone for a third time and a doctor said you were in danger if you did it again. Would you retire from competition?"

I snorted. "Absolutely not. And neither would you."

"Okay. All true. So then answer this: Why is Mimi retiring?"

"Sandy said it's her wife's doing. The wife is the one all impressed by the doctors."

"Would you stop riding if I asked you to?"

I shrugged noncommittally. Personally, I wouldn't let a faulty collarbone take me out of eventing. What else would I do with my days? And Mimi had been eventing for decades more than me, so she probably had nothing else in her life, either. This sport demanded everything. But Sandy had said her wife wanted her to retire. Pete would never be so foolish.

"You're not even going to pretend?" Pete laughed.

"What do you want me to say, Pete? I don't think I can answer it because I don't think you'd ever ask me to stop." But while my tone was flippant, the question needled me. What if I *did* have to stop for someone else's sake?

When I'd first started riding again after Jack was born, it had been hell. I'd never been afraid in the saddle before, but suddenly I understood why we wore helmets for every little ride, why even schooling cross-country meant air bag vests and safety stirrups, and the significance of wearing a medical emergency armband on course suddenly loomed large in my mind. If something happened to me, a small, perfect person would grow up without his mother. The very idea made my stomach turn every time I mounted up.

The terror passed as I grew stronger and riding began to feel as natural and normal as breathing again. I could put on my helmet now without that hideous thought—*This is the only thing between your skull and the ground*. But that was only because nothing had gone wrong. No bad falls, no broken bones. The danger was still there, I just hadn't had to face it.

There weren't eventing police out there stopping people from getting on the cross-country course against the advice of medical professionals. Mimi could make a comeback. But she'd have to get her wife's buy-in. Maybe she hadn't given up yet.

"She doesn't want to retire," I said, suddenly understanding Mimi—at least, I thought I did. "She regrets the decision, but it's too late to do anything about it. She *can't* do anything about it, because she made a commitment to her wife. And she's blaming us, because she can't blame the person she's retiring for. She's fighting back the only way she can. She hopes we'll look incompetent and that she can't deny Hannah the favor if Hannah wants her to take the horses back."

We had been standing here for such a long time, the exterior lights around the farm had switched on. I was suddenly aware of how very tired I was.

Instead of replying, Pete pushed back from the fence. "I'm getting stiff. This cold gets right into your bones."

"Let's grab some Epsom salts from the tack room," I suggested, "and we can take baths back at the motel room."

"Oooh," Pete said, nuzzling my neck. "Sounds sexy."

"Get off." I laughed, shoving him aside. "Obviously I mean *separate, alone-time* baths."

"Spoilsport."

"Get us our own motel room," I told him, "and we'll talk."

Jack loved it when I took a bath. He wanted in, too, which meant I had about ten minutes of peace before I gave in to his little hands slapping against the door and let him come splash with Mommy. I sat him on my thigh, my back against a towel on the tiled wall, and let him soak the bathroom floor. His fair hair curled against the nape of his neck and fell over his little ears in soft tendrils. I looped my fingers through it and brushed it against his cheeks until he laughed and swiped my hand away. This was the person I could give up horses for, I thought. No matter how much it hurt, Jack would always come first. I just hoped it would never come to that.

Marcus's nose appeared next, pushing the half-closed door the rest of the way open, and he padded over to the bathtub with his tongue hanging out. He licked at the water on the edge of the tub and gave me pleading looks with his big brown eyes.

So many children to please. It was a good thing the horses were back at the barn. I wouldn't be able to say no to them, either.

Marcus found a dry spot to sit, and I rubbed his head with one wet hand, wishing his red-brown patches weren't being swept away under a roan of white hairs. His beautiful face with its white stripe between chestnut eye patches . . . it was all turning gray now. Even if I didn't want to admit it, Marcus was getting older, and Pete had made noises once or twice over the summer about getting a new dog—so that we'd have a dog around the house when Marcus wasn't with us anymore.

"I can't bear the silence," he'd said, and although a house with Jack and Gemma in it was rarely silent, I knew what he meant. The absence of a dog was an echoing thing.

But how was I supposed to get another dog without making Marcus feel like he was being edged out? I understood Marcus; we were only children. We liked it that way. He would be hurt if I brought another dog home.

And anyway, I wasn't ready to consider a life without him. Not yet.

Marcus stayed in the bathroom until Jack splashed him, and then he closed his eyes once, twice, in deep disappointment at the baby, before retreating to the motel room. I heard the springs on our bed squeak as he jumped up onto the mattress, ready to curl up in a ball until someone offered to give him one last walk.

That someone was Pete. "Come on, boy, don't go to sleep yet," Pete said.

Jack stopped splashing and stared gravely at the door, as if he hadn't realized his father was on the other side.

"That's Daddy," I told him. "Daddy's taking out Marcus."

"Mawk," Jack squawked, and went back to splashing.

A warm bubble of happiness swelled in my chest. A few months ago, we'd thought Jack's first word was "horse"—until Lacey informed us babies didn't start speaking at six months. Obviously, we'd read that in the mountain of baby books currently housed in our living room back in Florida, but had we really absorbed everything we'd read? Clearly not. Still, I was pretty sure he was ready for that milestone now. And if Jack was about to go from baby squeaks to ordering our dog around, what a fun first word that would be!

After all, what mattered more than dogs and horses?

"You're up there on my list, though," I told my slippery little son. "Really high up there."

Maybe on top, sure. Who was keeping score on the things we loved, anyway? Only an insanely competitive person would do *that*.

When I was finally certain I'd soaked out as many eventing-weekend aches as possible, I tucked myself into flannel pajamas and got under the stiff motel-room covers. Gemma went into the bathroom for a shower. Jack sang to himself in his Pack 'N Play. I turned on the Weather Channel with the sound muted. A storm chaser was frantically pointing at a nearby tornado. I turned the TV off again and picked up my phone. I just wanted the forecast, for crying out loud.

The forecast didn't make me happy, and I was muttering to myself about freezing temperatures when Pete returned with a cheerful Marcus.

"Someone found a piece of pizza!" Pete announced as the beagle trotted into the room with his white-tipped tail wagging furiously. "And ate all of it before he could be stopped!"

"Oh, Marcus, what fun for you." I rubbed his floppy hounddog ears. "What a day!"

Pete glanced at the closed bathroom door and sighed. "You know, I was thinking," he said, sitting down to take off his shoes.

"Dangerous."

"I know. But seriously, I think for the rest of the stay, we should consider getting a second motel room. I think there'll be a vacancy here tomorrow, and it's not that expensive."

I stared at him. Pete was the one who had insisted we could only have one room. I decided I was too relieved to point out this hypocrisy.

"Yes," I agreed. "Please. Go get us a second room right now. I'm already in bed for the night, but Gemma can have it."

Pete held up a hand, laughing. "Whoa, there. I saw some people packing up their trucks tonight. I guess they're leaving tomorrow. Then, hopefully, we can score one of their rooms. I'll talk to the office before we go to the barn in the morning."

The water turned off in the bathroom, and I heard Gemma stepping out of the shower. I thought: *We live on top of each other back in Florida, but this is ridiculous.*

"Yes," I repeated. "Please and thank you."

Jack began to grouse in his Pack 'N Play, so Pete scooped him up and brought him to me for a bedtime cuddle as Gemma came out of the bathroom in a cloud of steam. It heated up the room deliciously. I wondered if we could get rooms with a door between us. The idea of missing Jack's bedtime was disconcerting and, for a moment, I squeezed him just a little too tight. He mewed and squealed, pushing at my chest.

"Sorry, sorry," I attempted, but he was furious and demanded to be handed off to Gemma.

She adjusted her nightshirt, tugged her wet hair into a bun, then took him, murmuring the soft nonsense phrases she used to soothe him to sleep.

I sighed and turned my attention to Marcus, who took all the attention I could give him, and still asked for more.

7

THE CLERK IN the lobby told Pete he could have a second room if there was a cancellation in tomorrow's bookings; he'd know after three o'clock. Pete raided the sad continental breakfast the motel set out and brought back tiny bagels along with even tinier packets of cream cheese as consolation. I ate my breakfast in bed, chewing moodily, while Jack fussed his way through a jar of pureed banana. The day was windy, and a cold draft snaked through the faulty seals around the window and raised goose bumps on my arms.

"I hate it up north," I said to no one. Marcus licked my elbow encouragingly.

He thought giving him some bagel would make it all better.

I gave him a big hunk, and watching him chomp it down in one gulp *was* pretty satisfying.

In light of the cold, blustery weather, Gemma stayed behind with Jack while Pete and I tramped out to the truck and drove the fifteen minutes to the farm.

The trees were trying to hang on to their yellow and red leaves, but the wind was making it difficult, and autumn leaves spilled across the road as we made our way from suburban sprawl to countryside.

At the farm, I sat in the truck for a moment after Pete shut it off, unwilling to get out and face the blustery morning. Our horses, muddy and bedraggled from their night of turnout, watched us with pricked ears from over the pasture gates. They didn't mind the wind and would have happily stayed outside in it, but what they *really* liked was food.

Joan's horses were already in; I spotted a groom pushing a wheelbarrow to the manure pile around back. Joan herself wouldn't be out yet. She was a successful attorney with some DC firm and worked from home, riding her horses on her lunch breaks and after work. As an amateur competitor who spent a few weeks on the Florida circuit every winter, she'd taken two horses to the top five in the Retired Racehorse Project, won the American Eventing Championships at Training level with a homebred Irish Sport Horse, and had completed the old Radnor Hunt International Three-Day Event back before its retirement—three times. In short, this attorney who rode part time had a more impressive résumé than I did.

Despite all this, I liked her.

At Hannah's recommendation, she'd been delighted to rent us her second, empty barn for the full six weeks of our stay, and offered two pastures as well. The place was quiet, private, and had a full course of fences in the arena, plus some cross-country combinations out in the fields.

And while the Eastern Shore, where Chesapeake Three-Day Event was held, was a decent drive away—for a small state, Maryland knew how to stretch its distances—we'd be stabled on the grounds for the entire event, so a long commute didn't really matter. Pete and I would camp in the horse trailer for the event weekend, while Gemma and Jack stayed behind and a hired groom took care of the horses who weren't competing. Assuming that Pete's new horses really weren't.

Pete left me in the truck and marched to the barn, head bent against the wind. After a few minutes I sighed, zipped my coat to my chin, and trudged out to the pasture gates to start haltering horses. By the time he had the barn doors open and was dumping grain in the feed bins, I was leading our horses in, two lead ropes in each hand. The four horses strewn behind me nipped and squealed at each other.

I ignored them.

"Jules," Pete remonstrated as I dragged the crew into the barn and let them dart into their stalls, "you should not be bringing in four horses at a time. Honestly, it's like you're twelve."

I ignored him.

Sometimes, like on cold mornings when you hadn't had enough sleep, and you'd been within the same six square feet as someone else for what felt like forever, it was just better that way.

With the horses eating and occupied, I began slipping into stalls and changing out the heavy winter rugs for their stable blankets. Clay fell from the blankets in moist, peeling sheets. "This is what I asked you not to do," I told Mickey as I shook out his messy rug. "Exactly one hundred percent what I asked you not to do."

He turned and rubbed his face on my arm in reply, leaving a pattern of white hairs on my sleeve.

I was just finishing up the changing of the blankets when Joan slipped through the barn door and came down to say hello. She was wearing fleece breeches and a thick sweater, and looked stylishly warm. I tried not to compare my jeans and battered old coat, which were insufficient for the weather and looked cheap, besides. I should have emailed Rockwell Brothers and asked them to send us some of the winter collection, but I'd deluded myself into believing it wouldn't actually get cold until we were heading home.

"So, you guys had a great weekend!" Joan announced, hands on hips like we'd neglected to share the good news. "Some good placings."

"Yeah, it was a nice event," I agreed, buckling the chest straps on Mickey's sheet. Most of our horse clothes were Briar Hill Farm blue, but this particular blanket was black; light gray horses looked exceptionally sharp in black, I thought. Mickey arched his neck to lip at my fingers. "This guy had a funky dressage test, but he liked the hills on cross-country. Rogue wasn't so sure about them, though."

"That's the ex-jumper, right? Pete's old horse?"

I nodded and leaned down to fix the leg straps in place. Mickey shifted to watch me, his mouth full of hay. "Stand still," I said reflexively, even as I moved with him. "You're acting like this is your first time wearing clothes. Yeah," I said to Joan. "Rogue was a jumper, but he needed to stretch out on cross-country and it's been a lot better for his brain. He just struggles with fitness."

"That happens," Joan said sympathetically. "So, you're going to Mimi's place today, right? To get Pete started with Hannah's two horses?"

I glanced at her, surprised she knew that. But of course, she was Hannah's friend. I wished we were on more neutral territory. I didn't like the idea of Joan and Hannah whispering about us, swapping stories and speculating about our personal lives.

Pete came out of the feed room and answered for me. "Today's the day," he said heartily. "I'm really looking forward to those two."

"I guess so, since you're competing them in the two-star," Joan said.

I looked at her sharply. She knew everything, didn't she?

"I think there are more discussions to be had before we make a final decision," Pete hedged. "But if we decide to take them to the three-day, the horses are fit and ready to go. Mimi's only been off them a short while, and she's had a student doing their conditioning work. I have a few weeks to get to know them."

My gaze swiveled to Pete. Wait. Was he really considering the two-star, or was he just stringing Joan along, since anything he said would get back to Hannah? I really wanted to believe it was the latter.

"I hope you're right and the horses fall right into place for you," Joan was saying. Did she sound a bit skeptical? Maybe she was on my team after all. "Because you'll have a big course to jump around at Pin Oak. And you know Chesapeake is no picnic, either."

"Well, I'm not too proud to bow out if I don't think we're ready, or if things aren't going okay on course." Pete glanced past Joan and smiled at me.

"Not too proud, maybe," Joan said, "but Hannah will be sorely disappointed if you start and don't finish. She's spending a lot of money on that weekend. If you take them to the starting box, you're going to have to ride them through the final flags, and do it well, Pete. You'll have to muscle up and get them around the course no matter what."

Wait, wait, wait. Retiring on the cross-country course before something went terribly wrong was a mark of true horsemanship. Joan was making it sound like a waste of money. Like cowardice.

Pete raised his eyebrows. "What are you saying?"

"Don't take them to Chesapeake," Joan said, looking at him like he was a fool for making her speak plainly. "Do I have to make it any more clear to you?"

We both stared at her.

"But—Hannah—" Pete began.

"Hannah doesn't know what she's asking of you," Joan said. "But I do, and I've told her. She's not listening. Hannah listens to Mimi in everything. Or, she did."

I couldn't take any more of this. "Joan, why would Mimi want Pete to take those horses to Chesapeake? She has to know it's a terrible idea."

"I don't think Mimi's been thinking clearly for a while," Joan said. "You know she only broke her collarbone because she was trying to prove a point to Sandy Sullivan, don't you?"

For the second time in less than a minute, we both stared at Joan, utterly speechless.

She shook her head. "They were racing down at his hunt's point-to-point grounds—"

"Racing?" I interrupted. "Those two were racing? At their age?"

Joan pursed her lips for a moment. I realized she must not be much younger than Mimi or Sandy. Finally, she went on. "They were racing, as they do every fall, and Sandy shouted for her to go around one of the fences because the ground was no good on the other side, but then he jumped it anyway and she did too. Sandy's horse made it without trouble, but Mimi's stumbled and pitched her over his shoulder. Diane was there and saw the whole thing. She told Mimi she was done eventing before the woman had been loaded onto an ambulance."

"Sandy left out that part," I said, annoyed.

"He's embarrassed," Joan said. "But everyone knows it. Those two have been egging each other on for decades."

Pete spoke up then. "Did Sandy tell her she shouldn't retire?"

Joan gave him a level look. "What do you think? And now he

regrets it, because Diane wants to kill him. They can't be within a hundred feet of each other now. She's out for his blood, and meanwhile Mimi is going to try everything she can think of to keep those horses. Even, and I'm sorry it's happening to you, try and get some poor rider into trouble."

8

A STONE FARMHOUSE with a little barn snugged up against it, a dressage ring with pale sand footing, a series of wooded paddocks connected by coops and dotted with cross-country fences . . . Mimi Pulaski's tidy little farm was cute, efficient, and betrayed an obsession with cleanliness I could only respect. There was nothing wrong with wanting perfection in one's personal equestrian center, and Mimi seemed to have achieved it. While the place wasn't big, it was clearly the home of a professional who took her job extremely seriously.

And what a relief, given how oddly Mimi had behaved already. Somehow, it seemed harder to believe a very organized person was also a devious villain who wanted to knock Pete out of the game so she could come out of retirement and take her horses back. I didn't like the story Joan had presented to me, with its neat little tale of obsession and a long-running rivalry culminating in one last, desperate bid to keep the horses—especially when it meant putting the horses into situations beyond their capability. I could understand trying to keep my horses at just about any cost—but would I send them cross-country in the hopes they'd be overfaced and have to pull up? If it was true, Mimi must be banking on Pete's reputation as a slow and careful horseman, because she had to be completely confident he'd pull up instead of pushing on, as Joan thought he should.

Or maybe she was just as bad as she seemed, and she was out to not only keep her horses but get Pete hurt or ruin his reputation at the same time.

I shook my head, as though to clear my mind. Focus on horses first, issue baseless accusations later. The Jules Method.

A tall bay horse was grazing in the front paddock as we drove up the short driveway and parked in front of the barn. Two rows of stalls set in an L-shape around a paved courtyard made a cozy little area to keep and groom horses. Under an overhang, Mimi was briskly curry-combing a crosstied horse.

Even from the distance, I could see we were dealing with a pretty impressive beastie.

"I think that's one of yours," I exclaimed, unbuckling my seat belt. "Holy cow, Pete, look at him."

Pete took a more measured assessment of the horse, but even he couldn't play unimpressed. The mahogany bay horse was tall, with sloping shoulders and sharp withers, a strong hind end, big platter-sized hooves. His head was slim and sensitive, and he turned it as far as the crossties would allow to get a look at our truck.

Mimi was a woman of average height, and she stood beneath this horse's chin with plenty of clearance when his head was fully raised. If this was the horse she'd launched off while racing Sandy, it was no wonder she'd broken her collarbone.

Pete bit his lower lip as he considered the horse. "That must be India," he said after a moment.

"Right, Star of India," I recalled, thinking back to the paperwork Hannah had sent us while we were still in Florida. "Named for that big white star on his face, I guess." He had a geometrically perfect diamond, like something you'd find in a children's book illustration, with a slim black forelock that swept off the plane above his left eye. "Lindsay said it was a colonizer name and we should change it," I added, remembering my occasional-working-student's assessment of Pete's new horses.

At nineteen, Lindsay was in her change-the-world phase.

She hadn't had a problem with the other horse's name, Once a Prince. She thought that was pretty cute, actually. So did I.

"We can't change it," Pete said. "He's not our horse. He's Hannah's."

"I *know* that," I told him impatiently. "I was joking."

But right now, Pete didn't have the mental capacity for jokes. I knew he was already imagining putting a leg over his new horse. I was anticipating a few rides on him myself. Everything about this horse promised athleticism and grace.

That symmetrical white star gleamed at us through his dark forelock as we walked up to the barn.

"It's a sapphire, by the way."

I glanced at Pete curiously.

"The Star of India. It's a huge sapphire."

"Not a diamond?"

"No. I guess whoever named him figured it was close enough."

Lindsay was going to hate that.

Mimi stood to one side as we walked into the yard, curry comb still in hand.

"You made it," she said, as if there'd been some doubt we'd show up.

Her eyes slid past me yet again.

That was fine. I'd just be a ghost and sneak around her farm without being noticed.

Pete and Mimi exchanged pleasantries while I wandered around the yard and barn. The space was clean and surprisingly empty. There were six stalls, but only two had bedding in them; the rest were swept and bare. The cobweb-free corners indicated they'd been cleaned out recently. Stripped and sanitized after their residents left? How many horses had Mimi lost with her forced retirement from competition? Hannah had suggested she had a horse of her own, but that didn't seem to be the case anymore.

I glanced out at the paddock, where the horse who must be Once a Prince was happily grazing on the lush grass this region seemed to grow so easily.

When we took these two, Mimi would have an empty farm. No wonder she didn't care for us. I'd probably chase me away with a pitchfork.

Although, I still thought the obvious dislike directed at me was pretty unfair.

I looked back at Pete, who was kneeling, running his hands down India's legs. Mimi was talking in a low voice, probably telling him the horse's history, any medical stuff to know about, that kind of thing. His expression was stern, but I could see the happiness in his eyes when he looked up and caught my gaze. He was already half in love with this horse, had been since the moment he saw them. Some horses were like that—the mere sight of them reached out and grabbed you by the heart.

That was good. Pete needed horses he loved. I was the one who declared every horse I took home to be a heart horse; Pete was much more pragmatic, considering the business side of the equation more strongly than I did. For all that I'd thought I was a horse business genius when I'd first come to Ocala at twenty-one, it turned out I was just a big old horse girl softie.

"Jules?" Pete called.

"Coming," I sang out, and headed back to the crossties, where Mimi was fitting a padded black bridle on India's shapely head. She managed to look right through me, her gaze flicking from the work at hand to the paddocks beyond and back to the horse without ever acknowledging my presence. I had to grant her grudging admiration for that. A strong move in the Disrespect Olympics.

Pete was checking the stirrup length. "Could you get my helmet? I left it in the truck."

"Of course," I told him. "Oh, and those stirrups are uneven," I added, pausing a few feet away and gazing at the horse head-on. "So you'll want to check both sides before you choose a hole to set them on."

That got Mimi's attention. She turned her head as quickly as her neck collar would allow. "My stirrups are *not* uneven," she snapped.

I bit back a triumphant grin. "Look for yourself." I spun on my heel and headed for the truck.

I went slowly enough to hear Mimi's muttered "Son of a *bitch*!" as she discovered she'd been riding off-center for goodness knew how long.

Star of India was an admirable horse. Even-tempered, with just a hint of spice when Pete put his leg on, big uphill movement and a flashy way of flicking his toes that would get the dressage judges salivating onto their score sheets—he had all the marks of a top competitor. He made fences disappear with one smooth motion, knees up and ears pricked.

I was a Thoroughbred person through and through, but some of these European horses were drool-worthy even to my begrudging gaze, and India was one of the (very, very) good ones.

But he wasn't easy. Pete was a quiet rider, but I knew him well enough to see the signs that he was working for every move he got—the way he'd slip back a heel to touch the horse's side, then nudge again harder, told me that India wasn't as responsive as our other horses. There could be a lot of reasons for this, ranging from ineffective training by Mimi (a possibility) to untreated stomach ulcers (a probability). I thought I understood, as Pete tried to gently ask for a shoulder-in at the trot and then had to resort to a more obvious request, why Sandy had warned her off a jump he was happy to take himself.

Well, there was no way Pete would agree to compete them at Chesapeake now. India needed schooling, and to be brought up to hair-trigger responsiveness on the aids, before he would be safe to take on a two-star course.

And it would be dressage schooling that he was lacking. It was always the dressage. Mimi came from old-school eventing: hot-headed off-track Thoroughbreds performing a dressage test like a bear doing ballet before the real work started on endurance day. But since endurance day was turned into cross-country day and dressage became a focus instead of an unfortunately fastidious warm-up round, riders learned to spend the extra time on their flatwork—or fade out.

I'd seen India's dressage scores. I knew what was going on here. And why Hannah had chosen the author of a dressage manual to take over her horses in Florida.

Mimi just didn't put in the extra effort to become a dressage queen, however temporarily, at events. And riding with her left stirrup a full hole shorter than the right couldn't have helped. How long had *that* been going on? Now that my initial amusement had passed, I was kind of worried about her. Someone should have caught the stirrup length issue. If not Mimi, then her working student. Where was that student, anyway?

Oh, it was Monday. Probably their day off. Or possibly already laid off, since we were here to take over the horses. I looked speculatively at Mimi, who was watching Pete ride her horse with a grim expression.

"Just you here today?" I asked.

No response. Not even a twitch.

Maybe she hadn't heard me?

I tried again. "Does your student have off on Monday?"

This time, Mimi gave me a cool look. "I fired my student," she said.

"Oh."

"Not a lot of work for her now." Mimi looked away again.

I decided maybe it was better if I didn't say anything else to her.

Things escalated in the arena. India tossed his head at Pete's polite request for a flying lead change, then planted his forehooves in the dirt and threw a little buck. We might be in for some fireworks now. I leaned on the rail, interested in Pete's response. The way he reacted to the horse's defiance would be a window into their future together. India had to want to work with Pete, not feel coerced into cooperation, but if Pete was too soft and the horse sensed a way out of working, he'd keep pushing back every time Pete asked for extra effort.

Pete simply sat still in the saddle, kept his leg on, and lifted his hands. No argument, no escalation, just a continued ask: *Will you, please?*

India took the hint and lifted his forehand in response. Slowly, almost grudgingly, he drew his energy up into his withers, then skipped lightly over the ground, his leading legs swapping position. He flicked his tail as he cantered on, clearly impressed with himself. I wanted to clap. His movement was graceful and light, everything his athletic build suggested he was capable of being.

"Good." Pete laughed, and eased up on the pressure in the

reins. India bounded forward, his ears pricked as he thundered up the long side of the arena.

"What an easy temper," I remarked to no one. "One tiny fit and then he's back in the zone."

"He's a horse in a million," Mimi said grudgingly.

I looked at her, but she was still watching Pete ride her horse.

If I wasn't mistaken, her gaze was wistful. I knew what it was like to see Pete coax the best from my horse in the dressage ring; he'd done it more than once when I was struggling with some movement in training. But I could see why it would be especially painful for Mimi, knowing that the rider chosen to replace her was going to score better and place higher than she ever had. I wished there was a way to let her know I got it; Pete was just so good at this, it was annoying.

Mimi didn't appreciate what I'd supposed was an empathetic expression. "You're loving this, aren't you?" she said.

"Loving—what?" I asked, caught on the wrong foot.

"Another feather in your cap," Mimi spat, losing her careful control of her temper. "Someone else's work in your barn. Everything I've done with India and Prince, years of hard work, and you two will get all the credit, all the glory." She started to shake her head, winced, and stilled. She put one hand on the collar, and I saw gnarled fingers, joints that didn't flex without pain. Mimi had been through the wringer; every ride had to cost her, but she'd kept on. Nothing had stopped her.

And then I knew for sure.

She wasn't going to retire. Her determination to return was written on her face, in every angry word.

I felt bad for her. I knew this woman could ride, and she'd devoted her life to eventing, and now it was going to be taken away from her. I had too many things that I loved to be comfortable watching someone be stripped of her passion. Jack, Pete, Marcus, the horses, my students, my friends, my farm, *eventing*—I needed all of them like oxygen. Even if Mimi had people she loved, who would she be when these horses were gone?

Mimi glared at me. She didn't want my sympathy. She wanted to hate me. Because I was a woman who could ride.

I didn't really blame her now, for all the dark looks and snarling glances. I'd be exactly like her, if I was in her paddock boots.

"You've done a lovely job with him," I said, unable to leave the silence hanging between us.

"He's a good horse," she said shortly. "Anyone could win with him."

Except you, I thought, and I wasn't proud of myself for thinking it.

"He needs the dressage score to win, though," I said. I didn't bother to say *Pete will get his dressage score up,* but I knew we were both thinking it.

"Eventing is not about winning, it's about *completing,*" Mimi snapped.

"Maybe it was twenty or thirty years ago," I replied. "But it's a new world now. We're stuck with it."

She didn't like that. "Modern eventing is broken. It's nothing like it used to be."

"Well, it's what we've got," I said. "And in modern eventing, you win some of those events you complete, or you go broke."

Mimi laughed, surprising me. "And do I look rich to you?" She gestured around her, inviting me to take a look at her six-horse barn, her tiny paddocks, and homemade cross-country jumps. "I'm a dying breed, and it's a shame people like you are what will replace me. I built this place with my own two hands, no sponsors, no lucky breaks. And for what?"

"Mimi," I began, keen to make her understand that none of this was personal, "I know it's awful losing horses—"

"No," Mimi interrupted. She turned her entire body to face me. "You have no idea what this is like. To be forced out, to be told you're not worth anything anymore—well, this will be you in thirty or forty years. It's a long time to wait, but you'll know what this is, eventually. And you'll know how wrong it is, too."

She turned on her heel and stalked back to the barn, leaving Pete and me alone at the dressage arena with the horse she would never ride again.

"Uh-oh," Pete said, reining back on the other side of the fence. "What did you say?"

I shook my head. "This wasn't me," I told him. "Not that it matters."

9

MIMI'S COLD WORDS put me in a bad mood as we drove the horses to Joan's farm. I was silent while we unloaded India and Prince, put them in their stalls with full hay nets, and hung around to make sure they settled in and drank a little water. Both seasoned competitors, they let the move to a new farm pass with just a few spooks and some trumpeting neighs that set every other horse off for a full five minutes. And then they dug into their hay nets and that was that.

Their easy acceptance of a new life annoyed me even more. Didn't they even wonder where Mimi was? Where was the loyalty?

I was being ridiculous and I knew it, but at the moment, all I wanted was to rush back to the motel and squeeze Jack close before he became just like a horse and imprinted on the next human to give him a square meal. If he said *Mama* to Gemma instead of me, I was going to lose it. What if Mimi was right, and in thirty years I was broken and put out to pasture and everyone who should have cared about me had written me off years ago, as the woman who cared more about horses than anyone who loved her?

Gemma wanted to get Jack out of the motel room, so we went to get them before we did evening feeding. On the way back to the motel, I sat and stewed in the passenger seat, while Pete tried and failed to talk with me about the new horses.

"What's the matter with you?" Pete asked as a heavy silence stretched between us. He swerved to avoid a squirrel in the road. "Jeez, the squirrels up here just do not care about cars."

"I'm in a bad mood," I informed him.

"You're going to have to be more specific than that."

"What's that supposed to mean?"

"I think we both know you are a woman of many bad moods. Is this one directed at me? Should I spend the evening alone?"

I sighed. "It's not about you. You're fine." Pete could be so sensitive. He always ruined a perfectly good sulk by getting his feelings hurt. "I'm just thinking about Mimi and her wife and having to quit horses and having nothing to replace them."

"Just a few small things, then."

"Don't make fun of me."

"I'm not." Pete patted my leg. "But you can't compare yourself to Mimi. The two of you are nothing alike."

He was very confident about this, but I wasn't so sure.

The winding road straightened as it came out of a thicket of forest and entered a tiny town. I looked at the shopfronts on either side. Most were closed and dusty, but there was an ice-cream shop and a little grocery store.

"Cute town," Pete said.

"Ca-tah-kin Creek," I attempted, reading a hand-painted sign on a shop window. "No, I missed a letter."

"Cah-*tok*-tin," Pete corrected me. "Have you been saying Catoctin Green wrong this entire time? Is that why the show secretary laughed at us when you picked up the packets?"

"It's possible," I grumbled. "I can't get any of the names right up here." The main river in this region was the Monocacy. I still hadn't tried to say it aloud.

"I've never once heard you stumble over a Florida name," Pete pointed out. "Apalachicola, Waccasassa, Micanopy, Caloosahatchee . . ."

"Those are child's play. Don't compare Florida words to Maryland words."

Pete laughed. "Most of the people I've spoken to up here can't even pronounce Alachua correctly."

"They're completely phonetic. You always emphasize the second-last syllable. Except when you don't. And you changed the subject."

"Well, are you still in a bad mood about Mimi?"

"No," I admitted. "I'm in a bad mood about words now."

"So," Pete said, "I guess that's something."

Gemma and Jack were waiting for us, already bundled up against the chilly weather and holding Marcus's leash as he sniffed happily outside the motel room. They piled into the back seat of the truck and we headed back to Joan's farm to do the evening chores. I kept turning around to tickle Jack, and felt bothered each time he turned his big eyes back to Gemma.

In the barn, I knelt in the shavings to unwrap Mickey's legs and peel away the brown paper keeping the poultice damp. I'd turn him out bare-legged for the night and most of the mud would dry and flake off, but the healing oils in it would still be tingling on his skin, working their magic.

A lot of equine sports medicine seemed to be witchcraft, even as science advanced and made riding ever more expensive. Special magnets, magic lasers, curative mud. Was any of it real? We didn't dare find out by skipping the treatments.

Anyway, yes, poultice absolutely worked. It was all the new stuff I used begrudgingly.

Mickey leaned down and sniffed at my hair, his hot breath tickling my neck. I smiled to myself as I unraveled the bandages, settling into this age-old routine.

And then I heard a weird, high-pitched cry from outside the barn.

Mickey jumped, and I shoved backward from him, my instincts in full control. He shied away from me and his hindquarters connected with the back wall, rattling the boards. The other horses, already tense from the strange noise, spun around their stalls in a panic at this new scary sound.

"What's going on?" Pete shouted, running out of the feed room. He saw me in Mickey's stall. "Was that you guys?"

"No," I said, pushing through the half-open stall door. I pulled it closed behind me, looking up and down the aisle for Gemma and Jack. "Was it the kids?"

I didn't see them.

Pete and I took off running at the same time.

Outside, a cold wind whipped through the trees as the sun began to sink behind the mountains. Joan's horses were already turned out, blanketed against the chill; they clustered near the water trough, kicking and shying. Something had upset them. The same shout that had startled our horses. "Where *are* they?" I cried, looking around the cluster of barns and outbuildings. "Gemma? Where are you?"

"We're here," Gemma called, coming around the corner of the barn with Jack on her hip. "We heard someone yell, and we went to see what it was, but we can't find anyone."

"It must have been Joan or her groom," Pete said, hurrying over to Joan's barn.

I looked at Gemma. "Did you hear where it came from?"

"That was the weird thing," Gemma said. "It seemed to come

from the backside of *our* barn. But there's no one behind it. I guess the wind is making sound travel funny."

"I hope no one's hurt." Gemma handed Jack to me, and he wrapped his little arms around my neck. "Hey, buddy," I whispered, feeling that warmth he always gave me seep through my cold bones. "Everything's okay, right, bud?"

Pete came back from Joan's barn, shaking his head. "The side door is locked and I don't want to pull back the sliding doors without a good reason. I don't hear anyone in there, though."

"The sound definitely was outside," Gemma said. "And I don't know how you'd have heard it from inside your barn, if it was in Joan's. The wind is too loud."

It *was* loud, I realized; the wind was moaning between the barns and roaring in the trees. It even whistled once or twice as I stood listening to it.

And it was cold. I wasn't even sure our horses should go outside in this weather. Maryland horses might be used to it, but our Florida horses were thin-skinned, even with rugs on. I shivered, and Pete slid his hand beneath my elbow, tugging me back to the barn. "Come on," he said. "Let's get everyone inside."

"I'm going to call Joan," I decided as we slipped through the side door and into the relative warmth of the closed-up barn. "Ask her if there's anyone out here we don't know about."

But the phone just rang and rang. Jack nestled into my neck as I tapped my thumb anxiously on my phone, willing Joan to answer. Finally, her voicemail picked up. I hesitated; was Joan a voicemail person, or would she just ignore it? Hardly anyone left messages anymore. But she was a lawyer, so she probably had to deal with them. By now, a few seconds of dead air were already recorded for her listening pleasure. I stammered a quick message about a strange sound and hung up.

Jack looked at me questioningly, wondering who I was talking to.

"Yes," I told him. "Voicemail! You'll probably never have to leave one."

He smiled.

Pete came out of the feed room with the horses' dinners stacked up in small buckets, and the whole barn erupted into hungry neighs. Jack strained and twisted his neck to see the horses.

"Back to Gemma you go," I told him, accepting the inevitable. "Mummy has to feed the ponies." She materialized beside me like a good witch and he reached for her eagerly. Whatever she murmured to him was lost beneath the impatient whinnies echoing from the stalls.

So much for weird noises, I thought, moving to take some of the buckets from Pete. We'd never hear them over a bunch of hungry horses.

I felt bad about leaving the horses inside all night, but the temperature was near freezing already, and it would be much colder by dawn, with a wind chill that was getting into the ridiculous region of the color chart. I just couldn't turn my Florida horses out in that kind of weather. So we promised everyone they could have turnout in the morning, loaded them up with hay, and flipped off the lights. All the humans were cold and morose as we waited for the truck to warm up. Even Marcus looked displeased; he curled up in a little ball against Gemma's leg and sighed, again and again, with that special beagle air of grievance. Only Jack clapped and grinned, seemingly delighted with the cold air. It must have been like a game for him, air that didn't cling to his skin with simmering heat, nearly liquid with humidity.

I didn't find the cold charming. Inspired by my dog, I made a dramatic show of looking at my weather app and being shocked by the results. "It's sixty-seven back at the farm," I announced, perversely determined to make the situation worse. "A lovely evening. And we're missing it to freeze our noses off here."

"It'll be cold there tomorrow," Pete predicted. "October cold fronts happen in Florida, too. You just don't want to admit it."

"A high of fifty," I conceded, flicking through the forecast. "And it will be windy, like it is here."

"Do you think it's the same wind?" Gemma began, and then she laughed. "Oh my God. I'm losing my mind."

"It kind of would be the same wind," Pete said thoughtfully. "If you consider it's caused by the same weather system."

"Let's go and get some food, Pete," I urged, putting away my phone and the unhealthy compulsion to tell everyone the windchill was twenty-eight degrees.

Warm air finally spilled from the vents, and Pete put the truck in gear. We were just driving past Joan's pretty farmhouse, all lit up and looking like a postcard, when the front door opened and Joan herself came running down the porch steps. She was wearing fleece pajamas under a winter coat. Even in that get-up she still, impossibly, looked put together. Like a woman running away from a murderer in a thriller novel, but keeping her sense of style intact.

Pete jammed on the brakes and cracked the window, letting cold air whistle into the cab. "What's up?" he asked, as if this was a normal neighborly stop.

Joan tucked the coat up close to her chin. "I got Jules's message. There shouldn't have been anyone else around the barns this evening; we fed up early, and we were done before you guys got here. Are you sure you heard someone shout?"

Pete looked at me. I nodded. "It was a high-pitched yell, like someone was surprised or hurt."

Joan shook her head vigorously, her hair falling over her

forehead. "I don't know what that could have been, but now I'm worried. I'll flip on the security cameras tonight, so, uh . . . don't do anything you wouldn't want caught on camera, okay?" She grinned.

Pete laughed. "We'll try to keep our clothes on."

"Shouldn't be too hard with this weather!"

"Don't get me started," I contributed, and Joan waved her hand at me.

I watched her run back to the house. "Do you think she has a secret control room with a bunch of monitors that show everything going on around the farm?"

"I don't know," Pete said. "Would you be jealous if she did?"

"I would," I said. "I absolutely would."

"I'll put it on the list," he promised.

We both laughed at that. The list, if it were ever printed out, would probably be fifteen feet long. The list was infinite and ever-expanding.

Like everything else.

We took a vote on the drive into town, and Mexican food won easily, so Pete drove us to a dark little dive just outside of Frederick where we could sneak Marcus in under a table near the door and no one was fussy about dogs, anyway.

I liked the joint; it reminded me of Ocala and some of the makeshift restaurants I'd grabbed tacos at there, places where it seemed like you were in someone's house instead of a restaurant, places where the dining area was carved out of an old feed store and there was still hay stuck between the floorboards. A server named Suzie, wearing sagging Wranglers and a fringed Western shirt, served us margaritas and iced teas and chips and house-made salsa, red-hot stuff that singed our chapped lips.

"I'm never moving back to the UK," Gemma announced, digging into the salsa. "You know we can't get Mexican like this there. And don't even get me started on the barbecue."

I slipped Marcus some tortilla chips and smiled at Gemma, heartened when she said things like *I'm never moving back*. I was going to need her for the rest of my life, or at least until Jack was graduating from college.

"So, what do we think that weird shout was tonight?" Pete asked.

Jack slapped his hands on the table.

It was the only answer any of us had.

"I really think it was a person," Gemma ventured at last. "And it sounded like a person getting hurt. Maybe someone stepping on a nail or something. It was quite a shriek, honestly."

"I don't want to play this like a Scooby-Doo murder mystery," I complained. "Don't we have enough going on without wondering who made the scream in the barnyard at sunset? This sounds like Joan's problem, and I like the way she's solving it. With lots and lots of security cameras."

"I was just making conversation," Pete said, giving me a look of such mild chastisement, I actually felt a little bad.

"Sorry," I muttered, tucking back into the chips and salsa.

"But we can talk about something else, if you prefer." He picked up his margarita and took a contemplative sip. "Like about the look I got from Rose Martin as you were trotting out of the jumping arena the other night."

"Rose Martin?" I sat up straighter, as if one of the current heroines of eventing was in the restaurant right now, evaluating my position on the chair. She *could* be, after all. "*The* Rose Martin?"

"That's right," Pete said, with a little smile that made me want to kiss him or kill him. I could never decide which. "*The* Rose

Martin was pretty impressed with your ride over the Intermediate course, judging by the nod she gave me."

There was a moment of quiet, made deafening by the roaring in my ears.

Rose Martin was a West Coaster, so she'd probably met Pete when he'd been on his California trip a few years ago. When he was playing dressage monk and working on his book between riding another trainer's horses. She'd come east for the Chesapeake Three-Day Event, and was staying in Maryland for the season to prep, like we were.

Pete ate another handful of tortilla chips and watched me wait for him to go on.

"Well, what did you say to her?" I demanded at last. "What did she say to you?"

"Nothing," Pete said. "She just gave me a nod, like I said."

"What *kind* of nod?" I was two seconds from lunging across the table and grabbing him by the collar.

"An impressed nod!" Pete shook his head. "Didn't I just say that?"

"Is that really the whole story?"

"Well, she had like five horses here. I don't think she had time to do anything more than nod."

"Pete! I need more information than that!"

Gemma was laughing, her shoulders shaking as she bent over the table. "You guys are ridiculous," she muttered. "So ridiculous."

Jack finally got his hand on the bowl of chips and upended it. Chips went raining across the table and onto the floor. Marcus was on them like a flash, crunching happily through as many as he could scarf down.

The server sighed and brought us a new bowl.

"Sorry," Pete said. "We'll leave a big tip."

"I can't believe you acted like Rose Martin had something to say about me and it was nothing but a nod," I grumbled, scooping up chips. Marcus licked my fingers.

"It was an impressed nod," Pete defended himself.

"No more," I warned him. "Not another word."

10

JOAN'S FARM WAS connected by a few farm lanes to a network of trails running into the Catoctin Mountains. She was always saying we should check them out, and midway through the week, we decided to take the big horses out for a conditioning ride, masquerading as a hack through the woods. The weather was finally easing up on us, and the sun had actual warmth in it as we tacked up Barsuk and Mickey. Gemma and Jack sat beneath a sycamore tree in Joan's fenced backyard, piling crispy brown leaves on top of Marcus, who was too busy napping on the cool grass to mind.

"Bye, Mummy and Dad! Have a nice ride!" Gemma called, waving Jack's hand for him. Jack opened and closed his fingers all by himself. It was adorable, and I felt my heart melt a little as I led Mickey to the mounting block in the center of the farmyard. Part of me wanted to stay and join them. Jack's first pile of fall leaves! He was experiencing new things with Gemma, instead of me.

"Are we okay, Mummy?" Pete asked, grinning. He was already on Barsuk, feet hanging below the stirrup irons. The gray horse cropped at the grass alongside the barn, eating like he'd never seen the stuff before and didn't know when he'd encounter it again. You'd never know these horses were turned out for fourteen hours a day.

"I'm fine." I sniffed and wiped at my eye. "I'm just allergic to Maryland."

"In October? You must be allergic to whatever the opposite of pollen is."

"Oh, leave me alone." I put my boot in the stirrup and hopped aboard Mickey. He walked away from the mounting block before I was in the saddle, as usual. I didn't have time to train him to stand still. That's what I told myself, anyway. I found the right stirrup with my toe and flexed my heels down, feeling that *this is right* sensation that overtook me every time I sat on Mickey. It was almost enough to counteract the pull I felt toward Jack, who had gone back to piling leaves on my beagle.

"You're just cute when you show emotions," Pete teased.

"You're cute when you're riding your horse, so let's go," I countered, nudging Mickey into a jog. The sudden command surprised him in a good way.

Mickey flicked his tail and tugged at the reins as we headed down the gravel trail behind the barns. I heard Barsuk's hoofbeats quickly close in behind us, nearly smothering the sound of Pete's laughter.

The morning hummed and rattled around us: a cool breeze in the tops of evergreen trees growing in dark clumps on hillsides, dry leaves scattering in our wake, small brown birds landing on the wire fences lining the farm lanes. The ground rose and fell on either side in undulating waves, a sea of chestnut and gold fields with the occasional island of emerald pasture, all of it interrupted periodically by farmhouses, their dignified brick and stone surrounded by stands of old trees. Ahead of us, the mountains waited, earth-toned slopes still patchy with orange and gold trees. The sky overhead was a pale robin's egg blue, feathered with fine cirrus clouds.

I took a deep breath of cool northern air. It was dry and crisp and nothing like the heavy, humid air of Florida.

It wasn't better. It was just different.

As the narrow farm lanes turned into wooded trails, hooking back and forth along the mountainside's gentle slopes, we let the horses choose their pace. They cantered up the steeper inclines and jogged or walked along the flatter sections of trail, turning their ears to listen to birds and squirrels and heaven knew what else. The trees closed in around us, and through their gray branches we could only catch occasional glimpses of the countryside we'd just ridden across. As we climbed higher, I started looking for a trail Joan had mentioned, marked on trees with a white blaze.

"Here it is," I said with relief, about forty-five minutes after we'd entered the woods. I was beginning to think I'd missed it. "Turn down this trail, Pete," I said over my shoulder.

Barsuk, close on Mickey's tail, would have followed us no matter where we went, anyway. He crowded against Mickey's hindquarters as we shuffled onto the narrower trail. I reined back Mickey as the trees suddenly opened up, and when I saw the low stone wall ahead of us, I pulled up and dismounted.

I did *not* want Mickey to think that was a cross-country jump.

Because below that wall there was nothing but treetops, and ahead was a clear view of the valley where we'd been staying for the past few weeks.

"Whoa," Pete breathed, and I heard him dismount, too. He walked Barsuk next to Mickey and stood by my side. Even well back from the old stone wall, we could look right across the countryside to distant mountains we couldn't even name. "Maryland is beautiful," Pete whispered, as if he was afraid someone would overhear him.

Florida, maybe.

He was right. The patchwork of farms spread out in front of us was gorgeous, fallow fields and autumn trees glowing in the midmorning sunlight.

"Can you see our farm?" I asked, trying to make sense of the twisting country roads and the dark trails of streams.

"I think . . . there?" He pointed, and I squinted in the general direction of his finger—there were farms out there all right, but any one of them might be our home base. This country was so *settled*, I thought, almost wistful. It reminded me of Ocala in some ways. Unlike the wilder stretches of North Florida where we lived, Ocala was largely established already, a grid of farms and businesses and communities. There was a comfort in that. Our High Springs nights could be very dark.

Suddenly a little farm complex jumped out at me: the farmhouse, barns, and pasture fences looked right. With my eyes, I followed the lane between pastures until it disappeared into a thatch of woods. "That's it," I told Pete, nudging his finger to the right a few centimeters.

"Ahh . . . you're right!"

We looked at the farm we'd left an hour ago.

Mickey and Barsuk chewed on the leaves from a branch hanging overhead and waited for us to get our acts together.

"There's Catoctin Green," Pete said. "I think I'm getting the hang of this, now."

"Oh, yeah, I see the cross-country course!" I laughed. "Talk about Beginner Novice. Those fences are tiny."

"This would be a cool place to watch an event from, if we ever weren't competing for some reason."

"And if we were in Maryland while we weren't competing, which we wouldn't be." I turned back to Mickey. "The trail goes down past the wall and loops back to the main trail we started on," I said. "Let's go that way, change it up a little, and then we'll go home." Where we'd have more horses to ride, then have lunch with Gemma and Jack, then drop them back at the motel for their naps, and then . . . The day spun away from me in a series of chores and appointments.

"Sure," Pete agreed, but he didn't move. He was still gazing across the farmland.

I shook my head at him. Farmer Pete, dreaming of the old country.

I'd found a high spot of ground to stand on and was just positioning Mickey alongside it, ready to mount, when Pete finally turned away from the overlook.

Barsuk grabbed one more tree branch for the road, leaves hanging from his mouth. Pete tugged a stick free but let him keep the leaves. "Hopefully those won't kill you," he told the horse, tossing the stick aside.

"He wouldn't eat a poisonous tree," I said. "Horses aren't stupid."

"And this isn't Florida, where half the species are invasive murder-plants," Pete agreed.

"I love Florida." I sighed, and hopped into the saddle. "Here, Pete, use this spot to mount."

"Do you really love Florida more than this?" Pete asked.

I circled Mickey, ducking a tree branch as I turned him back to face Pete and Barsuk. "Are you kidding? Of course I do. This is pretty. But Florida's home."

"Home is where the horses are," Pete kidded, walking Barsuk to the spot I'd used to mount Mickey. "Ho, buddy," he told the horse. "Stand up."

"Home is where the palm trees are," I retorted, although we only had a few palm trees around Briar Hill Farm, and most of them were down by the spring. Around the house and barns, we had live oaks—those ancient, gorgeous sentinels of the southeast—and water oaks, their pretty but dangerous cousins, dropping branches every time it rained and occasionally just splitting right in two.

Pete settled into Barsuk's saddle and we walked the horses side by side down the trail. It skirted wide of the stone wall and took us on a more moderate route down the mountainside. The trees and shrubs began to seem monotonous, and I felt a little chilly in the shade. I zipped my windbreaker up to my chin and hunched my shoulders, wishing we'd find another break in the forest. But beside me, Pete looked happy as a horse in a hay shed, looking all around him as if the woods contained some special beauty only he could see.

I mean, it was pretty, especially where the leaves were changing color, but wasn't it a lot of the same over and over again?

I was still watching Pete's expression with some suspicion when we found ourselves back on fairly level ground . . . and I realized we hadn't regained the main trail. A patch of sunlight ahead of us grew until it was obvious we were heading out of the cover of forest. I wondered how far away from our entry point we were. We'd been in the woods for over an hour and seemed to have been traveling north most of the time. If we had to turn around and go all the way back, we'd never recover this day.

Pete realized we were off course, too. "That's not where we came in," he said, frowning at four-board fences surrounding green pastures. A long, beautiful barn with an adjacent indoor arena appeared in the distance, along with an outdoor ring encircled by stadium lights. "But it's definitely a big equestrian center."

"I have absolutely no idea where we are," I admitted, "and I have no phone service. But maybe when we get closer . . ."

A few grazing horses near the barns turned to look over at us, and as I saw their intent, I gathered the reins more tightly.

Mickey began to jig-jog, excited for new friends, and the horses came galloping toward us. Barsuk squealed and bucked, and Pete hauled back on the reins to get his head up. Mickey started bouncing up and down, plunging like he didn't know whether he should rear, buck, gallop forward, or race backward. By the time the pastured horses reached the fence line, both our horses were in the middle of grade-A, prime shit fits.

And then everyone just stopped and stared at one another.

The pastured horses lowered their heads and blew hard through their nostrils.

Mickey and Barsuk did the same thing.

"All right, guys, have we established that you don't know each other?" I asked. "Because it's time to move on."

"Follow the trail?" Pete asked, cautiously turning Barsuk's head. The horse resisted at first, then plunged forward.

I sighed. "Wherever it may lead."

It looked like it led straight to that barn, actually. Well, at least whoever was running this place would know where the hell we were.

"One good thing," I added. "At least we know for sure this isn't Mimi's place."

She was the last person I wanted to run into.

11

RIDING INTO A stranger's equestrian center was not my favorite activity, but we didn't have much choice—if we went back into the woods, we were probably going to end up hopelessly lost and there would be search parties, local news coverage, embarrassing interviews with my mother . . . In short, not a good time. So we rode up the farm lane, the horses in the paddocks dancing alongside us, to the spacious entrance of the center-aisle barn. I liked the style of the place: open windows along each side, white paint with gray trim, a few decorative cupolas punctuating the clean lines of the metal roof.

"Classy," I remarked, and Pete murmured in agreement.

The barn itself was bustling with midday action. Rock music spilled out of the center aisle, and the ringing sound of a hammer carried that farrier rhythm we knew so well. A truck was backed up to the barn aisle's broad doorway, with a forge hissing on the tailgate. At the sound of our horses' hooves hitting the pavement, the farrier himself straightened up from his bent position, leaving a red-hot horseshoe hanging on the anvil. He pushed back his cap, revealing red hair above an unlined face. I'd place his age in the midthirties, but his skin was fantastic. Not at all what I'd have expected of a farrier.

"Well, hello," he said in a friendly tone. "Looking for Sean or Nadine?"

He sounded almost like he was from New York, which was interesting.

Maryland's chief accent, I'd found, was nothing. Absolutely no accent to be found.

"Uh, hi," Pete replied, glancing around with a sheepish smile. "Actually, no. We got turned around in the woods and ended up here."

"Oh, well, that's easy to do. You're not the first, actually. Need a rest? Feel free to stay awhile." The farrier grinned. "We don't bite, except for Nestle there in the first stall, and we just keep hay in front of him so his mouth is always full."

"We can just get directions and get out of your hair—"

"Yes," I said, interrupting Pete. I needed a restroom. "If that's okay."

"Crossties just down there," the farrier said, pointing into the barn. "Help yourself to a halter on a stall door along the way. They all belong to the school, so no one will get upset."

The school? I glanced at Pete, then shrugged and dismounted. Mickey shifted, looking around the unfamiliar barn warily, but I led him inside with my shoulders back and my chin up. *Confidence, big boy,* I thought, hoping my horse would pick up on my subliminal messaging. *No one here is gonna eat you.*

Except maybe Nestle. The chocolate-brown pony ran his long yellow teeth along his stall bars as we passed.

It was a lovely barn inside as well as out. The stalls on either side of the aisle were fairly new, stained wood front panels with black bars on top, well-lit from above, the windows open to the pastures beyond. Most were empty, but a few had horses inside; they looked up from their hay and nickered with interest at Mickey and Barsuk. Our horses fluttered their nostrils in reply.

Near the center of the barn, six crosstie bays faced each other, with a tack room on either end. The rubber mats had drains in the center, and there were heat lamps installed overhead for winter bathing. Racks on the walls held grooming supplies. Everything was impressively clean and tidy. Someone with a real organization complex ran this barn, I thought appreciatively. I pulled out my phone and took a few pictures to send to Lacey—she'd probably have similar racks installed at Alachua by the time we got back to Florida.

With Mickey crosstied in a borrowed halter worn over his bridle, I took a grateful break in a well-appointed bathroom and came out to find someone waiting to say hello. A dark-haired young woman, wearing breeches, argyle knee socks, and a heather-gray sweatshirt with LONG POND EQUESTRIAN TEAM stenciled across the front, looked at me with an inquiring expression.

We faced each other for a moment and then her gaze flicked to the horses. Back to me. Back to the horses—specifically, Mickey. I waited for her to ask me who the hell I was and why my horses were in her barn. The farrier was probably extending invitations that weren't his to give.

"Oh my God," she said at last. "You're Jules Thornton, aren't you?"

Behind me, Pete muttered something that might have been *Morrison*.

"Yeah, that's me," I replied, fighting back a grin. I loved being recognized outside of events. It didn't happen that often; I mean, I was an event rider, not a rock star. But every now and then, in the right place, someone knew my face and my horse well enough to pick me out of a crowd.

"Wow, um, I didn't expect to find you in my barn!" The woman blushed and put her hands up to her face like a teen confronted with a pop idol. She shook her head, smiling. "How does this happen?"

"We didn't expect to crash your party," I told her, "but we got lost in the woods and ended up here."

"Oh, the Catoctin Mountain trails. Yeah, that checks out. They're *so* badly marked. You wouldn't believe some of the things that have gone on out there. Um . . . do you want a drink? Water? Or, it's cold. Maybe a coffee or—a hot chocolate—um—" She was really frazzled.

I was delighted enough to put her out of her misery. "I think we're fine. We just need to figure out how to get back to our farm. And your place is gorgeous, by the way."

"Great. Thanks! Okay." She shook her head really quickly, like she was trying to get hold of herself. "Um, well, I'm Nadine. Nadine Casey. I'm the barn manager. You're at Long Pond . . . it's a boarding school for girls. My husband, Sean, is the head instructor."

"And I'm Kevin," the red-haired farrier said, walking up with a small horse trailing behind him. Her hooves looked fantastic, trim and shining with new silver shoes on the front. Kevin seemed like a real keeper. "And *this* is Star, and she's all shod up and good as new. Want me to put her away, Nadine?"

"She can actually go out, if you don't mind, Kev. Thank you. So much."

Kevin turned Star around and the pony followed him down the aisle.

Nadine looked back at me. "So, your farm . . . where did you say you're staying?"

We managed to get directions back to Joan's farm out of her. Luckily, a trail that wound directly behind the neighboring farm would take us back to the country lane we'd followed into the woods in the first place.

"Don't worry about trespassing, by the way. It's Rosemary Beckett's place," Nadine explained. "She runs a rescue farm, and she's a real sweetheart. Teaches horse management here part time."

"How nice," I said, not especially eager to meet this Rosemary, even if she was a real sweetheart. Rescue owners always seemed to want me to take on project horses that were really unsuited to my work. For free. I didn't blame them, not at all; I just wasn't at that place in my career where I could afford to train adoption-only horses that would go Novice at best. Maybe someday, but not today. I started to turn toward Mickey, saying, "Well, we should be getting back."

"It was really great to have you here. Sorry I was so—" Nadine paused as a teenage girl suddenly appeared next to her. "What, Abby? I'm with these people—"

"Sorry," the teenager said unrepentantly. "But the sign-up sheet for Mimi's clinic is full, and I wanted to put my name on it. Is there more room?"

"Oh, yes. Just grab another sheet of paper and stick it on the board, will you?" Nadine looked back at us. "Sorry, everyone wants to ride with Mimi Pulaski! Do you guys know her?"

I blinked at our hostess, leaving Pete to take over. "We do know her, yeah," he said.

Nadine waited a moment, expecting him to continue. When he didn't, she shrugged and went on. "She's a big supporter of our program here. We love having her out for clinics. Of course, since she broke her collarbone, we've had to cut the riding demo portion, which is too bad. But she's such an amazing horsewoman. It's so cool that you know her! I guess all the upper-level eventers know each other, though, right?"

"Right," Pete agreed, smiling back at her. "One big happy club."

"I don't know if you'd have time," Nadine said, "but we really could use a riding demo for the clinic . . . and I know some of my eventing girls really admire you guys."

"Oh, you want *us* to ride?" I blurted, surprised.

"I'm sorry." Nadine looked down. "That was presumptuous."

"No, it's fine," Pete said. "If it fits into our schedule, we could."

"Really? Next Wednesday afternoon, around two? The girls would love it, and I'm sure Mimi wouldn't mind. We'll be having a supper afterward in the viewing lounge, with some of the parents, and we'd love to have you join us for that, too."

I pictured myself riding under Mimi's instruction. She'd probably light a hoop on fire and tell me to jump through it.

Nadine caught my expression and blushed all over again. "Oh, jeez, you guys are too busy to come out here and ride for a bunch of teenagers. I'm so—"

"No, don't apologize," I interrupted, before she could say *sorry* again. "You just caught us by surprise. Trust me, we're no stranger to teaching teenagers."

"We'll think about it," Pete offered. "Wednesday around two, right? We'll reach out."

"Great, um—hang on." Nadine dug in her pocket and gave me a business card, a little crumpled and damp but still legible. "You can text me. Thanks again!"

I gave her a tight smile and turned to untie Mickey. "Let me just get your halter back to you," I told Nadine. "Time to go home, Mickey boy."

We were halfway back to Joan's farm before Pete said, "We're going to have to go to that clinic, aren't we?"

"This is the last time I go for a ride in the mountains," I grumbled.

12

IT WAS OFFICIAL—I needed more goods on Mimi Pulaski. There was no possible correlation between the steely-eyed witch I knew and the crowd favorite Nadine described, so the truth had to be somewhere in the middle. I suspected that, at heart, Mimi was just a vulnerable woman who had spent her life on horseback and was being forced to give it up for love—what an uncomfortable position to be in. It would make anyone slightly crazy.

It was either that, or she was a supervillain with the power to mask her true self among the impressionable teenage girls of Long Pond.

Because this was the horse business, I considered either answer to be just as likely to be true.

Lacey agreed. She'd called me up while I was cleaning up after our trail ride to share that Jordan, Lindsay, and Maddox had formed a drill team among the younger riders and were plotting to have them perform in the High Springs Thanksgiving Day Parade. "So far they've only had two crashes, and luckily those were at the walk. I told them no trotting in formation until they figure out the walking part."

"Lacey, do I need to forbid this?" I asked wearily. I did not want to call Lindsay and pull rank, but my students were used to riding with at most four other horses in the arena, all of them keeping to the rail while one rider at a time took a course of fences. They didn't have the rowdy, free-for-all riding background I thought they'd need to safely ride four abreast in a circle or trot those figure-eights where it looked like they'd crash but at the last minute they didn't.

"I think they'll scare themselves out of it pretty soon," Lacey said. "Ricky has already dropped out and he was the first one to sign on. Maisey's sticking with it out of the pleasure of showing up her brother, but come on, Maisey doesn't stick to anything for long. Remember when she was going to be a bareback performer?"

Honey was a wide, round-bodied pony and Maisey had slipped around her barrel like a Hula-Hoop the moment the horse stepped into a trot. There was no more talk of bareback performances.

"So what are you going to do about your new nemesis?" Lacey asked, having run out of co-op kid stories to share.

"Try to dig up some more info on her," I said. "But since I've already spoken to everyone I know about her, I'm not counting on big results."

Joan seemed like the most reliable resource for the information I craved, but I had to wait for her to finish her civilian job first. By the time she was dressed in breeches and boots and strolling down the farm lane, we were already mixing evening feed and Marcus was sitting at the end of the barn aisle, watching the truck to make sure we didn't get into it without him.

"As if I'd leave you anywhere," I told my beagle, stroking his long, silken ears. He gave me a lick and turned on his Soulful Look, which is a powerful thing in a beagle. I melted a little and dug into my pocket until I found a baby carrot for him.

With Marcus crunching the carrot in contentment and Pete in the feed room, I meandered across the farmyard just in time to catch Joan as she arrived. "Hey, stranger," I called. "Nice night for a ride, huh?"

"Jules!" Joan had the grace to act as if every time she saw me was the first and most delightful meeting of her life. "How has your day been?"

"Somewhat eventful," I confessed. "We got lost in the mountains."

Joan laughed. "If you can get lost in the Catoctins, never go out west, okay? I'd hate to see what the Rockies could do to you."

"No problem. I don't see any reason to ever go there."

"Well, you could go for vacation."

"Vacation?" I snorted. "Never heard of her."

Joan shook her head, still smiling. "You big-time pro riders. Someday you'll remember there's a world outside of eventing."

I highly doubted it. "Any updates on the phantom yell we heard yesterday?"

"Nothing, and I don't think we'll ever figure it out. Maybe it was an owl."

"An owl? What kind of owl shouts like a human?" The owls at Briar Hill Farm were legion in number, and they all called *Whooo?* when they weren't laughing like ghouls in the oak trees.

"Birds can be weird." Joan glanced toward her barn, impatient to leave. I was keeping her from her riding. "I should—"

"Before you go," I said quickly. "Mimi."

Joan lifted an eyebrow. "I told you she wasn't going to be your biggest fan."

"When we got off the mountain today, we ended up riding over to this school—"

"Long Pond? Sean and Nadine's barn."

"Right, so you know them. And apparently, everyone there loves Mimi. The kids are, like, her biggest fans. And I have to tell you, we didn't get a 'loves kids and small animals' vibe from her. So if there's a human heart beating under that armor, I would love to know more about it. I don't want to fight with her, and neither does Pete, but she's making that difficult. It would be nice to end whatever feud this is before she takes it public." If she hadn't already. I couldn't forget Sandy Sullivan telling me we were in for trouble with Mimi before we'd even met her. At least a few members of the Maryland eventing community knew that Mimi wanted to wage war with Jules and Pete Morrison.

Joan sighed and looked longingly at her barn. She wanted to ride, and I was keeping her from it. But Joan was at her core a professional, and I was a paying client. Slowly, thinking about every word, she said, "I think that Mimi's passion for her horses extends to teaching, but not to making friends with her competitors. You follow me?"

"That she's a lovely coach, but we're always going to be at war?"

"As long as you're in Maryland," Joan replied, shaking her head and smiling at the same time. "But, hey, look on the bright side. She's retiring from competition, and you're going back to Florida. Whatever little war she wants to start here, it can't chase you. If I were you, I'd keep away from her as much as possible. That way it's less about 'burning bridges' and more like, 'Mimi? Never really talked to her.' You know what I mean?"

"Yeah, that actually makes tons of sense. The less contact with her, the easier it is to deny whatever stories she might want to tell about me." This wasn't my first rodeo in the gossipy, backstabbing equestrian world. "So, keep my head down until we can get the heck out of your state? That's your suggestion?"

"Precisely. You're a fast learner." Joan winked. "Now, I better get tacked up or I'm going to lose what little daylight we've got left. Talk later, Jules."

I walked back to our barn, matching my footprints in the gravel to the ones I'd left behind on the way to intercept Joan. I was really glad I'd talked to her, gotten a second opinion on Mimi. If Joan was right, there was nothing I could say or do to change Mimi's mind about me. We just had to get through our Maryland stay while interacting with her as little as possible. And that meant we needed to forget about riding with her at Nadine's clinic on Wednesday.

But that didn't assuage my feeling of guilt, which wasn't entirely rational but existed nonetheless, for taking her horses away and leaving her so desperate to get them back, she was willing to risk another rider's safety. That was a big deal. Safety was paramount in the eventing community. No matter how we felt about each other personally, we took care of each other out there. This sport was dangerous, and no one wanted to see a fellow rider get hurt.

Mimi was crossing a line, and as much as I wanted to be angry with her about it, I also knew there had to be serious hurt driving such inappropriate actions.

I felt like I wanted to help her.

It was silly, I knew. I wasn't a therapist; I could barely handle my own problems and hang-ups. But the way I still struggled at times to leave Jack in Gemma's arms was a reminder that back in the spring months, when I was supposed to be happily climbing up that mounting block to resume my career, I'd had real fear keeping me from riding. What if I'd decided to quit competing? It wouldn't have been a decision I could easily live with. I'd always be straining to get back in the tack. I'd have done what I thought was necessary for my family, had it come to that, but I'd have been miserable for the rest of my life—or as long as my self-imposed prohibition lasted.

I'd have had to find something else, or go crazy. What else was there?

Teaching, that was all.

Mimi was a good coach, apparently. I wondered if there was something there.

Pete had set out the feed buckets, so I scooped up a few and started heading into stalls, dumping grain into bins while the horses crowded me, grumbling and pawing to tell me I'd taken too long. "I haven't eaten *my* dinner," I reminded them, pitching my voice to the barn at large. "But no one cares about that!"

"They really don't," Pete remarked.

I followed him back into the feed room with the empty buckets. "Rugs tonight?"

"I think so, yeah. What do you want to do for dinner?"

The idea of the evening stretching ahead of us, another restaurant or bag of takeout, then the trials of sharing that tiny space with Jack and Gemma, suddenly seemed impossible to deal with.

"I want to move out of our motel room. Did you ask management?"

"Ah, I forgot." Pete had managed to forget for the past three days. "Sorry. I'll do it—"

"Right now," I interrupted, before he could say *tomorrow.* "Call them up. I can't take another night in one crowded room."

"Okay, okay," Pete said, as though I was the unreasonable one. "Let me go outside where there's better reception."

"Don't take no for an answer," I warned him. "Or I'll go down there and forcibly evict someone."

"They frown on that," Pete said, leaving with his phone in hand.

I sighed and looked around the little feed room. With a space heater and a pillow, I'd be tempted to sleep here tonight. I'd done worse. We'd lived in a horse trailer, for heaven's sake.

On a whim, I pulled out my own phone and opened Facebook. I was a member of about six thousand equestrian-related groups, so what was one more? I joined a group that promised temporary stabling and housing for equestrians in the region and started flicking through listings.

A post caught my eye almost immediately—it was for an RV that could be set up anywhere around Frederick County. The beast was so big it was more like a two-bedroom apartment than a camper, with pop-outs that made a full living room and a tiled shower that looked downright glamorous. I admired the photos, then went to message the owner—and was surprised to recognize the name of the person listing it. Rosemary Beckett! That was the neighbor Nadine had mentioned, who ran that rescue farm next to Long Pond.

Would Rosemary be like every other horse rescuer and try to send me home with a couple of free horses from the grab bag? Probably, but I was just anxious enough to get out of our motel room that I was willing to risk it.

Hi! We're in Maryland for the eventing season and I met your neighbor Nadine today. Would it be possible to learn more about your RV? Looking for space ASAP!

And, Send. My phone made a satisfying whooshing sound.

I was smiling to myself when Pete came into the feed room, shaking his head. "Sorry," he said, "but they don't have anything this week . . . Why are you smiling like that? It makes me nervous."

"I found us a solution," I told him, handing him my phone. "Just look at the pictures."

He whistled as he flicked through the gallery. "That's quite a camper."

"It's a full house on wheels. I think it might be bigger than our actual house."

"Looks close. I don't suppose we can afford it, though."

"Oh, we can afford it," I said happily, taking my phone back. "Things are cheaper here. We're not in Ocala during hunter/jumper season anymore. And . . . here's a reply already!" I skimmed the paragraph from Rosemary Beckett. "She says it's ready to go and we could move in this evening. All she has to do is plug in the electricity."

"Where is this?" Pete was used to my snap decisions, so he barely blinked.

"Right next to Long Pond, where we ended up earlier today. It's called . . . let me see . . . Notch Gap Farm." Rosemary sent me the Airbnb listing for the RV and I flicked through the reviews. "Look at all the five-star reviews," I said, holding up my phone again. "None of them even include the word 'murder.'"

"Victims can't write reviews," Pete muttered, but he was already looking up our new landlord for himself. "Fine, I guess. Seems safe enough. What now?"

"We turn out the horses, then we go back to that motel and we get packed," I said, feeling triumphant. "Gemma will love having her own room."

Gemma was thrilled to find out we were moving to a two-bedroom; so thrilled, in fact, that it was mildly insulting. But we'd all sleep better, especially Jack, so she had the motel room essentially packed by the time we got back, and after we'd showered and put on clothes better suited for meeting landlords than our filthy barn togs, we drove over to Notch Gap Farm.

The night had fully closed in by this point, and the wooded lane to the farm was a little disconcerting. But after we'd rumbled over a bridge, the lights of a house and barn appeared through the branches, and then the whole farm spread out before us. There were wide-open spaces on either side of the truck, and a well-lit brick farmhouse sitting snugly beside a large barn.

Two figures came onto the front porch and waved.

"They seem friendly," I observed.

"Remind me how you found them?" Gemma asked.

"Friends of friends," I said before Pete could say anything.

"Cool." That was all Gemma needed to know.

I hopped out of the truck and walked up to meet Rosemary and a man who turned out to be her husband, Stephen.

They were the sort of people who instantly put one at ease, especially the kind-eyed Rosemary. *Absolutely zero chance they'd murder us,* I thought, as Stephen led me up a clay driveway between the barn and the house, waving for the truck to follow.

The headlights picked out a wooden fence at the top of a slope behind the house, with a farm lane turning off in either direction. Stephen walked me to the right, where the RV waited for us in all its sleek splendor. The interior and exterior lights were on, showing off a large front porch under a canopy and the chunky pop-outs that were fully extended. Next to it, the back side of an old barn loomed. The hillside fell away on either side of it.

"I love how the barn is built into the hillside," I said. "Are there stalls on two levels?"

"No, the horse stalls are only on the bottom level, where the land flattens out. This level has storage and the tractor, hay, that kind of thing. You can go in and see it tomorrow, if you want," Stephen offered. "But for now, here's the key to your home for the next few weeks."

"Thank you so much. You can't even imagine what it's been like . . ." I went up the metal steps and unlocked the RV. Inside was exactly as advertised, clean and fresh and spacious. "Oh my goodness." I sighed. "It's about time I had some good luck."

"Rough month?"

"I would say it's just more of the usual. You're a horseman, right? You get it."

The truck pulled up alongside the RV. Stephen turned and waved. To me, he replied, "My wife is the equestrian. I moved here from New York City to be with her. Best decision of my life, even if horses do still make me nervous."

"Let me give you a little advice," I said, watching Pete hop out of the truck. "It's not the horses you have to watch out for, it's the people."

"Funny," Stephen said. "My wife says the same thing."

13

THE NEXT MORNING, we all sat together in the RV's kitchenette for toast and a chat about how well we'd slept. There was a general consensus that the RV had changed our lives forever, and I suggested to Pete that we buy one back in Florida. We could use it for all those upcoming distant events he wanted to travel to.

"With what money?" Pete asked.

"Whatever we win at the many three-day events we're going to use it at?" I bit into my toast and smiled around it.

Pete snorted and dropped more bread into the toaster. Unbelievably, the RV fridge had come stocked with bread, butter, eggs, and milk. A little horse head magnet was stuck to the freezer door; pinned beneath it was a note that said we could order dinner from the Blue Plate Diner and it would be delivered directly to the fridge for us. Signed, Rosemary.

I felt like we were being hosted by a good fairy. I wondered what else Rosemary could solve for me. I wondered if Rosemary would have advice for how I should handle Mimi.

I wondered if she *knew* Mimi.

Nadine said Rosemary taught something about horses at the school as well, so the answer was almost certainly yes. I could ask Rosemary about Mimi, say that we were supposed to work with her on Wednesday but weren't sure how welcoming she'd be, because of the horse situation. Maybe she'd be more forthcoming than Joan about Mimi's backstory, which no one else seemed willing to share. Surely a woman who ran a rescue farm and stocked a rental RV with breakfast foods was more apt to offer actual advice, or even a personal olive branch, than simply shrugging and saying the woman didn't like me.

"What are you plotting?" Pete asked suspiciously. "You're being very quiet."

Gemma chortled. "Always a bad sign. Jack gets that from you."

"Nothing," I said. "Don't gang up on me."

"We aren't ganging up on you," Pete assured me. "We're just teaming up to make sure it's a fair fight."

I made a face at him, finished my toast, and went back to the bedroom—the luxury of a bedroom with a door!—to pull on breeches and warm socks. Another day of riding in the chilly Maryland wind was upon us.

Gemma and Jack elected to stay at the RV—"Jack has some cartoons to catch up on," Gemma explained gravely—so we left them to the comfort of the carpeted living room floor and headed out. Marcus, sprawled on the sofa, didn't even look up as we closed the door behind us.

At Joan's farm, every horse had the wind up their tail—every single one. We brought them in from turnout like we were handling crazed dinosaurs, bundled them into their stalls, and looked at each other wearily while they growled and banged through their breakfast.

"Let's go home and forget riding," I suggested.

Pete sighed. "If only."

Riding was going to be an adventure. As I swung into Mickey's saddle an hour later, I felt like I was climbing into a roller coaster. The cold wind was still whipping and Mickey launched forward as soon as my leg was over him, snorting and tossing his head when I reined back and demanded he stand. Pete got a similar response from Barsuk, who nearly skittered out from under him and raced past Mickey, his tail lashing up and down.

"I should've taught you manners when I had the time," I muttered, leaning back on Mickey's reins like an up-down lesson kid on a runaway pony.

Mickey shoved into the bridle, his jaw pushing against the restraint of his flash noseband. When that didn't make me ease up on the pressure, he tried other tactics: he jigged, he cantered in place, he resisted circling. I set my jaw and kicked him through all of it. What a waste of time! My big horse was seriously acting feral this morning, and it was all because of the damn weather. At the other end of the arena, Barsuk squealed and bucked. I looked up at the clear blue sky, the wash of colorful leaves scattering through the air as another gust of cold wind came rushing down the mountainside, and wished very much that I was back home in Florida.

Horses are simply too happy in the cold.

Not that I want my horse to be unhappy, but . . . oh, forget it. I think everyone knows what I mean.

"This is a dressage day and you are going to do dressage," I informed Mickey in a clipped tone, turning him toward the arena. "If it kills us."

"Maybe not the best sentiment," Pete drawled, cantering past on a wild-eyed Barsuk.

He gave up before I did, taking the gray horse in and emerging from the barn a short while later with India. I brought Mickey down to a walk, which was almost flat-footed after half an hour of arguing, and watched the new horse with interest. So did Mickey.

No one knew him yet. India and Prince were turned out in a small paddock together, and they'd only been ridden for short hacks around the farm lanes in the few days they'd been here. Pete had been planning on their first dressage schools today, and I thought he might actually use the cold wind to his advantage. The weather would sharpen them up, and he could praise them for quick reactions to seat and leg, something they hadn't been giving to Mimi.

As they approached the arena, I had a feeling there'd be a lot of quick responses today. The tall horse seemed even taller than usual, as if he was standing on his toes. The tips of his pricked ears were like a pair of satellites trained on Mickey and me.

I gave myself a moment to salivate over the horse, turning Mickey in a tight circle so we didn't get too far away.

God, he was gorgeous. Horses were gorgeous, weren't they?

Tears pricked at my eyes and I blinked them away, knowing I could blame the wind if Pete saw them, but perfectly aware I was having another one of those hormonal bumps that made me feel completely overwhelmed by the beauty of the natural world—specifically, horses. I never used to cry over them before, but having a baby had done all sorts of things to my brain. Mostly bad things. At least I had Jack.

The gate clanged shut behind Pete and Mickey tucked his butt under his back before scooting forward, snorting. I lurched along with him, barely keeping my seat. Ah, the endless beauty of horses.

"Enough of that! Dressage day isn't over yet! And I'm going to survive this day to see Jack at the end of it," I promised him. "Circles! Circles until you behave!" I spun that goofy horse around in an eight-meter circle until his walk grew flat-footed instead of springy. Knowing I had gotten as much good behavior as I could expect, I let him trot after that, but promised him a circle for every bolt. "Ten more minutes, and you can go in," I said, and Mickey snorted.

India gave Pete no such insolence. The mahogany bay gelding was on high alert as he scoped out his new surroundings, but he managed to walk on a loose rein without darting away. I watched Pete out of the corner of my eye as Mickey bounced around the arena, jealous of his new horse's quiet poise.

It took a few more circles, but finally I had Mickey's attention on me at the trot, his mouth softening as he reached down for the contact. I half halted him with an overexaggerated motion, slowing him nearly to a halt, then pushed him forward into another working trot. Mickey sprang forward happily, mouthing the bit before twisting his neck to one side and tugging on the reins.

One of those days, I thought resignedly, and circled him to the inside to work on suppling and softness. Ordinarily we'd be done by now, but today was shaping up to be an hour-long ride if we were going to get any real work done.

But at least I wasn't really noticing the wind anymore. All this work had me roasting hot inside my coat. If it wouldn't risk a meltdown from Mickey, I'd have tried taking it off, but removing a jacket on horseback was a training activity we'd never had to practice before.

Sweating, I wound Mickey through the arena, occasionally passing close to Pete and India. The new horse seemed to have settled into Pete's riding style without hesitation. It was a good thing we'd shipped him over right after that first ride at Mimi's farm. If I were the former rider and saw him going this well for someone else so quickly, I'd have gone out of my mind with jealousy.

India bowed into Pete's reins as if he'd been waiting for this day to come for his entire horsey life. Maybe he was a man's horse,

I reflected. Some horses just preferred men. Not a lot of them, obviously. I smirked to myself, and Mickey took advantage of my moment of absence to shimmy sideways and spook at something only he could see.

Well, I thought, squeezing my inside rein to get Mickey's attention back, it was also possible that Pete had been India's person all along. Sometimes horses just seemed to be waiting for their match.

And if that was the case—I pressed my left leg against Mickey's side as he wiggled out of his bend—then good, because Pete needed that. A horse who loved him and worked for him as his partner. Pete had been looking for that ever since Regina hurt herself back at the old farm. I knew he and Barsuk were a fine team, but Barsuk was the kind of amiable horse who would go nicely for anyone with soft hands and a kind way about them. Regina had been Pete's horse, his co-captain on course, and she'd even taken charge when she felt it was necessary. Relationships like that were special, and rare. But Regina was retired and expecting her first foal, so her thoughts had turned firmly away from human companionship. She lived out with my broodmare, Carla, and the two of them were engaged in some kind of complicated matriarchal relationship that only horses, and mares in particular, would understand. When Pete walked out to the fence to say hello to her, she looked at him as if he was a relic from her past life—curious about how he was doing, but not too curious, either.

I was rooting for India to be Pete's next great partnership, even if the horse belonged to an owner I didn't quite trust. India was young, talented, and ready to move up. And since he was already competing at Intermediate, Pete could skip years of work preparing him for upper-level competition. They just needed time to get to know each other.

"And I've got you as a partner," I murmured to Mickey, getting him to trot in a straight line for five strides before his attention was taken up by a lowing cow in the distance, "for better or for worse."

Just like a marriage.

We were just stepping into the canter for the first time when Pete slackened the reins on India's neck and turned the horse's head for the gate. "I'm going to hack him along the farm lane," he called over the howling wind. "Then I'm taking him in and I'll do Prince next."

"Be careful out there, please." I gestured to the bending tree limbs all around us. "Don't get dumped."

Pete grinned and waved. I knew he was resisting pointing to his apparently bomb-proof horse. He might be confident, but not enough to tempt fate. I took Mickey to the far end of the arena, away from the wind kicking in the trees, and circled him to canter.

Finally warmed up and focused, Mickey's canter rocked beneath me; his spine felt as round and supple as an archer's bow. I didn't make up that metaphor. I read it in Pete's book.

He had a way with words, my husband.

"Good boy," I murmured, stroking Mickey with my inside hand. "Good boy, good boy."

He picked up his head and looked out of the arena, past the line of shivering trees, and along the driveway running past the farmhouse. The movement killed his pretty gait and as he flattened, I sat down and asked for a trot. Then I took a good look at what had distracted him. A truck was driving toward the barn, silver and shiny, with a logo on the side.

It stopped at our barn, and the driver hopped out, looking my way. A woman with short dark hair, slight and slim, in breeches and a sweatshirt. Mickey pricked his ears at her hopefully.

"I think that's the girl from the school," I told him. "Yes, you dummy, we can go say hello."

He picked up his hooves double-time in his hurry to meet someone new.

This horse was like a dog sometimes.

"Hello," she called as Mickey reached the fence and leaned over it, nostrils fluttering with excitement. "I'm Nadine. From the school yesterday?"

"Hey, Nadine, I remember you."

She smiled. "Great. Rosemary said you moved out to her place last night. You won't regret it. She's, like, the best human."

"So far, I'm a huge fan."

"Good, good." Nadine stroked Mickey's nose; she didn't have much choice, the way the horse was shoving it at her. "Um—you're busy. I'll let you go."

"I have five minutes and you drove all the way over here. What's up?"

"Well . . ." Nadine seemed embarrassed. Her eyes flicked around—Mickey, the ground, the trees—anything but me. "I know I said to text me, but I was passing by, and . . . you know . . . the clinic next week?"

"Yes, the clinic." Mimi's clinic. "What were you thinking you'd have us do? If we're available, I mean." I wasn't ready to agree yet, although I had a feeling Pete would insist we be neighborly and do it. Especially with us living in Rosemary's RV and Rosemary being connected to the school . . . The horse community got wrapped up in knots so quickly. Meet one equestrian and you're well on your way to meeting them all.

"So, we were thinking—Sean and me, my husband, I mean—we were thinking you might do some riding demos on a few of our horses, and then Pete could maybe give a demo about dressage, with some exercises from his book? Most of our kids event, so they'd find the dressage/cross-country comparisons he does really useful.

We can rustle up some horses who have a few little quirks, nothing serious, and you could show them how to work the horses through them for a smoother ride. What do you think?"

"Absolutely," I agreed, feeling better about this clinic by the second. This could be a good thing! If Mimi had to work with us in a professional setting—in front of children, no less—she'd have to let go of her weird enmity for at least as long as we were there.

Maybe she'd even warm up to us.

Anything was possible in the great sport of eventing, right?

"Let me double-check with Pete," I said, "but I think you can count on us."

"Well, that's super," Nadine said, sounding relieved at getting that request out of the way. "Thank you! I know you guys are so busy."

"You picked the right week. Later would be a different story," I told her. We had Pin Oak the following weekend. "And hey, thanks for thinking of us."

"Um, well, *yeah,*" Nadine said, grinning suddenly. "It's really exciting to have you in the neighborhood, honestly. Do you like Maryland? Isn't it great here? Moving to Catoctin Creek was the best thing that ever happened to me. I met Sean, we got this riding school started, and everyone is so nice."

A cold wind raised goose bumps on my arms; I was getting chilled just having this conversation. I picked up the reins and prepared to send Mickey back to work so we could warm up again. "I love Maryland," I lied. "It's amazing here."

It wasn't *all* bad. But it wasn't Florida.

14

WE FINISHED WORKING the horses around four o'clock, then decided we'd go pick up Gemma and Jack to give them some barn time before we wrapped up for the night. Notch Gap Farm was just five minutes from Joan's farm, once we found the right winding country road, making it more convenient than the motel.

I'd expected Gemma to look a little wild-eyed after being confined to the living quarters with Jack, but instead, she came out of the RV smiling and holding him on her hip, looking fresh as a daisy.

"We've had the best day," she announced, kissing Jack's downy head. "We love the RV! And Jack got to play in the grass out here. Such a nice spot. Thanks for finding this for us, Jules."

I gave Pete a significant glance.

He shrugged back at me. "It's not like I said I didn't want to move into it," he reminded me. "So you can quit acting superior."

But I was the one who found the RV and booked it without waiting around, so I was the one who got the glory. Those were the rules. "I'm so glad you guys had a nice day," I told Gemma. "Ready to go to the farm for a little while?"

"Yes, this little man wants to help feed dinner, don't you, buddy?"

Jack beamed with delight.

The new route back to the barn took us through the town of Catoctin Creek, which was almost impossibly cute. I could appreciate it a little better now that I wasn't midway through an argument with Pete. We drove up a classic old Main Street with brick and wooden storefronts facing each other, getting quick glimpses of back streets dotted with Victorian houses and one 1950s-era diner sitting smack dab in the center of the town. I recognized the name from Rosemary's note on the RV fridge: the Blue Plate Diner.

The plate-glass windows and boxlike structure made the diner stick out among its Victorian neighbors like a sore thumb, but it was clearly the neighborhood hot spot. There was even a tractor in the jam-packed parking lot. I suspected the hand-painted ads for *Fried Chicken Night* and *Fried Trout* that were splashed across a few of the plate-glass windows had something to do with the crowds.

Both dinner options sounded amazing.

"Someone drove their tractor all the way into town to get dinner," I marveled. "Pete, can we borrow a tractor to drive to the diner? I'll ask around."

"It probably didn't take them long to get here," Pete pointed out. "See? We're already back in the countryside."

And he was right; just like that, we were passing a beautiful old house on the very edge of town, and then the brown autumn fields took over on both sides of the road.

"That sign in the last house's yard was for a bakery," announced Gemma, who had a sweet tooth the size of Big Ben. "A *bakery*!"

"Mmm." I imagined walking into a warm, bread-scented

bakery. Emphasis on the "warm" part. "I could really go for a chocolate croissant."

"Oh, me too," Gemma enthused. "Pete, turn this truck around."

"There's no way a bakery is open out here at this time of day," Pete said. "But tomorrow morning, maybe?"

"Yes," I told him. "Tomorrow's bakery day."

Back at our barn, we blanketed the horses and turned them out for the night, then ran through the stalls with pitchforks, doing a quick manure cleanup so we'd have less to muck out in the morning. Gemma played with Jack in the tack room, a simple game involving dumping out grooming totes and then putting the brushes away again. All of my wooden-backed brushes were scuffed now, but it was fine. Marcus sniffed in big, winding serpentines, his nose never more than a half inch from the ground.

I went outside in the blue dusk and looked at the moon, rising over the fields like a tangerine. The horses were grazing, noses close together as they stuck to their little herds, and for a moment the wind died down and the evening was utterly quiet.

Something out there made a horrifying shriek, and I turned and ran for my life.

"Pete!" I shouted, "Pete, that yell! Did you hear it?"

He slipped through the half-closed barn doors. "I heard it this time—but, what—"

The horses were looking around, ears pricked.

And then I saw something running close to the ground, barely visible in the gathering night.

"A fox," Pete said, his voice full of wonder. "Look at that!"

It scampered right across the farmyard in front of us, not fifteen feet away—small and skinny, red-coated, with a laughing black mouth. The fox glanced at us, and his stride stuttered for a moment; he hadn't expected anyone out here.

Then he picked up speed and disappeared into the bushes lining the stone wall of Joan's backyard.

"It was a fox all along? *That's* the sound foxes make?" I looked at Pete in astonishment. "You lived in England. You never heard a fox?"

"I heard foxes barking," Pete said sheepishly, "but I guess I never heard one yell like that . . . like a woman in trouble."

"Like a woman in *pain,*" I said, shaking my head. "Jeez. I always thought they were so cute, too."

Gemma came out of the barn, Jack in her arms. "Did I hear that yell again?"

"It was a fox," Pete said, pointing to the wall. "It must have moved into Joan's backyard."

"Oh, you know what?" Gemma nodded sagely. "Now that you mention it, that did sound like a fox. But I didn't know you had foxes in America."

We looked at Pete's cousin for a moment.

"Well, of course we—" I began, and then dropped it. "Let's close up shop and get some dinner."

"How about fried chicken?" Pete asked. "That diner's on the way home."

"I knew there was a reason I married you," I told him.

The crowds had gone home, tractor and all. The Blue Plate Diner was nearly empty when we strolled in just before seven o'clock. It was just as well, because we all smelled like dust and hay and horse blankets. I don't think anyone would have minded, though; the floor looked like a lot of mud-encrusted boots had already been through tonight.

A teenage girl with her fire-engine-red hair up in pigtails gave us menus and tall plastic cups of ice water. I could have done without the ice, but I thanked her and ordered a hot tea. Pete glanced at me with mild surprise.

"What?" I demanded. "I'm freezing inside and out."

The teenager gave me a curious look. "Are y'all not from around here?"

She used "y'all" in the country way, not the southern way. The twang was slightly different.

"Florida," I told her.

"A tea for me as well, please," Gemma said earnestly. "With sugar and milk? Thank you so very much."

The teenager blinked several times at Gemma's accent. "Mm-hmm," she agreed at last, and sauntered back to the kitchen. I could have sworn I heard her mutter, "Florida," as she went.

I was used to people giving me attitude for living in Florida, as if I was somehow responsible for all the insanity that went on there. When pushed, I tended to remind people that the insanity was usually caused by people who moved *to* Florida—and I didn't appreciate taking the blame. Floridians mostly wanted to do their work, go to the beach, and stay inside during the summer enjoying their air-conditioning.

"Please don't do your Florida speech," said Pete, who could read my expression and knew exactly what was coming.

I made a face at him and concentrated on tickling Jack's little hands while he played with the pyramids of half-and-half pods Gemma stacked up for him to smash down.

When the mugs came out, resting empty on their saucers along-side the little steel pots of hot water and a single bag of Lipton each, Gemma did her best not to make a face, but declared the teapot the wrong size for the tea bag and poured herself some water into the mug, dousing the tea bag. She glared at it until I asked what was wrong with the tea, and she said that the milk should go in the mug first and now everything was wrong. Apparently, for Gemma, there were strict rules about milk and tea mixing in the correct order. I pointed out that since the server hadn't brought us milk and it was doubtful the half-and-half pods actually contained real dairy, anyway, she couldn't be accused of any tea shenanigans by the English Tea Authority.

"It says real dairy on it," Pete said. "That's literally the name of the brand."

"They sit out on the table all the time, so how could they be milk?"

Gemma watched the brown cloud of tea billow through the hot water. "We have all kinds of milk that don't go in the fridge at home," she informed me. "You don't have to keep everything cold all the time, you know."

This was a sore spot between us. I'd caught her putting eggs on the counter instead of in the fridge several times. I kept nearly every kind of food in the fridge, but that was a reaction to many years of living in poorly insulated places with lots of mice. Still, eggs went in the fridge. And so did milk.

"Nothing goes bad from being cold," I retorted, while Pete sighed and leaned his elbows on the table, hands over his face.

I was only bickering because I was hungry, so when the fried chicken came out, on glorious heavy diner plates, accompanied by mashed potatoes doused in gravy, I concentrated on putting food in my mouth as quickly as possible.

"Oh my God," Gemma moaned. "This is better than KFC."

"Are you kidding?" Pete demanded. "This is better than anything I've ever had, in my life."

"Y'all enjoy," the teenager said, who had come back for that "is everything okay" check and found us elbow deep in our food. She threw a few more napkins on the table and gave Jack a little pat on the head. He picked at the peas on his plate and smiled at her.

The food filled us quickly, and we were already slowing by the time our plates were half-empty. By now the restaurant was all but cleared out, just a few older couples on the other side—they'd made a beeline for the farthest tables when they saw we had a baby in a high chair, and I didn't blame them. Jack had liberally scattered peas and French fries on the floor around him, and was busily smearing grape jam on his shirt, when a young woman wearing a blazer over her black trousers and white shirt came out of the kitchen and did a slow circle of the room, saying hello to the other diners and chatting for a moment, before finally reaching us.

She gave us a slow, easy smile, seemingly unconcerned with the circle of chaos around the high chair. "Y'all enjoying?"

"Amazing," Pete replied. "The chef should be given a puppy and a chocolate cake."

She laughed. "Well, I'll let him know. Although it's not his recipe—that honor goes to Nikki's aunt."

"Nikki?" I asked, surprised she thought we were locals. "Sorry, we're not from here."

"Oh, I know," she said, still smiling. "Nikki's someone you *should* know, though. Most out-of-towners meet her pretty quick. She has the bakery and restaurant at the end of the town. I'm just the manager here; Nikki's the Catoctin Creek restaurant mogul who owns the place."

"The bakery!" Gemma exclaimed. "We're going tomorrow."

"You'll love it," the young woman assured her. "She's a genius. Try the cranberry-walnut muffins."

"Two restaurants in one town," Pete remarked. "I'm impressed."

"Well, she inherited the Blue Plate, but Nikki's always had bigger dreams than frying chicken, if you can believe it. Definitely try her place down the road. And you'll meet her there. She lives upstairs, so the staff can just about never get rid of her."

"That's my kind of management style," I quipped as the manager headed back to the cash register to check out one of the older couples. "Always on property. Always watching the staff."

"And you wonder why we can't keep help," Pete said.

"Who can't I keep? Lacey has worked for me for almost ten years, if you don't count the part where she moved to Pennsylvania. She came back, which says something. Lindsay came back, too. People love it when I micromanage them." I dipped a fork into my green beans. "I'm boss of the year."

Jack slapped his little plastic plate and sent mashed potato flying.

Pete sighed. "And I'm tipper of the year," he said, looking at the mess around the high chair. "Especially if we want to be allowed back in."

"Oh, we're coming back," I assured him. "I might be from the south, but they don't make fried chicken like *this* in Florida. Not even at Publix."

Pete was so in love with his dinner, he didn't even bother correcting me about Florida not technically being part of the South, like he usually did.

That's how I knew the food was pure magic.

Gemma took Jack to the restroom for a quick cleanup before we left, and Pete stayed at the booth for a moment, phone in hand to answer some emails. I pushed myself up and headed to the parking lot, ready to start walking off the enormous dinner.

Catoctin Creek dozed around me, a little town that clearly turned in pretty early. I watched a black cat hop into the dumpster behind the diner, ready to rustle up some fried chicken of its own.

A car door slammed and I glanced over my shoulder. The woman walking up to the diner was on the angular side, hair tucked back in a tidy braid, wearing a tweed suit with little brown boots. Something told me she'd been wearing the same clothes since the

1980s. She looked my way, put her hand on the door, then looked back at me.

She turned and came over.

"I can't give you directions, if that's what you need," I said.

"No, I live here." She studied my hat. "Briar Hill Farm?"

"That's right. In Florida, though."

"You're Jules Thornton-Morrison, aren't you?"

The fans just kept coming. "Yeah, that's right," I said again.

She nodded. "I've heard a lot about you. I'm Mimi's wife, Diane."

"Oh . . . uh . . . hi." Flustered didn't even begin to describe it. "Nice to meet you?"

Diane gave me a tight smile. "Listen, I know things are tense between you guys and Mimi. I've been getting an earful every night. Just—stay the course, all right?"

"You're on our side," I said. "Because you want Mimi to retire."

"I'm on my marriage's side," Diane said ruefully. "I know none of this is your fault, but it would make things easier for me if you continued to be the enemy."

"Because that way she isn't blaming you for her career ending," I guessed.

"Exactly. I'm just buying myself some time . . . I know she's not going to quit horses, I'm not crazy. But I need her to find a replacement for eventing. Something that's equally fulfilling. Does such a thing exist?"

"I don't know if it does, but I was thinking the same thing. I'll help if I can."

"You're helping by being the evil interloper stealing her horses," Diane said. "Anything more than that is too much to ask."

"Well, I'll see what I can do," I said. "About being evil, and everything."

Diane smiled. "It was nice meeting you, really," she said. "I just have to pick up my order before they close."

"Goodnight," I said. "Good luck with Mimi."

Diane chuckled. "Yeah. Same to you."

I was half-asleep before we got back to the RV, and Jack was passed out for the night. I put him to bed while Gemma and Pete showered, then took Marcus out for a walk. The whole place felt so homey, it was almost a shame we'd only be here a couple of weeks.

But then again, maybe we'd be tired of it by the time we took off for the Eastern Shore and Chesapeake Three-Day Event.

Either way, I settled onto the tiny couch with a sigh of contentment, a little whiskey sloshed into a glass with some ice to help with digestion—a trick Pete had taught me—and waited for Pete to finish with Marcus's walk. I was surprised when he poked his head in the door and said, "Come out and say hello to Rosemary?"

I couldn't exactly say no, even though I was very comfortable and hadn't planned on getting up again before it was time to brush my teeth and fall into bed.

We'd met briefly on the night we moved in, but otherwise my only impression of Rosemary Beckett was of a kindly note-writer who left breakfast in the fridge. Outside, I found a smiling woman with dark wavy hair, a little older than me and dressed for comfort in jeans and a heavy plaid shirt. She was holding a bottle of wine. "I brought this over for a welcome gift," she said, offering it up in both hands. "I hope you're comfortable in the RV."

"Oh, my goodness." I took the wine bottle from her. "You've already been so generous. We really appreciated the breakfast food waiting for us. It's so hard getting everyone out the door in the morning, so that was a treat and a time-saver rolled into one."

"When Stephen said he wanted to have an RV available for friends and people in town, I said we'd have to make sure they were set up for living so far out in the country. You can't get food after seven o'clock here—that's when Trout's Market closes in town—and then you only have until eight to get something at the diner. So when people arrive late, like you did, I worry you won't have any breakfast . . . anyway, we stayed at some cottages in Ireland last year and every single one of them provided eggs and bread and milk, so I thought I would just try that. You like it?"

"Love it," I assured her. "Too kind. And we ate at the diner tonight . . . incredible."

"Fried chicken?" Rosemary asked, that ready smile twinkling. "Like nowhere else on earth. My best friend Nikki owns the diner, and that recipe is closely guarded."

"We heard about Nikki, too. The bakery is hers, I hear. Anything special we should try?" I wrapped my arms around myself; the wind had died down, but the night was frosty.

"The bakery's her pride and joy, and the muffins are to die for—but listen, I'm keeping you out in the cold. I'll head back to the house."

"I'd ask you in to try this wine," I said, "but the baby's asleep."

"I wouldn't dream of waking the baby." Rosemary stooped and rubbed Marcus's ears, just the way he liked it. "Just one thing, before I go—if it's not too much of an imposition—"

"Please, what can we do?" Pete asked politely, while I pondered the potential of an imposition. I didn't love that word.

"I have a horse rescue here, you might know . . . and there's a horse I think has a lot of potential."

I covered a snort with a cough. Straight to trying to get me to take a horse off her hands.

Pete frowned at me, then turned back to Rosemary. "What

kind of potential?" Like he thought Rosemary had the next eighty-dollar champion in her barn.

Although she might. Stranger things had happened.

"Well, she can jump," Rosemary explained. "Usually I keep rescues for life. The horses I bring back here are generally traumatized in some way and not really suited for everyday boarding-barn life. It's really rare for me to adopt one out. This one . . . she's different."

Of course she was. "What makes her different?" I asked.

"She has a lot of presence, and she's *very* athletic." Rosemary chuckled ruefully. "Quite a jumper."

I caught her meaning immediately. "Oh, so you can't keep her in?"

Pete cleared his throat.

I shrugged at him.

Rosemary just looked at me for a moment, chagrined. Finally, she asked, "Okay, how did you know?"

"Very athletic is usually seller's code for 'a lot of trouble,'" I told her. "And saying 'jumper' in that tone implies you haven't actually asked for all the jumping you're getting. I get that you're not in the business of selling horses, but some things are universal."

"Well, she's a bit of trouble," Rosemary admitted. "But I swear I'm not trying to dump her on anyone. That's not the way I do business."

"No one could think that of you," Pete assured her. "I'm sure she's a lovely horse."

I couldn't help feeling curious. "You think she'd make a nice event prospect?"

"She can jump the moon," Rosemary said. "And her movement is gorgeous. She's too young and green for the students up at Long Pond, but I really think she'd thrive in a competition home.

I wonder if you'd find some time to take a look at her for me. Tell me what you think."

"For sure," I agreed, thinking, *Why the hell not*? "Maybe Sunday? I think our afternoon is pretty open, right, Pete?" It was one of our only event-free weekends in Maryland, and we'd been planning on hacking the horses in the morning and taking the afternoon easy. If we were already going to be hanging out around the farm, riding Rosemary's athletic mare wouldn't hurt.

Might even be fun.

"Sunday's good," Pete said.

"Perfect," Rosemary replied, smiling at us. "So how about in the afternoon? I'll make us a nice Sunday supper, and you can look at Fling before we eat."

We watched Rosemary's flashlight beam take her back to the farmhouse.

Marcus settled down on the mat in front of the RV steps, clearly happy with the cold, but I was shivering. "Let's go in," I told the beagle. He thumped his tail at me.

"Thinking of adopting a new horse?" Pete asked.

"You're getting two new ones," I reminded him. "Maybe I'd like a new toy, too."

"But you don't even like mares," he said.

"Maybe I can change," I told him.

I didn't really believe it. But Pete had enough horses now. It was my turn to build up my string, and if Rosemary's wonder mare was my next big thing, I'd have a great story for the blogs to pick up.

15

OUR HORSES TROTTED through life without knowing I was getting to check out a new horse on Sunday afternoon, or that Pete was quietly running up against the entry deadline before he had to tell Hannah that he wasn't going to compete the horses at Chesapeake, even if they did qualify next weekend at Pin Oak. I didn't know his plan, and didn't think he should just let her pay that hefty entry fee. If he warned her, got the conversation out of the way, she could get a refund and let them pull competitors from the waiting list. Everyone would win. But when Pete spoke with Hannah about the horses' progress, he didn't bother stopping her from talking excitedly about the upcoming three-day event, and I didn't ask why.

Pete and I came to a silent, mutual understanding: he wasn't going to talk about it, and I wasn't going to nag him about it. I was annoyed, of course. Anything I couldn't control annoyed the hell out of me. But even I had to admit the new horses were going very well for him, and thought he should probably be less enthusiastic in his reports to Hannah if he was actually planning on pulling them out of the event.

Through a jump school on Friday, a dressage school on Saturday, and a succession of slow hacks on Sunday morning, our horses enjoyed the warming weather and the sunlight on their backs. Gemma and Jack came to the barn every day to play in the perfect weather, while Marcus slept cozily in yellow patches of light in the tack room, soaking up the warmth. Everyone in our little bubble was content. All of Maryland seemed to be happy. The pastures grew greener, while the orange and yellow flowers in all the gardens thrust out new blooms. It was like a short second spring.

I texted Lacey to boast about the magic combination of short-sleeve weather and not sweating, something that only happened rarely in Florida.

She texted back *Can't talk. Judging an art competition to see who can draw the best horse with poultice on the wash rack wall.*

I shouldn't have left her alone with all those kids. She was turning back into a teenager.

"This is the last hurrah," Joan proclaimed, pushing up her shirt sleeves as she rode with us on one of the last hacks of the morning. "November will be so gray and dreary, we'll start to forget what colors even look like. That's when I start dreaming of my Florida trip."

"Will you be down there this winter?" I asked, prepared to offer her stalls at market rate. We had some space and could always use the cash. But not many people wanted to board their horses so far north of Ocala; we were a solid hour from the big showgrounds. For some reason, folks who were perfectly content to live an hour from shows while at home were only interested in renting stalls within ten minutes of the showgrounds when they came down to Florida. Or that was what it seemed like to me.

"In January," Joan said. "I stick it out here as long as I can."

"Got a place to stay?" I ventured, and she nodded.

"I always rent the same place in Ocala," she replied. "Pool, dressage arena, paddock for the kids. It's like heaven on earth."

Well, we didn't have a pool, if that was the deciding factor. I glanced at Pete and he gave me a little grimace in reply; he knew what I'd been thinking.

But we didn't need a pool when we had a gorgeous freshwater spring. I wondered if there was something there, some way to leverage the spring and the trails we'd been cutting through the woods around it as a draw for winter boarders. Then again, did I really want more people around?

I sighed. The constant conundrum: balancing the earning potential of our land against the desire to have a home to ourselves. Isolation must be a privilege of the rich.

After our ride, Joan took her horse back to her own barn to untack, and we curry-combed the saddle marks off our two in the crossties.

"Excited for our date with Rosemary?" Pete asked teasingly. "After you ride the 'athletic' mare of your dreams?"

"I sure am," I replied. "I'm hoping she makes some down-home dinner, like pot roast."

"Or cabbage," Pete suggested drolly. "The Old Country could run strong in her. Joan said her family has been living on that farm for more than two hundred years, and everyone here seems to be of German descent. We should probably have a backup dinner in the fridge, just in case."

I snorted. "Actually, I hope the whole meal is just an entire slow cooker full of cabbage and all the windows in the house are closed tight." I shook my head at him. "Come on, man. Are you still mad at me about the mare? The mare we haven't even looked at yet?"

"I was never mad at you." Pete unclipped the crossties from

Prince's halter. "I just think you're going to be disappointed. Because you don't like mares."

"Are you kidding?" I called after him, as he led Prince to his stall. "I freaking *love* mares!"

"You've given away nearly every mare you've ever owned," Pete retorted.

"I only gave away Margot, and that was because she had a special bond with Lacey."

"That's one of three," Pete said. "My point stands."

I hadn't really planned on buying Rosemary's mare. Another green horse, eating on my dime and racking up competition bills while I painstakingly brought her up through Starter, Beginner Novice, Novice? Not what I needed. But Pete was pushing my buttons. He thought I couldn't make a good partner for a mare? I was going to have to prove him wrong. I didn't have any choice in the matter.

We prepared for our afternoon with Rosemary with care. Clean breeches; tucked-in shirts; one of those cute stretchy belts with a D-ring snaffle for a buckle for me, and the more traditional and dignified leather belt with the brass buckle for Pete. I brushed off my boots with a polishing wipe and did the same for him as he stood outside in the afternoon sunshine, waiting for me to announce he'd passed muster.

Mentally, we'd both agreed that we wanted to look our very best for our generous landlady. In our line of work, a smart rider quickly learned that open-handed benefactors were the single most important kind of person. When it came to money-making careers, eventing had to come somewhere in the all-time-bottom-five choices. We worked hard for every dime we made, but we were paid entirely by enthusiasts. How's that for a lack of security?

Rosemary and Stephen Beckett were not only providing us with a nice place to stay for a reasonable rent, they were also feeding us dinner (approximate retail value, sixty-five dollars with tip, unless they were actually giving us cabbage), and Rosemary was potentially offering up an inexpensive event prospect. That was becoming less and less common in the booming horse market. Nowadays, finding a cheap retired racehorse took a lot of connections and the ability to live with a lot of risk. The old routes were slowly closing as costs rose on everything from hay to hoof oil.

If Rosemary's mare really was an athlete in a rescue's clothing, I wasn't going to let this shot go.

And I always felt like a better rider when I dressed the part.

"Are you guys taking Marcus with you?" Gemma called as I put away the saddle soap wipes. "He whines when you leave him with me in the afternoon. He knows you're doing fun stuff without him."

"And you want a nap without a dog whining through it," I observed. "Go on, admit it."

"Well, if Jack's going down, there's nothing keeping *me* awake." Gemma was unrepentant.

"Fine, get me his harness." Gemma could have the moon if that was what it took to keep her happy.

Marcus literally tripped down the stairs, nearly tumbling tail over long hound-dog ears in his eagerness to join me. I had to tug on the harness to stop him from landing on his nose.

Gemma smiled beatifically at us before shutting the door, no doubt eager to make it to her nap date with my son.

I turned to Pete, who'd been outside waiting while I got Marcus into his harness. "Ready?"

He held up our helmets, one in each hand. "Ready."

It was a lot of fuss for a two-minute walk. We followed old

stepping stones set into the hillside to the side gate. Inside the grav-eled barnyard, Rosemary was standing beneath the barn overhang, texting someone.

We'd been too busy to come down here and take a look around, so I took it all in with interest. I wasn't used to historic buildings; Florida wasn't very kind to wood, what with the hurricanes and humidity and termites. Most buildings that survived more than fifty years were concrete block. This barn, though, had to be counting its years in the triple digits. Beneath an overhang, a stone wall held sliding doors into the underside of the barn, alongside a person-sized door and an antique, crooked window. Everything looked very old and handmade.

Rosemary looked up from her phone and waved. "Well, hello! Welcome to my barn! What do you think?"

"I feel like I'm at a farm museum," I confessed, closing the barnyard gate behind us. "What are the stalls like?"

"Come in and see," Rosemary said, gesturing to the open sliding door behind her. "Probably darker than what you're used to, but they spend the nice days outside, anyway. And most of their nights, too. We used to keep them in half the day, but now I keep them as close to twenty-four-turnout as I can."

"We're trending that way, too," Pete said. "It really cuts down on ulcers and anxiety. The only problem is keeping them stalled at events."

"There's always a problem," Rosemary agreed.

Inside the barn, the air was thick with a rich, pungent aroma: a blend of hay, shavings, molasses, and a faint tang of manure. I was used to wide-open Florida barns with aisles and windows and a near-constant breeze to air things out, so the scent took me aback at first. But as I walked around, I could see the stalls were pristine. It wasn't bad horsekeeping that gave this barn its odor, it was the design and the sheer age. The low timbered ceiling, the stone walls with their crumbling mortar, the small, crooked windows set into the walls on either side: it was built to absorb warmth and keep things inside, not bring the outdoors in.

It wasn't a barn I'd love to work out of, but I could guess it was probably very cozy in the cold winters.

The design was clearly intended to get as much use out of the relatively small space as possible. A narrow aisle ran along the front, so that horses and people could move around inside when the sliding doors were closed. Two short rows of stalls ran from the aisle to the stone wall at the back, with spaces for eight horses. Off to the right, a door led to what must be a feed room. That was it. That was the whole barn. For the purpose of keeping rescued horses safe and cozy during snow and storms, it was plenty.

Two stalls were occupied, the horses within eating hay with that contented crunching sound all horse people loved. I looked them over. One horse had a single stall guard to keep him in, while the other horse had two blocking the door—so it wasn't hard to guess which one was Fling.

From where I stood in the doorway, she looked small, but typey—a Thoroughbred who had stayed under sixteen hands.

"A pocket rocket," I murmured, making my way down to her stall.

The horse in the corner stall, a massive black Percheron, chewed his hay and watched me with pricked ears, his brown eyes quiet and unperturbed.

The Thoroughbred stopped chewing and stared at me. A crescent-shaped sliver of white showed at the back of each dark iris.

Uh-oh, I thought.

There was nothing good for me about horses with exposed

white in their eyes. As a child, I'd always been told that when the horse's sclera was showing, that meant the horse was so sensitive and spooky they always had their eyes open a little too wide.

Was this true? I had no idea. I saw lots of riders very happily compete horses who showed the whites of their eyes. And yet it continued to make me nervous. Maybe this was the closest thing to a superstition I believed in.

I was considering it might be prudent not to try this horse after all when she suddenly moved closer to her dual stall guards, pressing her quivering nostrils through the gap between the webbings. A small white strip between her nostrils was enough to make me think, *Oh, cute,* and then she lifted one dainty foreleg, holding the hoof up, trembling, a foot off the ground.

"Oh, Fling!" Rosemary laughed from behind me. "She's begging for a treat. She doesn't paw, thank goodness, but she lifts that hoof like she's been taught to shake hands."

"That's really cute," I admitted, even though whoever taught horses dog-tricks was playing with fire. A raised hoof could become a stomped head in no time at all. "Do you usually give her something?"

"I do," Rosemary confessed. "I know it's just cementing the behavior, but honestly she already does it so consistently I don't know any way of training her to stop. And sometimes tricks are useful at fundraising events."

"I'm sure," I agreed. Rosemary handed me a horse cookie, and I slipped it to the mare, who instantly dropped the foreleg and took the cookie with greedy lips. Next to us, the Percheron caught wind and made an eager whicker of his own.

"Here you go," Rosemary told him, handing the Perchie a treat. "And that's why I only brought in one horse to be her friend this afternoon. Otherwise, they'd tear the barn down until they all got cookies."

I laughed. "No problem. Can we see her out?"

Rosemary haltered the mare and brought her into the golden light spilling over the barnyard. Her chestnut coat glistened as she stepped nervously around the dark-haired woman, clearly confused about our reasons for disrupting her usual afternoon routine. Although her coat was already getting a little shaggy in preparation for winter, there was that bright metallic sheen on her shoulder and haunches where the sunlight struck her red coat just right, giving her a look of a copper penny gleaming in the light.

Dynamo had the same coloring. Yes, yes, I knew that "chestnut mare, beware" was a thing. But I was a sucker for a red chestnut.

I walked up and down as the mare circled, comparing her to my retiree back home in Florida. Dynamo took me from a high schooler hoping to event to a professional rider with an enviable career, and he'd done it all as a less-than-perfect horse: small, close-coupled, long-backed. Some Thoroughbreds were built like gazelles, some were like tanks; Dynamo was the latter. Fling, on the other hand, came somewhere in between. Small, but not too dainty. Well-proportioned for her height, but good bone.

I liked what I saw. Wide eyes and all.

"Do you have tack for her?" I asked Rosemary. "Or mine's in my truck."

"Sure do," she replied. "Just a minute."

Rosemary tied Fling to the barnyard fence and hustled to the barn, disappearing through the door at the end.

Fling looked around warily and blew out one long, suspicious breath, the air rattling in her nostrils.

"Mm-hmm," I said to her. "That's what I expected."

Pete sidled up to me and we looked at the mare for a moment, who seemed to be consulting her internal guidebook on what to do when left tied to a post.

The options were probably either *Be good* or *Freak out.* I had my money on the latter. That white sclera glinted as she looked around, swinging her head back and forth.

"What do you think of her?" Pete murmured. "A little small, maybe?"

"Dynamo isn't tall," I reminded him.

"Taller than this mare, and he didn't have what you wanted at the end."

I pressed my lips together, annoyed. "It wasn't that he didn't have what I wanted," I said. "Dynamo was more than enough."

"Not to go where you want—"

"Here we are," Rosemary announced, coming out of the barn before I could snap back at Pete. She had a battered jumping saddle in her arms, girth and bridle tossed over top of it. "An oldie but a goodie, and it fits her nicely. I'll get her tacked up and you can hop right on in here."

I noticed in her wording there was no indication she'd be showing us the horse under saddle herself. Usually, this was a red flag, but I decided to let it slide. Maybe she didn't do a lot of riding. After all, if this horse had so much potential as a sport horse, she could have made some money for her rescue by training and selling the mare on her own.

Fling wasn't easy to saddle. She sidestepped back and forth, forcing Rosemary to move quickly to avoid getting stepped on. I was aching to get this horse into a set of crossties with a wall on either side to gain some semblance of control. The psychological benefit of it alone—

"Sorry she's such a wiggle-worm," Rosemary gasped. "I should probably tell you she's very nervous under saddle. But I think it's just anxiety because she doesn't really know what to do. She needs a sensible rider and a steady program."

"Don't we all," Pete murmured.

I stepped forward as the mare gave Rosemary a hard time about tightening the girth, intending to take her by the halter and remind her that humans are the dominant species, but before I could get there, Fling took matters into her own hooves. With a sharp, practiced toss of her head, she broke the snap on the lead rope, darted backward, then somehow shoved that energy from Reverse to Drive and shot forward.

Her bascule, as she soared beautifully over the barnyard fence, was a sight to behold.

And so were her muscled hindquarters as she galloped up the farm lane, head high and mouth open, whinnying for her pasturemates.

Rosemary made a small, dismayed sound, but didn't move.

We watched as Fling leaped the pasture fence and went thundering up the slope toward the astonished herd.

I was very glad Rosemary's saddle was the one on her back.

"Well?" Pete muttered to me. "Still interested?"

I'd counted at least a dozen things I'd do differently with that mare if Rosemary wasn't the one in charge. Nothing against Rosemary or her horsemanship. It just wasn't what this particular horse needed.

Did I have what that horse needed?

Please. Of *course* I did.

"Actually," I said to Pete, "yes. Very interested."

16

"WHEN ARE YOU going to ride that new horse of yours?"

The daily question. Well, daily as of the past three days. But it was already tiresome.

I made a face at Pete over my coffee tumbler. After an elaborate sip, I replied, "When I feel like it."

"Very professional of you." He grinned to assure me he was joking. So funny, my husband. "If you're feeling sort of, maybe, almost like it—I think today might be a good day. Not windy. Kind of warm. Fewer excuses for her to act out."

I thought about my new mare's tail flicking in the air as she leaped over Rosemary's barnyard fence and headed for the hills. Should I have taken her based on that confident flick of the tail? I didn't even ride the horse after Rosemary trudged up the hillside and brought her back to the barn. I just said I'd take her. Rosemary had smiled from ear to ear as she assured me I would not regret it.

I didn't want to regret it.

And so I wanted to get this first ride *right*. Which meant doing it on my schedule, and so far, my schedule didn't include getting on her. I wanted to watch her a little more. See if I could figure her out.

Or maybe I was just stalling.

"Unfortunately, I'm still full from Sunday dinner," I told Pete. "Can't do it today. It's dangerous to ride on a full stomach."

"Today's Wednesday," he pointed out. "And it's *swimming* on a full stomach. Which has been debunked anyway."

"We ate two helpings of chicken and dumplings followed by lemon meringue pie, Pete," I reminded him. "I'm a changed person. I'm not who I was before that meal."

"You and me both, to be honest." Pete patted his flat stomach, and I resisted the urge to poke him in the belly button.

Instead, I glanced down the barn aisle, past the open stall doors. This close to lunchtime, there was a horse looking over each stall guard, waiting for us to show up with their midday grain. The only door that was closed, the only pretty head that was missing, was my new chestnut mare's.

Little Miss Fling had proven pretty quickly that a flimsy old stall guard was not going to keep her inside. She wasn't too worried about the paddock fences, either, although there was less I could do about that.

Rosemary kindly trailered Fling over to our barn for us on Sunday night when we went back to feed dinner, staggering from the enormous home-cooked meal Rosemary put before us. She'd said she used to cook for her neighbors, back when Long Pond was still a farm, and she missed the opportunity to set out big spreads for farmer appetites. Apparently, Pete and I ate more than her city slicker husband. I didn't know if this was a compliment or not, so I just smiled, had seconds, and groaned when I saw the pie from Nikki's bakery.

Now, I wondered if Rosemary had deliberately plied me with

food so I couldn't resist her offer to drive Fling back to the farm immediately, effectively removing any time for me to start doubting my spur-of-the-moment decision.

In the three mornings since Fling's arrival, we'd gotten to the barn and found Fling in three different places: on Monday, in the barn aisle; on Tuesday, wandering around outside; and this morning, in a paddock harassing poor Flyer and Mickey, who were trying to huddle together under a tree while Fling tossed her head and pinned her ears, squealing at them.

Mickey had looked at me with a piteous expression, as if to say, *Mom, I don't know what she wants!*

Ah, life with a mare. I called Lacey to ask for her advice, since she had such a good relationship with Margot. Lacey told me to just go with the flow. Fling lived where Fling wanted. She was a free spirit, Lacey said. Free and wild and—

At that point Lacey's speech just deteriorated into giggles, and I hung up the call. She called me back ten minutes later to share that Lindsay had bought purple and green sparkle hoof polish and the kids were currently painting the hooves of every horse in the place.

"Do you want us to save some polish for Fling?" Lacey asked in an innocent tone.

So, Lacey wasn't helpful.

As much as we would love to go with the flow and support Fling's free spirit, we needed horses to stay where we'd put them. This was a basic safety issue. And since she wouldn't stay in a paddock, and we couldn't just keep her in a box stall, the only option I could think of was a round pen with high walls. I'd seen one at Long Pond; I considered asking Nadine if we could borrow it for a few weeks. But the isolation would probably freak the mare out.

I sipped my coffee moodily, knowing there was no easy solution but annoyed I couldn't just fix it. I'd been sitting at the little table outside the barn, soaking up the morning sunshine while the horses ate their breakfast and Gemma showed Jack how to push toy trucks in the clay ruts of the barn lane. Pete was inside, tidying up the barn aisle. Fling had taken a few blankets off their bars and scattered a loose hay bale around before she'd gone outside to bother the boys. Pete was growing less enthusiastic about my Maryland souvenir by the day.

I refused to regret her. My official opinion was that Fling needed time—time to settle in, find a friend among the other horses, and learn that no one here was interested in shoving her around. I had no doubt Fling had become a jumper out of some need to survive, so she'd come around once she realized we were on her side.

Pete disagreed. "She needs to be worked," he said, once he'd marched out and given me an accounting of everything he'd had to clean up. "I guarantee that will be what fixes her."

"You *guarantee* it?" I shook my head. "No. I don't think that's it."

"Come on—what do you think she's looking for when she jumps out? She doesn't know why she's here. Give the horse a purpose. Don't give her any more time to think up new ways to cause trouble."

Fling moved like an athlete, with the kind of grace and ability that ought to be bottled up and sold to dressage judges like a drug. I just had to figure out how to get it in the bottle and keep it there until I needed it.

Pete was watching me hem and haw. Finally, he asked, "Unless you want me to ride her first?"

I put down my coffee tumbler on the metal table with a rattle that attracted the attention of every horse in the barn.

He lifted an eyebrow at me. "Coffee finished, or are you just mad at it?"

"Finished. You know what? Let's get Fling tacked up and I'll ride her right now. Will you hold her, please? I know she won't cross-tie yet."

Pete looked delighted at having goaded me into trying out my new horse. He stood up. "Yes! Let's go."

Fling's first ride absolutely warranted a jumping saddle, the one with my deepest and most secure seat—which also happened to have a silly little grab strap hooked across the pommel. Lacey had put it there as a joke one day after Flyer sent me into the dirt during a temper tantrum, and I'd left it because sometimes a little extra security wasn't the worst thing in the world. I eyed that grab strap now as Fling leaned into Pete's hands, one foreleg lifted as if she was going to paw the shavings.

"Don't," Pete warned her in his deepest tones. "Be a nice girl."

She shook her head and rolled her brown eyes, the white sclera widening.

I'm not a nice girl, her movement said.

"I know you aren't," I told her, adjusting the girth and running my fingers along the running martingale to make sure it sat at the center of her chest. "I didn't bring you here because you're nice, either. I brought you here because you're bad."

Pete sighed dramatically. "Now, why would you tell her that?"

"I want her to know she's free to be herself," I said. "Lacey's method. Hand me my helmet, will you?"

Pete reached around the barn door and found my helmet. He put it into my hands with an uncharacteristically serious expression on his face. "Do *not* take any chances," he told me.

I was a little touched by Pete's words. Annoyed, too, because he was avoiding the conversation about how he was clearly planning on taking a chance with Hannah's horses, but still, touched.

Obviously, I didn't take them seriously. I didn't necessarily *take chances* while I was riding, but I didn't turn them down, either. If I had to work Fling through a temper tantrum, that was just part of the job. What did he think, I'd feel one little crowhop coming and dismount? Maybe hire a cowboy to ride her, or hand her over to a rodeo?

No, of course not. Pete was just being protective. It was nice—as long as he didn't do it too often.

Marcus joined us on the way out to the arena and chose a comfy spot under a picnic table along the fence, while I followed Pete and Fling to the mounting block. A soft breeze fluttered the leaves on the trees and caressed my cheeks, and I gave myself a little stretch and shake, feeling good. Feeling ready.

Fling glanced back at me, tail swishing.

I met her eye, trying to gauge her mood. She wanted to do this, right?

"I don't think she'll stand here all day," Pete called, wiggling the bit in her mouth to keep her attention. She flicked her gaze back to him and nipped at his hand with a noncommittal gesture that said, *If I'd wanted to draw blood, you'd know about it.*

"I wouldn't expect her to," I told Pete, and with that I stalked over, hopped onto the mounting block, and jumped into the saddle before she had time to think about what I was doing.

Fling tensed all over, her muscles going rigid.

"We've got a freezer," I said to Pete. Pete immediately wagged her head back and forth, and as soon as the motion loosened her neck, he walked her forward. Slowly, the tension in her back released. I was glad he was at her head, giving me time to find my stirrups and settle into her walk without having to worry about fussing with her mouth or steering. She leaned against him like a racehorse in the paddock, all nervous energy and expectation.

"Steady, big girl," he told her, wiggling the bit with every stride.

"Nothing scary going on. Just having a walk around the arena." He looked back at me over his shoulder. "I'll take you around for a lap, okay? And then we'll see where she is mentally."

"Sounds good." Fling's ears flicked back at my voice, then forward again, then swung around to take in everything in the arena, like she was searching for some phantom satellite signal. *Fling, the aliens miss you.* She focused on the jumps, the trees, the picnic table, Marcus. She snorted and drew back as we came within a dozen feet of the picnic table and the snoozing beagle in its shadow.

"It's a dog," Pete told her. "A very sleepy dog."

I dropped my heels and settled deeper into the saddle, my calves well away from her sides. If she was going to explode from a touch, it wouldn't be mine.

Pete went on jiggling the reins, wobbling the bit in her mouth, turning her head a little in, then out, trying to keep her muscles in motion, rocking her weight from side to side. An old truism of horses: *If you can move their feet, you're still in control.*

Fling snorted at my dog, loud enough to make him lift his head and blink at us. I saw the interest spark in his brown eyes. We were walking a horse around? Pete was involved? Sounded like a job that should include Marcus. I watched him prepare to stand up, drawing in his front paws.

"Marcus, sweetie, please don't shake your ears," I told him, but what's the one thing a beagle had to do every time he thought about standing up?

He shook his ears.

Beagle ear-shakes are like little earthquakes; Marcus had his face scrunched up and his ears went flying back and forth and the license tags on his collar rattled together in a perfect storm of *Hey let's scare your spooky horse.* Fling snorted again, loud enough to wake the dead this time, and then promptly shifted into Reverse. I tipped forward onto her neck, my hands and knees catching me, as she started running backward—a gait most Thoroughbreds seem to have perfected to the point that maybe it should be included in the horse breed books as an additional gait. *Thoroughbreds can walk, trot, canter, gallop, and run backward.*

Luckily, Pete was coming with us, his hands still on the reins. "Whoa, whoa, whoa, whoa," he repeated, each word a puff of air that Fling felt free to ignore.

I was still balanced on my knees, with my hands right above that grab strap Lacey had given me, and suddenly I had an idea. I leaned forward, shifting my weight to just above her withers, slipped my right hand around the grab strap like a bronc rider ready for the chute to open, and told Pete, "Let go—right now!"

He jumped to one side, and I took the reins, drew them hard against Fling's neck, and tossed my weight to the right.

The scrabbling mare was terribly off-balance, making her shoulders easy to manipulate. With her balance abruptly thrown to the right, she staggered sideways in a half pirouette, her weight hurled onto her hindquarters. I took the opportunity to thump her in the ribs with my heels, knowing it would be easier for her to go forward than backward while she was essentially crouched on her hind legs. My left fingers were in her mane; my right fingers curled around the grab strap. The reins were free and open, giving her no reason to rear. Fling had all the space in the world if she wanted to go forward.

She used it. The wide-eyed chestnut mare launched herself into a canter with that huge, insane bound that could maybe be a Thoroughbred's *sixth* gait, and we were off to the races.

"Good girl," I told her as she cantered for the rail, clearly considering its height as she locked onto it with pricked ears. "But we're going to turn, so here we go!" I used the indirect rein trick again, pushing her to the right with the left rein hard against her neck, and she followed the shift in balance, her gait suddenly flowing smooth as a stream of water as she picked up the track and cantered around the arena on the rail. "There's a good girl. New rule: we always fail forward, okay? No more backward. Forward."

Fling's chestnut ears flicked back to me and she seemed to take a breath. Then another. Her neck slowly lowered, the tense bulge in her muscles disappearing. When she was snorting with every stride, I decided she was relaxed enough to come down to a trot, and then a walk. They weren't balanced transitions, of course, and there was lots of head shaking and tossing, but we made it.

She put her head down and sighed as if she'd just shrugged off the weight of the world, and all she wanted now was a nap.

I looked over at Pete, standing in the center of the ring with his arms folded across his chest. His expression gave nothing away. Impressed, and he didn't want to admit it?

"How'd we do?" I called.

"Not bad," he allowed.

I smirked at him. "I think she went great. And now we're going to do some proper work."

Pete gamely hung out on the picnic table, Marcus sitting happily at his side, while I rode Fling for another fifteen minutes, trotting and walking her in big loops around the jumps and along the rail. The mare took a few opportunities to spook at jumps or a scary-looking hunk of dirt, and I gave her the space she wanted. She didn't seem like she was actually scared of anything, just making a point—she hadn't asked for this life, and she wasn't prepared to say she liked it.

Not yet.

But I had a feeling she'd settle in just fine once she had some balance and brakes and understood what those jumps were for.

Fling liked jumping. That wasn't the issue. I just wanted her to do it over jumps, not fences and stall doors.

It would come. A content horse wouldn't try to leave all the time. I was sure of it.

I looked down at her pretty neck, her red mane rippling over her crest, and thought maybe having a mare wouldn't be so bad.

Marcus barked suddenly, and she hopped to one side, then regained the track.

"Good girl," I said, glancing up to see why my beagle was barking.

A truck that looked oddly familiar was pulling up alongside ours. Pete's gaze followed mine, and as I realized who was getting out, I sat down in the saddle.

Fling lurched down to a walk.

For God's sake.

I was having a nice morning. Who wanted to bet Mimi Pulaski had shown up specifically to ruin it for me?

17

I DISMOUNTED CAREFULLY and walked Fling back into the barn, leaving Pete to handle Mimi's arrival. But she seemed determined to get my attention. She stalked right into the barn after me and stood near the wash rack while I stripped Fling of her tack, Pete holding Fling's lead rope and watching the newcomer nervously. I kept my mouth shut and my focus on my horse.

Mimi gazed at Fling as if she were an oasis in the desert, and it occurred to me that her property must seem very lonely without any horses on it. Unless she had been off teaching lessons somewhere, Fling was probably the first horse she'd seen in over a week. The very idea was painful. I wished Mimi would give me an in, so that I could help her. The problem was that actually helping other people didn't come naturally to me, and her aggressive nature was triggering all my worst tendencies. I sympathized with Mimi, but I also wanted to get into a screaming match with her. It was a difficult position.

"Nice mare," Mimi said after a minute or two of silence. "She doesn't crosstie?"

"She will," I said crisply. "She just came in from Rosemary Beckett's rescue."

Mimi looked startled. She probably didn't know we were living at the Beckett farm. Then she rearranged her face, angry again.

"I heard you're gate-crashing my clinic at the school tomorrow," Mimi snapped. "I want to know why."

"I should give you my phone number," I said. "Then you could have just texted me to ask."

"I was in the neighborhood."

"I wouldn't call it gate-crashing," Pete said, doing a much better job of keeping his tone calm than I was. "The barn manager asked me to come and talk about dressage. It's just adding a slightly wider focus to the whole event."

So diplomatic, my husband. Maybe he could run for office next. I turned on the hot water to hose the arena dust off Fling's legs and hooves. The mare startled a little at the sound of water rushing in the pipes. I lifted my eyebrows at her. "Really, mare? You don't know about hoses?"

"And for Jules to do the riding demos?" Mimi was demanding of Pete. "Where did that come from? Whose idea was that?"

"Well, *you* can't do them," I reminded her sharply, finally forgetting in my irritation that I was supposed to be finding a way to help her, not offend her. "Because you have a broken collarbone that will shatter into a billion pieces if you fall off."

Mimi turned her laser-gun eyes on me, but I turned my back on her and made a big show of testing the water temperature with my hand.

She talked to my back, anyway. "They don't need riding demos, and I will handle dressage. It's not like I'm new to this sport. I've been in eventing for forty-some years. I think I can instruct children in how to do their Novice level tests."

"I know you can," Pete said, "but the thing is, I just wrote a book about it. So I imagine they want my perspective as a recent author. It's just a little novelty for the schoolkids."

I cautiously sprayed Fling's hooves with the water. She looked at me in horror but decided to allow it. "Good girl," I told her. "Nice clean feetsies."

"A book!" Mimi snorted. "Your generation is all alike. I'll bet it's a bunch of huggy-feel-good nonsense. What do you do, give your horse an organic cookie every time you half halt?"

"If that's what works for that horse," Pete joked, but Mimi took him seriously.

"You people are ruining this sport. *Ruining* it!"

Fling took a step backward to get away from the shouty woman just as I was getting the hose up close and personal under her tail, one hind hoof treading on my toe in the process. I groaned and pushed her off. "So heavy, mama," I told her. "Lose some weight, why don't you."

"Now, don't hurt her feelings," Mimi jeered. "Protect the horse's precious little ego!"

"Oh my God." I was over it. "Why are you even here? You weren't invited, we aren't friends, and you're being disrespectful, so how about you get the hell off this farm?"

"Jules," Pete murmured. "Please."

Even Fling gave me an astonished look.

Welcome to Jules-ville, Miss Mare.

Mimi held her ground. "I came here to tell you not to show up at that clinic tomorrow. I'm not teaching those kids if you're going to be there screwing them up."

"Oh, I'll be there," I assured her. "And Pete will be, too. And we're going to correct all the jacked-up old-fashioned nonsense you tell them!"

Her jaw was so tight, I might have been afraid she'd crack a tooth—if I'd cared one way or another what happened to her. Any goodwill I had toward Mimi was thoroughly used up. I took a threatening step in her direction, and for a moment Mimi looked like she might let me get all the way up in her face, but then she took a step back. She glanced down the barn aisle like she was gauging the distance to her truck.

"Then I'll cancel," she said scornfully, "and *you* can tell those kids why I didn't come."

She marched out of the barn, her boot heels clicking on the concrete.

I looked back at Pete. He gave me an *Are you satisfied?* look.

"She won't cancel," I told him. "Although a girl can dream."

Pete flicked the end of the lead rope around Fling's nose, giving the anxious mare something to play with. She reached for it with her lips, popping them together. "I thought we weren't going to start a war with Mimi while we were in Maryland," he said.

I just rolled my eyes.

The day passed in a comfortable way, horses ridden and horses bathed, the glorious October sunshine trying its best to make a Maryland convert out of me. Lindsay checked in from Briar Hill, where she and Maddox were living in the house while we were away, to let me know there'd just been a huge thunderstorm with gusty winds that knocked down two trees across the driveway. Maddox, it transpired, thought chain saws were just the most fun he'd ever had.

"I don't think my insurance covers Maddox chopping off a leg with a chain saw," I said, feeling faint, and she said he'd already handled the trees, cleaned the chain saw, and put it back in the toolshed.

"Lindsay," I said, "I cannot have teenagers using chain saws on my farm."

"We're both past our eighteenth birthdays, *Mom,*" Lindsay said. "That's the age of consent with using dangerous power tools. And anyway, Maddox's dad came over and showed him how to use it."

"You could have led with that!" I trusted Clay; even if he was a rock star, he was pretty capable.

"This way was much more fun," Lindsay said.

I told Pete we were never leaving home again.

"We'll see how fast you jump when the US Equestrian Team comes calling next time," Pete said, and I ignored him, because I didn't want to admit how right he was.

A blustery wind came over the mountains at sunset, bringing a reminder that it was autumn after all, and we led the horses to pasture with their tails and heads held high, looking for excuses to misbehave. I took Fling to the paddock where Mickey and Dynamo were turned out and added her to the mix, hoping that since she'd sought them out on her last overnight adventure, she'd choose to stay with them tonight. The geldings had already galloped off to the end of the field to stare at the mountains and switch their tails back and forth, acting as if the wind was carrying strange messages from the west only they could decipher, and Fling didn't seem to see them. As soon as I turned her out, she made a quick little circle, gathered herself, and leaped over the fence.

"Dammit, Fling!" I shouted, the wind tearing my words away. She galloped up the lane without flicking so much as an ear in my direction, and ducked into the barn aisle. I heard a shriek. And this time, it wasn't the damn fox.

That was Gemma.

I took off for the barn at the same time as Pete, our boots slamming on the hard clay. I rounded into the barn a few strides ahead of him, terrified of what I'd see. I stopped short, astonished.

Gemma had clearly been caught in the aisle and was holding Jack close against her hip, back against a stall wall, her eyes wide and surprised as Fling reached out her pretty head and touched him with her muzzle—first his feet, then his stomach, then his head.

I hated seeing babies close to horses—those adorable pictures of horses nuzzling infants in their strollers made my muscles clench. Horses were unpredictable flight animals who put their survival ahead of anything else; nothing would ever stop a horse from flinching and reacting explosively if something frightened them, and if that sweet little baby was in the way, well, that was just too bad, wasn't it? I'd told Gemma to keep Jack away from horses when one of us wasn't around to oversee things.

But now Fling had taken things into her own hooves and here she was, giving Jack the snuffle of a lifetime.

Jack giggled, the sound abrupt and beautiful, and Fling's ears, already latched onto him, somehow locked in even stronger. She breathed him in with her flared nostrils, tracing her muzzle back to his little sneakered feet.

Jack wriggled in Gemma's grasp and kicked Fling right in the nose.

"Ooooh!" Gemma gasped, sliding along the wall to get away from her. But Fling just drew in a long, rattling breath, surprised but undaunted. She really wanted to keep Jack as a pet.

I'd had enough, though, and so had Gemma. She kept sliding along the wall until she was out of Fling's reach and then ducked into the tack room. I bounded up beside Fling and grabbed her by the halter, thankful I hadn't been trusting enough to turn the mare out bare-headed. Jack drew himself up along Gemma's side and shouted, "*Mawk!*" with enough intensity to send the mare bouncing backward. I had no choice but to go with her.

Once she'd settled, Pete handed me a lead rope and I asserted something like control again. "You scared me to death, mare," I told her, showing her my open hand. She blew at it and chewed thoughtfully, a horse's sign that their brain was returning to regular mode.

Gemma and Jack came out of the tack room, Jack still squirming and calling for "Mawk." Marcus trotted up to see if he could be of service. "Look," Gemma said, "there's your Mawk."

Jack twisted and looked down at the beagle. "Mawk," he said sorrowfully, shaking his little head, and he pointed at Fling.

Pete laughed. "I think 'Mawk' is just a stand-in for whatever four-legged animal Jack wants for himself," he said.

"He needs a pony," Gemma said, grinning. She brought Jack back over and let him put his hand on Fling's warm neck.

"Mawk," Jack said happily.

"I need a drink," I announced to the barn at large.

18

PETE GOT OUT of the truck first. He'd found a spot next to Mimi's truck in the small parking area in front of the Long Pond stable. I was glad we were close to the barn, because the pretty weather of the past few days had blown away overnight, replaced with a gray sky and cold wind that raced right through my jacket and jeans. There were no horses in the outdoor arena, which was the best news I'd had all day: it meant we were doing the students' clinic in the indoor arena.

"Please promise me you'll behave," he said, taking his clinic bag from the back seat. He'd shoved his barn copy of his dressage book, which was a little dusty and torn at this point, in with the extra bits and spurs and assorted pieces of leather he carried with him to these types of events.

"I always behave," I assured him, reaching for the book. I wanted to admire the jacket photo for a moment—Pete, on horseback, back home at Briar Hill Farm. The sight of those green trees spreading a shady canopy over his head gave me a stab of homesickness. I was ready to be done with the browns and reds of autumn, thanks very much. Florida was calling my name louder and louder every day—every *hour*.

"Can it be the day after Chesapeake Three-Day already?" I said, handing back the book. "I want to be packing the trailer for home."

"You will complain all the way through that, too," Pete said. He tucked the book away and zipped the bag, then led the way to the barn door.

I followed, wondering if Pete was worried about the upcoming events. Our quiet period ended this weekend, with Pin Oak first and then Chesapeake two weeks after, and he still hadn't said no to Hannah's request that he take India and Prince to the three-day event. We were running out of time. He'd ridden those horses for less than two weeks at this point. He surely couldn't be thinking of riding them at Chesapeake? Yes, they were going well, but I still wanted him to choose the safe option, the logical option, and tell Hannah he was scratching them out of such advanced competition until we'd had a few months with them in Florida and he was better acquainted with the horses—and they were more confident in him.

I could see how he might have gotten away with taking them to Chesapeake a few years ago, but we were parents now. We had to consider what would be safest, not just for us, but for Jack. It was the sort of thinking that Mimi was struggling with now that her wife wanted her safe on the ground—was I the only one, out of the three of us, who had fully absorbed this lesson?

Nadine came out to greet us, wearing her usual combo of gray riding tights and Long Pond sweater. She was holding a clipboard and had a frazzled look about her, like the day had been tough so far and was about to get harder. Poor girl; if Mimi was determined to show us up today, then she was right about the second part.

"Hi guys," she called brightly, her tone much more cheerful than her expression. "Mimi is already in the indoor ring. She has a few guinea pig riders doing some gymnastics jumping. Jules, can I get you on the horses to illustrate some jumping exercises? I have a couple horses tacked up and waiting for her lesson to end, and then I can go over what each one is having trouble with and you can show the kids some ways to help, okay?"

"Sure," I said. "Sounds fun."

"I figure after that, you can take over, Pete. If that works?"

"That's fine," Pete agreed. "Is there somewhere you want us to wait while Mimi wraps up?" *Somewhere out of Mimi's way*, he meant.

"Oh, you can join them in the arena," Nadine said, blissfully unaware there was a feud between her clinicians. "There's plenty of seating."

"Perfect," I told her. "Thank you for having us."

Pete glanced at me as we walked after Nadine. "Should we tell her to possibly expect a scene?" he murmured.

"Oh, there won't be a scene. She's all talk."

"What about you?"

"I'm going to be good, honest."

He grinned. "That's right. You want to be *helpful*."

"I doubt today's the time or the place, but yeah, I do."

"Well, let's hope she agrees on the time and place thing," Pete said.

I wasn't sure Mimi would really behave herself with us. But despite the potential for embarrassment, I wasn't too worried. Teenagers loved drama. If we provided them with some, they'd love us forever.

The indoor arena was a vast and airy space with plenty of room for an entire jumping course. I felt instant envy as we entered. These kids had it made. There were two grandstand-style seating areas in the near corners, which were both half-filled with clusters of school-girls. They looked over their shoulders as Pete and I entered through the main doorway, and I saw some heads draw together, whispering.

A sense of unease came over me. I was used to teaching at Ala-chua and having my kids all around me, gossiping and whispering constantly, but they were *mine*. There was something unpleasant, almost as bad as a high school flashback, about walking into an auditorium full of strangers and seeing them take me in for the first time. I hadn't really enjoyed high school, not because I was an outcast or anything, but because school got in the way of riding horses. Being back in the school environment shouldn't have both-ered me . . . but there was something here, something that gave me the heebie-jeebies.

I was glad I wasn't walking right out there and teaching, be-cause I needed a few minutes to get my head straight.

Pete and I quietly took seats in the ground row of the closest grandstand as Mimi stood a few dozen feet away and illustrated to a youngish-looking girl on horseback how she wanted the reins held. Judging by her crouching stance, she was talking about the jumping position. I realized after a moment that she was trying to teach the girl a following release, which seemed like a rather lofty goal for a tween. The combination of balance and timing was pretty refined, and I wouldn't have expected anyone in my barn, with the exception of Maddox and possibly Lindsay, to move on from the simpler crest release for some time.

As a few minutes passed, my initial estimation proved cor-rect. The girl on horseback crumpled her forehead in confusion. "Okay," she said, "but what if I just fall forward over her neck?"

"You can't be leaning on her neck to jump in the first place," Mimi said. "And that goes for everyone." She turned to face the grandstands. "If you're leaning on the horse, you aren't ready to jump. Got that? You're just *not ready*! You have to get back to basics, and figure out your balance, and *then* go over fences. I know you guys think jumping horses is all that matters, but you are all, and I mean all of you, not half as good as you think you are. Go back to basics."

"Oh, so mean," I muttered to Pete. "They'll hate that."

I expected moans, but instead, everyone started clapping and whistling.

I looked at Pete in surprise. His eyebrows had gone up, and he looked around the crowd with interest.

"Wait a minute, they *like* being abused?" I demanded. "What's going on?"

Pete rubbed his face, partially to hide a grin I didn't like. "Jules, have you ever listened to yourself talking to your students?"

"What's that supposed to mean?"

"I think it means that you and Mimi might be more similar than you think."

That just kept becoming more and more apparent to me. Too bad Mimi hadn't noticed.

Then I realized she'd spotted us, and I sat up straighter, ready for the fireworks to begin.

Mimi's jaw jutted out. She considered us for a moment, her eyes narrowing. Then she beckoned to me. Obviously to me, not to Pete—those steely eyes said it all. Beside me, Pete stiffened.

Neither of us were prepared for Mimi to announce, "And here to demonstrate the *perfect* following release, Jules Thornton-Morrison!"

But I certainly wasn't going to back down from a challenge like that. I tripped right down to the arena, a smile on my face. I was going to make it easy for Mimi. Unfortunately for her, though, she wasn't going to make the point she was planning on. If there was one thing I excelled at, it was a fine following release.

So I made my way across the arena to Mimi and the student and her horse, noting the nice footing as I went. Fiber and rubber. Spared no expense, these girls' school types. I hoped they appreciated how good they had it, but I knew they didn't. Self-awareness wouldn't kick in until they were paying their own board bill.

The student had already hopped down from her horse and was happy to hand over the reins, avid interest on her face. She was probably about fourteen—I was developing an eye for this sort of thing after the past few years of herding tweens and teens around—and had the slim, greyhound look so many of my really hungry, talented students sported.

"The horse's name is Red," she told me.

"Hello, Red," I said, taking the reins and patting the school horse on the neck. He gave me a cool appraisal with his big, chocolate-brown eyes, and chewed at his bit. "What do you like to do for a living?"

"He's just a lesson horse," the girl answered for him.

"Oh, so like a genius who has to deal with a million different riding styles and abilities?"

She glanced at the ground. "Um."

Yeah, I thought. *I'm that kind of instructor.* Pete was right. Again. Damn him.

I asked her, "How often do you ride Red?"

"Three times a week," she said. "And every day in summer. I lease him for the summer term."

"And you jump him?"

"Three-six courses," she said, lifting her head again and giving me a challenging look.

"Good for you," I said mildly. "Three-six is big. So, you ought to be able to manage a following rein by now, but it's not something we coaches teach a lot of younger kids."

The "younger" annoyed her, as I knew it would. "I know I can do it," she informed me. "I'm the best rider in my age group."

A few hoots from the audience. She scowled at them while Nadine made hushing noises.

"Want to see it in action?" I asked. "And then we'll get you doing it, okay?"

"Go on and mount up," Mimi urged, clearly impatient to see me screw up.

I glanced around for a mounting block, then thought better of it. *Let's give the kids a show.* I kicked my foot into the stirrup and hopped into the saddle while barely disturbing its position on the horse's back. Since Red was only about sixteen hands, it was hardly a struggle, but the kid who leased him had the grace to look impressed. I wasn't lacking style.

"Okay," I told the kid, "let me trot this lad around the ring a couple times to make sure we know each other, and then I'll jump him. It would be rude to ask him to go over a fence and risk his balance like that for a rider he doesn't even know."

"Sure," the kid agreed, stepping aside. "That makes sense."

I felt out Red's mouth, which wasn't exactly soft putty like my horses' but was at least not two bars of iron with teeth on either side, like one could justifiably expect of a school horse. He probably didn't carry a lot of beginners at a place like this. Red softened for my hands after a moment's reflection, ducking his head and chewing on the bit. "There you go, buddy," I told him, giving him a nudge into the walk with my seat. "You're all right, aren't you?"

I made sure Mimi had to step aside as I walked him toward the rail. I figured if I was going to get anywhere with her, I'd have to assert myself first. Like stepping into a round pen with a rude colt—they needed to know I was just as tough and scary as they were before we could be nice to each other.

Red had a nice side-to-side swing to his walk, and once we were on the rail I found he had a pleasant, balanced trot. He got a little heavy in front, but I still thought he was a solid day-in, day-out hunt seat horse. I wondered how he was going to carry himself over a jump. Sometimes these horses made me feel like they were going to put their noses into the dirt after every fence—and those were horses who made it hard, even a little scary, to ride with a nice, soft following release.

I wondered if Mimi knew that about Red already.

Probably. Hence the smirk. She knew I'd want to ride defensively and stay back, which wouldn't be as textbook-beautiful as I'd ride a horse with an uphill approach and a clean, classic knees-up jump.

"Let's pick up our nose a little bit, buddy," I muttered to Red, giving him a couple meaningful nudges with my calves and, when that didn't go far, a tap with my heels. He did pick up his head at that, looking a little affronted, and he fluttered his nostrils in a snort as we came around the arena and faced the chattering peanut gallery in the grandstands.

"Ah, you like attention," I realized aloud. "That helps. We'll jump *toward* the crowd." And I sat down for a few strides, collected him as best I could, then bounced him into a lop-eared canter.

Red stretched happily toward the grandstands, then dilly-dallied along the long side of the arena, heading away from the audience. I could feel the difference in his balance as soon as the kids weren't in his line of sight, and it gave me an idea. As we cantered back toward the stands, I shouted out, "Okay, when we head for the jump, I need everyone to cheer for Red as loudly as you can! Want to give me a taste of how loud you can go?"

I saw Pete's eyebrows rise, and Nadine looked startled as well, but the kids were all for it. How often were they told to make noise in the indoor arena? And what did kids like better than being loud? There was a flurry of stamping and whistling and applause. Red's ears shot forward and his stride lengthened. In the middle of the ring, Mimi folded her arms and looked downright furious.

"Atta boy," I told him, giving him a quick pat on the neck. "Now you're ready to hop a fence without falling over it!"

I looped him back toward the jumps in the center of the ring, picking a line that faced the grandstands. It was nice and easy, set at two-foot-six with about five strides between the two jumps. A nice hunter standard. The arena held the fences easily, but I knew most horses would feel a little claustrophobic on a diagonal line like this, heading toward the wall.

No worries, though, because I wasn't here to stretch Red's stride. Just the opposite; I wanted to collect him. It could be a tall order for a face-first hunter schoolie, but I had faith in Red. We would make this work.

He tugged on me just a little as we turned toward the first jump—a good sign, I thought. He was interested in his job and, more than that, he was pretty interested in all those yelling kids at the top of the arena. The noise in the ring was getting louder and louder, echoing off the walls, and his ears pricked toward his raving fans, just beyond the jump course.

Time to compress that energy so I could wield it like a weapon. I wiggled the bit in his mouth and sat down in the saddle, adjusting his stride by slowing my hips. He sat back, unused to someone who could control him from the seat, and gave me a beautifully balanced canter right up to the base of the fence.

Leg, I thought, and gave him a good push.

Pop! Red hopped up with a heroic effort, and I slid forward with his momentum, letting the curve of his spine carry me just out of the saddle as my elbows followed the soft tug of the reins. Never touching a hair on his neck, my hands slid forward and then back again as I sat on the other side of the fence, maintaining a soft feel of his mouth so that he knew exactly who was guiding who on the landing side.

The smile that split my face was real. "Good boy!" I told him, giving him a congratulatory rub along his neck. "One more."

He bobbled a little and came up again with a canter stride that was flatter than before, but I tugged his nose back a stride before the fence and he put in another round, scopey jump. Again, I gave him a textbook release. It really wasn't hard. Red had all the right buttons; his kid just needed to learn where they were and how to press them.

The grandstand went wild. You'd have thought I'd caught the winning touchdown, or kicked it, or whatever those football players did. I saw Pete clapping as we cantered past, and Nadine waved a little, like a starstruck fan. I didn't know how Mimi reacted, because I didn't look her way.

"What a good job, Red," I told the horse, and then brought him down to a walk. "What a star he is," I said to the kid, when we got back to her. I kicked my feet free of the stirrups and dismounted, holding out the reins. She took them and looked at Red, then back at me, clearly wondering what I'd done to her slowpoke school horse.

"Here's the thing," I said, turning so the audience could hear as well. They hushed up and leaned forward. "The key to a following release isn't necessarily all about your position. It's about how you set up the horse, as well. When you don't feel like he's going to fall on his face, you don't have to prop yourself up on his neck to stay in the saddle. So think about getting the right jump, and the right position will follow."

"But how did you do that?" Red's kid asked plaintively. "I've never seen him jump like that. He usually just plops over the jumps. Should I kick more, or—"

"Oh, no. It's not kicking. It's just more leg, and some collection."

"I don't know how to collect him."

"Well, honey, here's the truth. You need dressage."

The girl made a face like I'd suggested she needed Jesus. The reaction in the grandstand wasn't much better.

"Trust me, dressage makes everything better," I told them. "And good news! Pete is going to give everyone a little dressage pep talk and you'll learn some good ways to incorporate it into your riding, okay?"

There was a general murmur of assent. But I knew I'd basically just told them they were going to have to work at riding the way they had to work at math or science, and no kid wants to be told that.

"Sorry, guys," I said, shrugging. "That's just the way it is. I didn't like it either, but you'll get over it."

I started back toward the grandstand. This was Mimi's lesson, after all. I still hadn't given her so much as a glance, but I could feel her eyes on my back.

I sat next to Pete and nudged him with my arm. "How about that little Red, huh?"

"You really perked him up." He pointed at Red, who was now trotting with a decent swing in his step as his rider pointed him toward a crossrail—evidently she found the two-six line a little intimidating for the lesson she was supposed to be learning. "I think he's going to give her a nice jump."

Red looked past the jump, toward all of us sitting on the grandstand, and I swear he looked right at me and winked before he jumped the crossrail like it was a three-foot fence of fire, nearly tossing the girl out of the tack, then landed in a pretty canter and even threw in a lead change at the end of the ring.

"Did she get the release?" I asked, trying not to laugh.

"I think she might have," Pete said. "She's certainly on her way to something."

"Teach them how to balance their horses with some little half-ass half halts," I told Pete, "and they might have a chance even if Mimi is teaching them that dressage is the eventing end of days."

In the center of the ring, Nadine was thanking Mimi for showing everyone how to do a more effective release over fences. "And a special shout-out to Jules for acting as our demonstrator, too," Nadine said, clapping. "She'll be doing some training fixes for us next."

The crowd cheered again, and I decided that for today, I liked Maryland just fine.

For dinner, the adults went up to the lounge overlooking the arenas, where the school culinary department had laid out a nice buffet of warming, rib-sticking country foods: turkey, gravy, cornbread, that sort of thing. I had expected something more formal, a long table and everyone conversing in stilted party talk. It would have made things complicated, with Mimi still fuming at me for doing a nice job in the riding demo.

Pete settled into a little table near the windows, evening light streaming in. It was early for a meal, and ordinarily we'd be turning the horses out right now, but a groom from Joan's barn was handling that for us tonight. I picked at my food, not particularly hungry. Pete's gaze flicked from me to Mimi, who was standing alone with a plate of cornbread. She wasn't touching it; it was too early for her to eat, too. Everyone looked uncomfortable, actually.

We were a party of confused horse people ripped from our native habitats.

I pushed my chair back. "Might as well go and talk to her."

Pete looked alarmed. "Here? Now? What are you going to say?"

"I'm going to tell her she should ask for a full-time position as a riding instructor," I said.

"What? Where did *that* come from?"

"I'm just a genius, Pete. I think of things." I marched over to Mimi, who held her plate of cornbread to her chest as if it was armor.

"I'm not going to shove you," I said, grinning.

She looked down at her plate, then back at me. "I didn't think you were." But she didn't move it, either.

"Listen, Mimi." I lowered my voice. The hum of conversation between Sean, Nadine, and the parents who had come up for dinner was just enough to keep things private between us. "I talked to your wife last week."

Her nostrils flared, and a crease between her eyes deepened into a chasm. "Why did you—Diane would never—"

"Chance meeting at the Blue Plate," I explained. "Listen. I know you're having a hard time with retirement, and I don't blame you. But—"

"You don't know anything about it," Mimi hissed. The anger in her voice took me aback, and that was all the time she needed to shove the plate at me. I took it without thinking, startled, and while my hands were full she stormed across the room and left, slamming the door behind her.

The buzz of conversation came to a stuttering halt and I felt the eyes of everyone in the room on me. Some curious, some confused, some concerned.

It was all the same to me. Flushing with embarrassment, I

turned around and held up the plate of cornbread. "She wasn't hungry," I said. "So . . ."

Nadine glanced at the door. "Oh, I should make her a to-go box," she said, but the sound of a diesel truck roaring to life put an end to that idea.

I crept back to the table where Pete sat, trying valiantly to hide his amusement. I put down the cornbread. "Got you this," I muttered.

"Yum," Pete said. "Cornbread."

19

THE HOURS BETWEEN the clinic and Pin Oak seemed to fold in on each other; one afternoon we were playing to a crowd, and then suddenly we were packing our things for the last horse trials before Chesapeake Three-Day Event. I was competing three horses, and now, so was Pete, which meant we had a full trailer-load to haul the hour or so to the showgrounds at Pin Oak Farm.

Everyone we'd talked to had said we'd love Pin Oak's cross-country course. It was apparently some kind of Maryland tradition. And I had to admit that even as a lifelong Floridian, I'd heard of the venerable Pin Oak Farm plenty of times. The fall event was large enough to sprawl over three days instead of just a weekend, with dressage on Friday, cross-country on Saturday, and show jumping on Sunday—like the larger winter events in Florida. And for many riders, it was the final tune-up before the three-day event in two weeks' time, so we were riding in good, and ambitious, company.

My mood was pretty serene heading into the event weekend. I had my new horse under saddle, which was always exciting, and the last week of nice weather had sweetened my mood toward

Maryland. A girl could get used to riding in short sleeves and still somehow not being a sweaty mess all the time. The cold, gray day that had settled in on Wednesday was replaced by golden sunlight by the time we left on Thursday afternoon. Gemma and Jack sat in the back seat of the truck, playing with toy horses. "Mawk," Jack said happily, trotting his horse along the armrest of his car seat.

I looked out the window with a sense of something close to contentment as Joan's paddocks slid by. I'd turned Fling out with her mare for the weekend and my chronic jumper seemed to be content enough to stay in one place at last, either because she was settling into the safety of the herd, or because she had done some work to occupy her brain—maybe both. Her chestnut coat gleamed copper in the slanting sunshine.

Near the cluster of trees that marked the farm driveway, something caught my eye and I clutched Pete's arm. He braked, and in the trailer behind us, the horses protested the jerky hauling job. But I was glad he'd slowed down. "Look, Pete!" I breathed, pointing. "The fox!"

The fox looked up at us from the center of the driveway, his red ears pricked with interest. Then he trotted off into the woods, twitching his brush of a tail as he disappeared into the bushes. Here was the fox who had been skulking around our barns for the past few weeks, giving us a saucy little sendoff before we went to Maryland's most celebrated horse trials.

"That fox is our good-luck charm," I told Pete. "He's saying, *You're going to do just fine at Pin Oak.*"

Pete eased the truck forward again, and the kicking horses settled. "You know we have red foxes in Florida, too."

"I've never seen one," I said. "Don't ruin this for me. The fox is good luck."

Marcus popped up from his bed on the floor behind the truck's center console and gave me a lick on the ear. "The fox and the hound," I told him. "But you're going to the horse show, and the fox is staying here."

Lacey texted as the pastures turned to cornfields and we picked up speed on the main road. *Things are going so great without you. Can't believe we only have two more weeks of freedom.*

I snorted and tapped a quick reply. *Just for that I am coming home early but not saying when.*

There was a moment of peace, then Lindsay texted to say, *Mom I heard youre coming home early does this mean I can't have parties at the house anymore??*

Lacey chimed in with a few messages about how happy all of the kids were now that I was gone.

"Your phone is blowing up," Pete commented. "Everything okay?"

"I'm being harassed by the worst people in the world," I said, and I texted both of them to leave me alone so I could focus on my very important job of jumping horses over logs. *If I don't jump these horses over logs who do you think will do it? Civilization would collapse without people like me doing the hard labor!*

I got back laughing-face emojis interspersed with skulls from Lindsay, and a few grinning devils from Lacey.

"The Two Ls are harassing you again, huh?" Pete asked as I groaned and tossed my phone into my purse.

"I guess I'd be worried if they didn't," I admitted. "Mean is our love language."

"They've done a good job watching the place for us." He took his foot off the gas as we began to overtake a tractor taking up most of the road ahead.

"Well, let's reserve judgment for when we see the place. I hope the sparkle paint has worn off the horses' hooves by then."

He chuckled. "What about the poultice art on the walls?"

"There's no way Lacey left that up even overnight. She's too much of a clean freak about her barn." Pete's phone buzzed, and I glanced at it for him. "You have a good-luck text from Hannah," I said. "Want me to answer it?"

"No, leave it unread," he said. "I'll call her when we get the horses settled at the showgrounds. We need to have a talk ahead of this event, anyway."

I looked at him. Pete kept his eyes on the tractor, slowly rumbling away ahead of us. It was massive, with tires about as big as a horse. No one could get around it until we reached Catoctin Creek, still a mile away. "What are you going to tell her?" I asked him.

"That I won't take India or Prince in the two-star, even if they qualify this weekend."

I exhaled in relief—it felt like a breath I'd been holding for nearly two weeks, ever since the new horses came to our barn. I knew Pete was figuring him out, but every horse had their own quirks, and he'd found India in particular was tricky—the horse knew quite a lot, but he *thought* he knew everything, and that sometimes gave him the confidence to defy Pete and go his own way. It never seemed like he was being aggressive or naughty, it was just that he was a young and cocky horse who sometimes wanted to do his own thing, and he knew he had the athleticism to do it.

That was what made me nervous, and not only about the three-day event but about this weekend, as well. India needed to trust Pete to be the leader. After all, Pete got to walk the cross-country course beforehand. India didn't.

Prince was a little more workmanlike; he had a lot of jumping ability, but his dressage was plain as mud and it was clear that was where his scores held him back. Pete and I had already discussed whether the horse would be happier as a show jumper. It just didn't seem worthwhile to push him through the tough, potentially dangerous work of cross-country and a dressage test he clearly considered drudgery when the big jumper classes would play right into his strengths. But that was a conversation for Florida.

Ahead of us, the tractor turned into a farm lane and Pete slowly put his foot down, speeding the truck up. A line of frustrated drivers began passing our rig.

"Are you going to make her a counteroffer?" I asked. "Sweeten the deal a little? You could take them to Glen Hill in November."

"For now, I'm just going to tell her we're in our feeling-out period and whatever happens at Pin Oak, it's not going to be enough for me to confidently take them to Chesapeake. Pin Oak is a top-level event. She'll remember that. I hope."

I thought she'd listen if Pete was very clear and laid out all the facts about safety for both horse and rider. There was no room for hesitation between horse and rider on an Intermediate-level cross-country course, and that went double for a major three-day event like Chesapeake. The questions asked of teams out there would be tricky to the point of confounding at times. From what I'd heard of Pin Oak, we might even find complex questions out on their course, too.

"Are you worried about the course this weekend?"

"I'm prepared to scratch or retire if I don't like the way the course works out. It might even be a way to get Hannah on my side, if she's still pushing back about Chesapeake."

"You'd have to ride badly before you retired," I mused. "Or people would question why you retired. It's not a bad idea."

"Okay, *pretending* I'm having a bad round might be going too far," Pete said, laughing. "But I'm going into this with no ego, and I'm prepared to play it safe. I want these horses for the long haul. They're quality."

From the back seat, Gemma spoke up. "Hey guys? I think we left the cooler in the trailer living quarters."

"Oh, no." We'd packed all the snacks—for Jack and for the rest of us, too—in that cooler. "Is Jack hungry?" I squirmed in my seat to reach around and look at him. He gave me a big smile and held up his toy horse.

"Not yet," Gemma admitted. "But I am."

"Why don't we stop quick in Catoctin Creek and we can grab some of those ham-and-cheese croissants from Nikki's bakery?" I suggested.

"The ones with raspberry jam?" Gemma brightened.

"Yup, those are the ones." Jam and cheese and ham shouldn't work, but it did. "Pete? It's just ahead. Snack stop, please?"

Pete picked up my hand and kissed the back of it. "Since you said please."

20

THE STABLING AT Pin Oak Farm was temporary but comfortable. We were placed on a western-facing row of stalls and the warm light poured in through the bars and doorways. There wasn't a scrap of shade but the temperature was below eighty-five degrees so it felt like winter to me. The Marylanders and assorted northeasterners were melting, but my horses hadn't even considered growing a winter coat yet and my regular, lightweight riding clothes were perfect for the balmy temperatures.

"Climate change is killing this sport," someone muttered as he walked by with a bale of hay, sweat pouring down his face.

I could hear the sound of clippers a few stalls down as a horse received an impromptu body-clipping session.

Kit came over to help us on Friday morning. They'd been boarding nearby and only had to travel a few minutes to get here. She was wearing a sun shirt and her cheeks were pink.

"Did you acclimate to Maryland or something?"

"I mean, technically I'm new to Florida," she said, grinning. "Remember I was in Aiken last winter? We had an ice storm and everything."

"That's disgusting," I said, fully aware everyone else on the showgrounds thought today's heat was equally disgusting.

"So, did you order the unseasonable heat?"

"Maybe I did, and maybe I didn't. All I know is, I promised the eventing gods whatever they wanted if they got me through the next two weeks in Maryland in one piece."

"And we all know you have a direct telephone line to the eventing gods." Kit spun around and surveyed my stable row. She nodded at the stalls of well-groomed horses and I knew what she was thinking: *Jules Thornton has a very nice life.*

She wasn't wrong.

"Well, thanks for coming over," I said. "Do you think you could hand-walk Mickey? I need to get the manure stains off Rogue, and then I'll cover him with a fly sheet and hope that keeps him from sleeping in his own poop for a few hours."

"Having a gray horse is such a nightmare," Vane announced as she strolled up to join us. She almost exclusively groomed a green-stained gray, as Big Dan was in a long-term relationship with manure.

I sighed, looking between my two grays, and Pete's gray in the stall right after them. Where had all the gray come from? I would swear horses were all bay or chestnut when I was a kid. "It wasn't my intent."

"It never is," she said, "but I won't ever let Kit buy another gray horse."

Kit looked over her shoulder, Mickey's lead rope already in hand. "I don't buy them for their color, Vane!"

Vane shook her head.

I was on my knees in the wet grass, scrubbing off Rogue's green spots with purple shampoo, when a panting dog alerted me that we had company. I glanced up and saw, without much surprise, that Hannah Grayer and her spotted Great Dane had already arrived.

"You're here early," I observed, looking for a tray of coffee cups or a bag from a bakery in her hands, but I was left disappointed. What kind of owner didn't bring snacks? "The Intermediate horses are out walking. Pete has India and Vane has Prince. Their first dressage test isn't until almost nine, so we have a little time—"

"Oh, we came early on purpose. Wanted to bring you breakfast," Hannah said cheerfully. She looked over her shoulder. Suddenly, a sturdy granddaughter appeared in the morning mist, carrying a large donut box. "And there's coffee on the way, too. Kids can be slow." She laughed.

Okay, bless you, I thought. Hannah was back on top as the greatest owner of all time. "Oh man, that's great. I just need to finish cleaning up Rogue here." I gestured at his purple knees. "Beautiful once he's clean, you know?"

"He's a very nice horse," Hannah said. I watched her eyes rove over him. She liked what she saw. "I look forward to watching him go. What time's his dressage?"

"Ten twenty," I replied. "He's going in Prelim." I wondered if Hannah was interested in buying more horses. With Fling added to the roster, I was going to have to form some new syndicates to buy future horses. I was tapped out.

"And what about India? How is he feeling today?"

"Seems fine . . . he ate up his breakfast," I said, turning back to Rogue's dirty knees. "And he was happy to go for a walk. I'd say he's feeling good. Same with Prince."

"Think he can win his division?" She was talking about India still. I had a feeling Prince was a little bit of second thought when compared with the mighty Star of India.

I shrugged, not wanting to accidentally contradict anything Pete might have said to her. "I really can't say. Anything can happen out there. And it's their first time together. Pete's done well with him at home, though."

"I'd like to see him win," Hannah said, "since he's not going to be at Chesapeake to do the two-star."

"You talked to Pete about it?"

"First thing this morning."

I kept my eyes on Rogue's knees. "You know, it might be a few times out before he really syncs with Pete as his new rider. Since he's only had Mimi before. Her style is *really* different. But you know that, it's why you picked Pete to take your horses to the next level."

"Of course, but—"

"Just the fact that he is *barely* squeaking into qualifying for Chesapeake with Mimi should be a warning that he isn't really ready at all," I went on mercilessly. "We usually like our horses winning before we move them up a level or take them to a three-day. Not putting in the bare minimum to qualify. Barely qualified is barely safe, I'd say."

Hannah was quiet; I glanced up at her and saw she was taking my words seriously. Thank goodness. "I never thought about it that way," Hannah said eventually. "I just assumed that if the horse is allowed in, if they have the points to get in, then they're contenders."

"I'd say no—in horse sports, it really doesn't always work that way." I stood up and surveyed Rogue's knees. Were they tinted slightly purple? That whitening shampoo could leave a stain of its own. I picked up the hose and began another rinse, continuing my speech. "In this sport, safety has to beat out everything else. A winning, experienced horse with more than his share of qualifications is going to have a better shot at getting around the course safely than a horse who has just squeaked into qualifying. Okay, what do you think? Are his knees clean enough?"

"I think so," Hannah said distractedly. "Thanks for telling me that about the qualifying, Jules. You're very direct, aren't you?"

"That's my best quality," I told her. "Well, that and the fact that I'm an incredible rider."

Hannah laughed. Impressed laugh, or get-a-load-of-this-girl laugh? She pushed the box toward me. "Have a donut."

I had a donut. I had several donuts. They were very cheering. Hannah gave a plain one to her Great Dane, who gobbled it up in one bite and looked for more. Inspired, I gave one to India when he came back from his walk, and he devoured it.

Maybe the donut put India in a fine mood, because he gave Pete a straightforward and professional dressage test from the first salute to the final.

Pete was so pleased that he gave India a heartier pat than usual and the horse spooked forward as they were on the way out of the dressage arena. A little laughter rippled through the people hanging around the arenas. Pete gave them a good-natured grin as he drew back on the reins and brought India back to a walk.

But the judging was already finished, so a little spook between friends was fine. A few minutes later, we found out they were waltzing toward the cross-country phase on a 28.2 penalty score—not too shabby, and not entirely out of the running for a top-tier finish, depending on how the weekend shook out.

Hannah promised India another donut for being such a good boy. Pete told her if she unbuckled his noseband, he could have it right away, but she said no, she thought India would prefer to enjoy his donut without a bit in his mouth. So I gave him a handful of carrot-flavored horse cookies instead. I really didn't think he'd notice any difference. For horses, treats were treats.

I'd been holding Prince while Vane walked Mickey in the background. We did a complicated horse switch—Pete dismounted and took Prince's reins from me, I took India over to Vane and swapped out his reins for Mickey's, and Kit walked around on Big Dan in the warm-up and watched, clearly laughing at us.

Vane made a big show of shaking her fist at Kit, then patted India and told him to follow her back to the barn.

I mounted Mickey and walked him in a slow circle around Hannah while Pete took Prince off to the warm-up area. The bay horse moved slowly, with a clear lack of enthusiasm.

"It'll be a different story tomorrow when he's heading to the cross-country warm-up," I guessed.

"Do you think he dislikes the dressage?" Hannah asked me.

"It's boring," one of the granddaughters said, flopping the Great Dane's ears up and down. "No one likes dressage."

"That's what Prince thinks, too," I told her. To Hannah, I said, "It just doesn't come naturally to him. I'm sure Pete will have some exercises to try with him once we get them home, to see if it makes things better for him, but some horses just aren't born for the dressage."

"He's a natural jumper though," Hannah said worriedly, as if I might be suggesting Prince was no good.

"Plenty of room for a good jumper in our barn," I assured her. "We already love Prince. We'll figure him out, I promise. I have to go warm up Mickey now, but I'll come back and watch his test with you, okay?"

Mickey moved nicely, breath snorting through his nostrils, ears flicking occasionally back toward the tree where Hannah and her granddaughters were standing. I knew he was thinking about those donuts. When we came back to watch Prince do his test, he snuffled around the kids while they giggled and poked him in the nose. These girls were very used to horses.

"He wants a donut," I told them.

"He has to wait," the youngest kid crowed. "No eating with the bit in the mouth!"

"You guys are strict," I said. "No way I'd be this mean if you weren't here to lay down the law."

The girls laughed riotously. They made me miss my barn kids. I wondered what kind of trouble they were planning for this weekend. Just a few more weekends without me. And then it was back to work for the winter eventing season.

I gave Mickey another turn around the warm-up, then came back to Hannah and the girls so we could watch Prince make his way through the dressage test. He wasn't as sharp as India, but I could tell he'd come out with a respectable score. He wouldn't be in last place, anyway.

Pete was much more gentle with his pat after the final salute to the judge, and when he walked over to us, Hannah assured Prince he could have a donut, too. "There are enough donuts for everyone," she told him, stroking his neck. "As soon as we go back to the barn."

"But first, Jules rides," Pete said. "You ready for this?"

"Obviously," I drawled, picking up my reins. I put on a good show, but I was tense on the inside. Entering the arena under the judge's eye got easier, but it was never actually *easy*.

This test was about sharpening Mickey up before the big competition at Chesapeake, and as he puffed himself up on the way into the dressage arena, I was glad we were here. He needed the mileage, but maybe I did, too. I felt my legs lengthening along his sides, my shoulders coming back, and my chin raising as we faced down the judge in her white gazebo. This was a high-class event, and there was no substitute in all our hours of training for the real thing.

I saluted the judge, and our test began.

It wouldn't really end until Sunday afternoon two weeks from now, when the final show jumping course was finished, and we would be free to pack up for Florida and home.

21

CARBS ARE IMPORTANT for energy, or so I reasoned as I took another dive into the donut box in celebration of Mickey's excellent test. I barely had time to wipe the sugar from my lips before Vane had come back to get me into Rogue's saddle for our Prelim test. I patted my stomach tentatively before loosening my belt a hole. It didn't help.

Pete gave me a sympathetic grimace, but what did he know? He could still eat donuts all day.

Hannah, on the other hand, saw my expression and gave me a bottle of water.

"Things feel different after you have a kid, don't they?" she said, gesturing for me to take a sip. "Nothing goes back to exactly where it was before."

"It seems like bodies should be arranged better than that," I replied. "And also, I don't think anyone told me my entire metabolism would change."

"No one tells us anything," Hannah said. "Not until you're initiated into the club. It was the same for me, and that was forty-some years ago. But what can we do? Drink a lot of water and keep on riding, Jules. You'll figure it out."

Vane looked me over with a critical eye as I settled into the saddle, but luckily she didn't comment about my tight breeches. Maybe they didn't look as bad as they felt. I tugged my jacket down anyway, feeling weirdly self-conscious.

"You should put on some lip gloss," Vane informed me. "I finally got Kit wearing some light stuff that doesn't make her too nuts . . . you want me to get it out of her purse?"

"No, no, no lip gloss. I'm not a dressage queen." I gathered Rogue's reins and flicked a few loose hairs from his lowest braid under the saddle pad. "No makeup for me, thanks."

"If you were a dressage queen, I'd be applying red lipstick and the longer-than-long mascara," Vane pointed out. "I'm just talking a little pink on your lips so you don't look like a big white ghost with a black hat on."

"I *like* looking like a ghost," I insisted stubbornly. "That is my competitive edge. That and being the superior rider on these grounds."

Vane snorted. "I'm sure."

Pete came over, done riding for the day and ready to annoy me—I mean coach me—for my other dressage rides. Kit was at his side, smirking at Vane.

"Are you harassing our groom?" he asked me.

"No," I replied. "Our groom is harassing *me*."

"Vane," Kit remonstrated, "you know Jules doesn't understand makeup. She's a feral wolf-child."

"Yeah," I told Vane. "I'm a feral wolf-child."

"You're just difficult," Vane said. "And you *like* to be difficult. That's all it is."

I glanced at Pete with the most innocent expression I could manage. "Is that true?"

He shrugged and turned toward the arena. "I think we have a dressage test to finesse, dear."

"Sorry, Rogue," I said, nudging the horse to follow Pete. "Boring day first, cross-country day next."

Rogue didn't seem to mind. He danced his way through his dressage test with so much grace, I started to wonder if a body snatcher had switched him with another horse. It turned out to be his best score yet, and I couldn't help a triumphant grin at Pete as we left the arena.

He saluted me in return, then smiled at a fellow trainer who came up to pat him on the shoulder. "Nice ride by your student there," the woman said.

I nearly fell off Rogue. *Student?*

"Thanks," Pete said, making sure his voice carried to me. "She was nothing before she met me."

I was *so* going to divorce that man.

Pete turned back to me and winked.

Okay, the divorce could wait. But only because he was so damn cute when he winked like that.

After dressage wrapped up and the horses were fed their dinners, the stable area grew quiet. A few people were camping, and they were sitting near their RV sites, grilling and enjoying the unseasonably warm evening. I had a craving for a hamburger with flame marks on it and half a bottle of ketchup dumped over it, but the breeches I'd worn this morning were already strained and I needed to wear them again for show jumping on Sunday, so no beef for me. Back in my early twenties, I could have eaten an extra-large value meal and not felt bloated; now I had entire weekends where I'd have to let out my show breeches if I ate more than a salad.

I was just heading for the truck when I heard my name called out. I turned and saw an older man in breeches. *Super-yay*, I thought bleakly. It was Sandy Sullivan. I wondered what he wanted this time.

"Hi," I said nervously as he drew near.

"Hello again, Mrs. Thornton-Morrison," he said.

"Jules is fine," I reminded him.

"Jules," he repeated, smiling like we were old chums now. "Yes, well. Good job getting those horses out of the three-day event. This is a much better spot for them to close out Maryland."

"Yeah," I said. "I know. Thanks for telling me about that ahead of time."

"Of course. And, I wanted to tell you—you know, I saw your cross-country round at Catoctin Green a few weeks ago."

"Yes, I remember." He had invited me to go hunting. I'd been flattered. Apparently the moment hadn't meant as much to him.

"Damn fine," said Sandy Sullivan, nodding appreciatively. He glanced up at the sky. "It's been very dry, hasn't it?"

Was his mind wandering? Great, I was going to have to call an ambulance for the great Sandy Sullivan. Everyone in Maryland would think I'd given him the vapors. I'd find myself at risk of being marched out of the state before I could finish what I'd come here to do. And suddenly I found I wasn't in such a huge hurry to leave Maryland. I had horses in good spots after dressage, a big event for Mickey in two weeks, and I wanted to play this out.

"No rain," Sandy said encouragingly, as though I was now worrying *him* with my confused silence.

"It has been dry," I agreed cautiously. "Good footing, though."

"It won't last. It's going to rain tomorrow."

"Well, maybe not that much—"

"India has a quirk you should know about," Sandy said. "He doesn't care for rain. He's had a—ah—bad experience in the rain."

"A point-to-point experience?" I guessed.

Sandy dipped his head as if to acknowledge the point. "So you know about that."

"It's come up. You and Mimi, out racing in the rain? Was that really a good idea?"

"Old fox-hunters," he said, shrugging. "We both made some bad choices that day."

I wished his intentions were clear. "So you're saying India is . . . afraid of rain?"

"She wouldn't have fallen off a different horse," Sandy said. "But India was giving her trouble because of the weather."

"Sandy, why don't you talk to my husband about this horse?" I asked impatiently.

"Oh, I wouldn't . . ." Sandy trailed off, and his expression became sad. "Pete looks so like his grandfather."

I nodded. That much was true. And another piece of the puzzle I'd been struggling with since we came to Maryland finally slid into place. Sandy's weird warning was at least partially because he felt guilty about getting Mimi hurt on the point-to-point course, but the reason he was coming to me with it all—that was because he missed Pete's grandfather. They'd been friends.

I felt for him, but at the same time, I really needed him to come to the point.

"Is Pete going to get into trouble out there? You need to tell me."

Sandy turned to leave, his bad leg swiveling beneath him. I was noticing a pattern with these older riders. They all had a limp. Something to look forward to, I supposed.

He looked up at the sky again and shook his head. Over his shoulder, he said, "He's not going to get into life-or-death trouble, I wouldn't think. But he might find the horse is a lot stickier than he's been led to believe. Tell him to keep his leg on, Jules. And be ready for anything."

That was terrible advice. The worst advice. Because, of *course* Pete was going to keep his leg on and be ready for anything. That was literally how cross-country riding worked. You did those two things, you prayed to the eventing gods, and you gave your horse room to figure things out. Sandy might as well have said, "Tell him to keep breathing with his lungs." Obviously, man.

I watched Sandy limp away and wished that the people of Maryland didn't have to be so esoteric and weird. I missed Florida, dammit. Where, yeah, everyone was weird, but they didn't go around scaring people the night before cross-country. Because now I had to go and tell Pete that India was apparently afraid of the rain.

Well, maybe I'd get lucky. Maybe the rain in the forecast would just dry up, fizzle away, and never come here. It could happen.

22

SUNRISES CAME UNFAIRLY late in October, making it harder and harder to get out of bed in time to feed. And, of course, it was even worse on event weekends, when we set our alarms for anywhere between three and five in the morning. So, I was getting used to starting the day by staying buried under the covers for a few minutes, cursing the black sky. But when I opened my eyes on Saturday morning, the darkness pressing down on our little bedroom seemed particularly impenetrable.

I took a breath and tried to figure out where I was.

Maryland. In an RV. On a cross-country day.

With time and place fixed in my mind again, I flicked the window blinds aside. Rain, streaking down the RV window. Just a few drops at first, but then more and more, until a steady downpour was hammering the glass. As if it had been waiting for me to wake up before it really got rolling.

Was it too much to ask that I have a nice, sunny day for *one* cross-country round in the state of Maryland?

"Could you make this one fast shower and we're done?" I whispered to the eventing gods.

The rain rattled overhead, but there was no other answer.

I sighed and reached for my phone, checking the time. Four fifty, an unholy hour, and also just ten minutes before my alarm was set to go off.

I sighed again, louder this time. No point in keeping this frustration to myself now.

Beside me, Pete stirred and rolled over. "Whassthasoun?" he murmured.

"It's raining."

"Raining," he repeated, voice husky with sleep. "Ugh."

We lay there for a few minutes in silence, listening to the rain drumming on the RV's roof. It wasn't like a Florida rain, quick and blowy and showing off.

This was a northern rain. Steady. Persistent. Unending. I could tell by the way it fell straight down. This rain was here for the long haul.

"On cross-country day," Pete said eventually.

"Yes."

"Again."

"I think it must be a law here."

I turned off my alarm before it started beeping. Then I held the phone for a moment, trying to decide whether to get up or not.

Here was the constant temptation when we woke to bad weather: maybe we should, perhaps, just . . . go back to bed? Kit and Vane were staying at Pin Oak in their horse trailer. I could text Kit, ask her to feed the horses, and we could just scratch. Forget about driving down there in the pouring rain, forget about galloping on the slick clay hills, just go around lunchtime, pick them up, and drive back for a quiet weekend.

We'd given up events due to bad weather a few times. But in

Florida, there was almost always another event to make up for a missed one; the winter season was packed with shows to the point where schooling shows were actually held on weekdays because everyone was too busy with rated shows on the weekends to get in any schooling time for their young horses. And, of course, we were at home, not paying for farm and RV rental just for the privilege of being within driving distance of Pin Oak. It made me feel like we had to get the full value of our stay.

But what if the footing was terrible? This Maryland clay made me nervous. It got slick and gluey. Plus, there were the hills to consider. Florida horses weren't conditioned on ground like that. We'd gotten around Catoctin Green okay, but this was a bigger course—and this rain was coming down harder.

And then there was India to think about. I'd told Pete about Sandy's visit, about blaming the rain for Mimi's accident. He hadn't been convinced. "The horse needs better reaction times to the aids," he'd said. "Mimi was operating on such a delay with him, she was really completely ineffective. He's more responsive to me, even after a couple of weeks, than he would have been that day—especially if they were galloping at racing speed over jumps, in the open."

All of his points were sound. It could be that Sandy was just feeling so guilty over Mimi—and fearful of seeing his friend's grandson injured—that he'd decided the rain was the problem. Pete had no fears on that point, though. "It's going to be fine," he'd said firmly, and that was the end of the discussion. Sandy Sullivan was shelved, and I hoped he'd stay that way.

But now, with the rain pouring down in buckets, I felt a fresh wave of worry wash over me. I worried about Pete more than I used to. Another side effect of motherhood. I stayed under the covers, fighting the urge to pull them over my head.

"Well." Pete sighed, pushing back the duvet. "I guess we better get going."

Naturally.

I picked up my phone again and looked at the assortment of weather apps, trying to calculate for myself when the radar would clear.

It didn't look good. Rain was swallowing up the East Coast, and while it wasn't to Pin Oak yet, it would be there in . . . oh, half an hour.

"Where was this rain yesterday when we were going to bed?" I grumbled, tossing the phone back on its ledge and sliding out of bed.

Pete was already in jeans. "I don't know, Ohio? I think it's still there, actually. This is a big storm system."

"I hate the north," I told him. "And if you say Maryland is technically a southern state, I will throw you out of this RV. We don't get rain like this in Florida."

"Have you been in a tropical storm recently?"

"At least they cancel events for tropical storms!" I retorted, but that wasn't strictly true. Sometimes the events simply went on. "Rain with a name" had to be pretty intense to interrupt the eventing community in Florida.

He threw me a sweatshirt. "Jules, my dear and sweet and gentle wife, I promise we'll go home very soon. But first, don't you want to make Maryland regret ever offending you with rain?"

"When you put it like that . . ." I tugged on the sweatshirt. Time to make Maryland pay. We crept out of the RV, careful not to disturb Gemma, Jack, or Marcus.

A gray dawn was slowly trying to get its act together as we drove into the stabling parking area. We slid out of the truck into a sloppy mess of battered grass and slippery mud, which only got thicker as we made our way around the well-trodden stable area.

I picked through the mud in a pair of Hunter boots I rarely wore in Florida—rubber boots were too hot most of the year, so I found it easier to just have damp feet and a change of socks and shoes during the summer storm season. I could feel the clay tugging at my heels with every step. The horses would feel it, too, and how much would that slow them down near the end of the course, when their hooves were heavy with clay? Alex once told me that on a muddy track, a horse could be lugging five extra pounds' worth of dirt on his hooves and legs. To a horse extending himself to his utmost, those things mattered.

"Should've stayed in bed," I murmured, and Pete gave my hand a quick squeeze.

"It'll be fine," he said.

The horses nickered eagerly when they saw us, ready for breakfast. Pete tramped over to the show office to see if the course had any changes thanks to the ongoing rain. While he was away, I fed the horses their grain and started filling hay nets, trying to keep the hay from tumbling onto the wet ground. Even inside the temporary stalls, the atmosphere was moist and getting wetter by the minute, as if the water was going to start oozing up from the ground and envelop us all.

Pete came back and said they were keeping an eye on the course. "That's all they'd say, though I saw some officials heading out there in one of those four-wheel-drive golf carts."

"Maybe they'll call off the competition? We could just pack up and go home."

"I don't think so. We'll put in big studs and get around just fine," Pete told me. "Stop worrying. You're not good at it."

"How dare you! I'm good at *everything* I do."

"Well, then, stop worrying so your incredible talent doesn't make me start worrying, too."

I made a face at him and hopped off the tack trunk I'd been perched on. I knelt next to it, my heels sinking into the mud as I opened the trunk so I could dig around for the biggest studs we had. I found four. "Where are the rest?"

Vane came over with a raincoat on while I was hunting for them. She held up a plastic bag. It was labeled JULES'S STUDS DO NOT TOUCH with masking tape and Sharpie. With a barn full of sticky-fingered kids, you had to label things with threatening messages or your whole life would go missing. I abruptly remembered Kit borrowing them, with permission, for a cross-country school the week after Catoctin Green.

"You want giant studs?" she asked, grinning.

"Giant studs are the only thing on my mind," I told her.

"Can't relate," Vane said, handing over the bag.

Pete shook his head.

Vane stuck around to help us tack up. Twenty minutes later, we had horses booted, saddled, and studded up for their cross-country runs. Mickey was pulling at the reins, excited and ready for action.

Vane led out Prince, who looked mildly interested in his surroundings, stepping carefully on his studs as he went from the deep bedding of the stall to the paved aisle. All in all, his expression said, a nap would be better, but he'd give the outside world a try. If he could figure out how to walk. He lifted a hoof high and set it down again with a tentative gesture.

"You're on high heels today, buddy," I told him. "Trust me, you'll want the help."

India looked decidedly unhappy with the weather. He hung back in the stall, his ears fixed on the raindrops falling across the doorway. Standing in the rain, I pulled Mickey back and glanced in at Pete, who was gazing at India with an expression of mild chagrin.

Almost as if he was thinking about whether the horse was *really* afraid of the rain.

"We should pop rain sheets on them," Vane suggested. "You have any? I'll grab them."

"First tack trunk," I told her, taking Prince's reins.

She ran back to the tack stall and threw open the trunk, digging out two rain sheets. "Any more hidden in there?"

"Probably not," I said, "but Mickey can make do with a saddle cover. He doesn't mind some rain."

Pete looked up at that, as if I'd said something disparaging about India, but he took the rain sheet from Vane and threw it over the horse without a word. He clucked to walk him from the stall, but India tensed, then shook his head and balked, his ears falling stiffly to either side as if he was afraid the rain would pummel down inside them.

"I bet you go out in the rain all the time," Pete told him, shaking the reins gently. "Quit acting like you're a big princess, now."

India snorted and put his head down to the ground, blowing suspiciously at a mud puddle just outside the aisle. We waited, standing in the bucketing rain, while Pete's big, brave event horse snorted at puddles. Mickey's coat was soaked through already, and the saddle cover was dripping with water.

"That's right," Pete said, patient as could be. "You can jump the puddles, India. I won't be mad."

The rain tapered off a bit, from a downpour to a steady patter. My raincoat began to leak. I stuffed my gloves deeper into my pockets, trying to keep them dry and tacky for as long as I could.

India stepped over the puddle but kept his head low, his ears off to the side. Something about his ears bothered me. He held them as if someone had been careless with a hose during a bath and gotten water into them.

We walked to the cross-country warm-up a short distance from the barns, where a few other wet and hearty souls were already cantering around. This event only ran through Intermediate, so we would be the first ones to tackle the course.

Vane stood Prince under a tree while she texted Kit, making sure her rider was managing okay without her. I didn't know how I'd ever thank Vane enough for taking care of us. Three horses and two riders in one division were too much to manage without our own grooms.

Pete was the first out, so he hopped into the saddle and I took a towel to his boots, rubbing off the mud that clung to the soles before he could dirty his stirrups too much. The clay clung to the towel in globs. "I don't know if being dark-colored will be enough to save your clothes," I told him. "So, maybe don't fall off, okay?"

"That's usually the plan," he replied dryly.

His tone was the only thing that was dry at this point.

I mounted Mickey, my boots sliding a little on the stirrups, and I leaned down to knock the mud off my boots with what was left of the towel. When it was just a mud-covered blob, I looked around to make sure no one was watching before I tossed it on the ground.

"Litterbug," Pete chided.

"We paid something like three hundred bucks per entry," I reminded him. "They can afford a ground crew to clean up after us."

"People like you are *why* entries are so expensive," he joked. "Easy, buddy," he said to India as the horse shifted unhappily. India was still holding his ears out sideways, shaking his head constantly as if the rain was making him crazy. Pete held him firmly in the reins, but I could see the concern in his expression. He knew something wasn't right.

He put a knot in the end of his reins and turned India toward the warm-up area. It should have been grass, but it was already looking like a broad sea of mud.

India looked at the scene with pricked ears, then flattened them again. Pete reined back for a minute to take in the scene, which set the horse to jigging in place. The ground beneath immediately began to turn to goo.

"Settle down, silly," Pete said with a sigh. "Okay, Jules, I'm going to just trot him and see if we can burn off some of these nerves. I know you don't need to start yet, but can you hang out nearby?"

"I'll stand Mickey under the groom tree," I said, pointing to a nearby tree where a dripping collection of helpers was clustered, trying to find some shelter from the rain. They were mostly unsuccessful, since the tree had already shed most of its leaves for the winter, but somehow its bare branches looked more appealing than just standing out in the open field.

The other grooms and coaches already hanging out beneath the tree stepped back as Mickey splashed over, making room for us with interested expressions as they looked over Mickey. "Hi," I said to the group at large. A few girls said hi back, and one youngish groom made a crack about the weather being nicer back in Florida, just to show she knew who I was. In the back, I noticed Rose Martin stood bundled up under a raincoat, dressed to ride and evidently waiting on her horse. I wanted to talk to her, especially since Pete said she'd complimented my riding at Catoctin Green, but the circumstances were less than ideal and I decided to wait until we were in Florida, and both in better moods.

I smiled back at the groom and then turned away, anxious to keep an eye on Pete. Even though Pete was the best rider out there— personal bias aside—and fully capable of riding India through some kind of tantrum, India was going around acting like a bear with a headache, shaking the bit in his mouth, overreacting to every move

Pete made, and flicking his tail back and forth as if something ir-
ritating and itchy had crawled beneath his skin. His ears still hung
to either side of his head, cupped toward the ground. He did perk
up a little at the canter, and slowly his ears slipped into a half-mast
position, turned slightly back toward Pete. He began to look normal, like a nice, fit horse who enjoyed his work. Maybe everything
would be all right. Maybe ten rides or so with Pete was enough to
build up the horse's confidence in his rider, and he could tackle the
course despite whatever traumatic experience in his past had left
him so worried about something as natural and simple as rain.

"That's a nice horse Pete's got," Rose Martin said, suddenly
standing next to me. "Is that the India horse Mimi Pulaski was
riding?"

"Sure is," I admitted.

"I thought she was aiming him for the three-day," Rose said.
She tucked damp hair beneath a Kentucky Three-Day Event ball
cap, dark with rain. "Is Pete going to ride him in it?"

"Seemed unwise to take a new partnership onto that course," I
replied. "We have plenty of time to take him to a three-day. He has
Once a Prince in here today, too."

Rose nodded, looking pleased. "I like to see people think like
that. Using their heads to make decisions, instead of just going all
out because they can."

"Pete's very measured. He doesn't get carried away."

"I've heard that." She paused, then said, "You know, it's a
good thing the rain is lightening up. Mimi couldn't get that horse
around a course on a rainy day. He's never finished in the rain,
not once."

Something in me seemed to break free and float away. "What?"
I looked at Rose in shock. "What do you mean, he never finished?"

"She didn't tell you, did she?" Rose nodded her head knowingly.

"Man, what is it with horse people? Why can't we just set each other up for success?"

I couldn't say anything.

"Mimi couldn't figure it out," Rose went on. "He'd go crazy in the rain, pull and plunge and dart out from under her. Sticky at jumps and nuts in between them. She used to call him her fair-weather horse, like it was a joke, but I know it bugged her. When she took that fall we all figured it had to do with the rain. Anyway, well, Pete already has him going better than she did, so hopefully—"

Pete had India pointed at a schooling fence.

A tapping on my helmet told me the rain was picking up again.

I watched India's ears fly out to the side.

"That horse got water in his ears once and he never got over it," I said.

Rose made a noncommittal sound. Then she said, "You know, you might be right."

We watched in silence as India threw up his head on the way to the fence, hauling on Pete's hands. But Pete had to keep his leg on, because a bolt toward a fence was an act of fear, and the horse was liable to slam on the brakes at the last moment.

Raindrops, as fat and heavy as the tropical downpours that fell in Florida, hammered through the bare tree branches and rattled against the hats and raincoats and grooming buckets of the assembled audience. They fell on the wet horses in the warm-up and slid down the clear rain covers on riders' helmets. They drummed steadily into the puddles skirting the warm-up fences, gray lakes filling in the depressions made by so many horses on takeoff and landing. They blurred the view of the trees and hills and first formidable fences of the cross-country course.

The course announcer said something unintelligible and then

the PA system cut out, silenced by the heavy, relentless onslaught of rain.

India skidded to a magnificent sliding stop in front of the fence, nearly pitching Pete over his shoulder. He darted sideways as soon as he had his hooves beneath him—he had excellent purchase in the mud with those monster studs Vane brought over, I noted—and flung himself hard to the right, twisting and bucking. Pete sat it all, the reins slipping through his fingers until he was gripping the knot. With effort, he got the horse back to a halt.

They stood still for a moment as the rain came down and the horses whirled around them. India dropped his head, his ears flattened. The rain turned his mahogany coat so dark he was nearly black.

"What's Pete going to do?" Rose asked me.

"Get off, I hope," I said, but I wondered if he would. Dismounting and starting fresh the next day was not Pete's thing. He was the type of quiet, methodical rider who always wanted to work through a problem immediately, whereas I had to call it a day before I risked losing my temper. Pete could turn baby steps into one giant leap like no other trainer I knew.

But today, when the trouble was falling from the sky . . . how would he even begin to solve India's problems?

He couldn't fix a horse he didn't understand. There was something deep and troubled in that horse's mind, a fear that something as natural as rain could be a deadly enemy. This was going to take time, trial, error.

"Hop off, Pete," I muttered. "Come on, man."

Pete put his heels against India's side and leaned forward slightly, evidently ready for the horse to plunge forward.

India went backward instead, scrabbling so fast his hindquarters crashed into the practice jump and sent it tumbling over. There was a general pandemonium in the warm-up as other horses scattered in terror and India went running for the stables, his saddle empty and the knotted reins slapping against his shoulders.

Pete picked himself up out of the mud and waved to me with his whip to let me know he was okay.

His clothes, on the other hand, were almost certainly not.

23

WE WERE BACK at the barn with all the horses—including India, who had been captured with the help of several junior riders and an alert official on a golf cart, which subsequently got stuck in the mud and had to be abandoned—when the competition was called off for the day.

Of course, we didn't know right away because the PA system had shorted out in the downpour, so Pete had been about to mount India again, muddy clothes and all, when a show office runner came through the warm-up area shouting the news. It turned out that while we'd been involved with India's drama, the first two horses on course had slipped badly, and a third fell but wasn't injured, at which point the officials realized the cross-country course was too dangerous for further galloping. Even the big studs couldn't contend with this much rain in such a short period.

"We could have stayed in bed after all." I sighed, reining a confused and disappointed Mickey back toward the barn.

Kit rode alongside us, mounted on Big Dan, who looked as though he'd been born in the rain and lived for the mud. His eyes were gleaming, and his walk was more like a swagger. "Well, look on the bright side," she said. "We can go home and sleep all afternoon."

"You can, maybe," I said. "I have a kid waiting for me at home, and he can't play outside."

Kit gave me a look that said *Tough break.* "At least you don't have to ride out there."

"No doubt." I really was relieved. It wasn't often I had absolutely no desire to run cross-country, but this time, my instincts had been right about the footing.

Plus, we didn't have to solve the mystery of India today. We had time to work with him, figure out what part of his brain was broken, and learn how we could fix it. In Florida, we'd have no limit to the number of days we rode in the rain. It could be literal immersion therapy.

Pete helped me pack the trailer. He was quiet, and I knew he was thinking about India. I'd told him what the woman under the groom tree had said, and he'd looked skeptical . . . but he was coming around. The sideways ears were really what gave it away. As soon as the rain started falling, India acted like a baby who had just gotten water down his ears during a bath.

Horses frequently came with inexplicable baggage. If Mimi couldn't get him around a course in the rain, then the problem must come from deeper in his past, maybe back when he was a little foal living in a pasture, long before his eventing career. We'd probably never know exactly what caused his behavior, but that didn't mean we couldn't help him work through it.

"Cookies every time it rains," I suggested to Pete as he hung a hay net in the trailer.

"I like that idea."

"For the horse, I mean."

"Oh. Well, I like that, too."

"But you're saying we need cookies now, right?"

"I think we do."

I walked over to the concession area, where a lone food truck was still providing cold, wet competitors with coffee and hot chocolate, and bought a couple packages of Famous Amos cookies.

"Did you know Famous Amos was from Florida?" I asked the guy working in the truck.

He lifted an eyebrow. "No, I never heard that," he said. "Wish I was in Florida right now, though."

"You and me both," I said, but as I walked back to the stable through the pouring rain, I realized I wasn't as homesick as usual.

It must be all the rain.

We loaded up the horses and Pete got behind the wheel. By now it was noon, and we'd been up for seven hours, and yet somehow, the rain was still falling heavily. I switched on a news and traffic radio station. A reporter informed us that the George Washington Parkway was closed in both directions due to flooding.

"Where's that?" I asked.

"DC, I think," Pete said.

"Never been. Have you?"

"Once when I was a kid." He thought about it. "That's where I saw the Star of India, actually. In a museum down there. Heh, that's kind of funny."

I wondered if we should be taking Jack to Washington, DC. Was that something all parents should do? Surely he was too young now, though. I wasn't sure what a ten-month-old would get out of seeing the White House or a display of sapphires. I decided a field trip wasn't on the coming week's docket.

Maybe next year.

Yep, I was already thinking about next year. Even though I'd been swearing off Maryland for the past month, and we'd just been washed out of our last prep event, all the arguments in favor of hitting the road for new courses must have been making their way into my skull.

The reporter described multi-hour backups on I-95. "Thank goodness we're going west," I said. "Unless he's just not bothering to report on anything outside the city."

"Is this like a hurricane we didn't know about or something?" Pete asked, gazing across the soggy field where the trailers had been parked for the weekend.

"Just rain," I replied, having researched this earlier. "Just weird northern rain."

"Jeez. Well, I hope that—" He stopped, like he was afraid to say it out loud.

"What?"

"I hope we don't get stuck," Pete said, looking at the field of horse trailers around us. "Or anyone else. We're all so heavy and the ground is soaked."

"No, we won't get stuck." But the fact was, now I was scared we might. Pete! Why did he have to go and say it out loud?

"Don't look now," Pete said, "but I think the Martin barn just got stuck."

He was right. A few trailers away, Rose Martin and her working student were out of their truck and looking with dismay at the mud flung up on the sides. Their back tires were mired about four inches deep. I noticed the trailer tires had sunk into the mud, too. The weight of the horses had driven it down in the soft ground.

We had four horses in the back. What was that, nearly four thousand pounds?

"Pete—can you get us out of here?"

"Hang on," he said.

Pete put the truck into reverse first and backed very gently. The truck growled in response and hesitated ever so slightly as the mud grabbed the wheels.

I clutched the seat cushion with both hands as if that might help the situation. "Come on, truck."

"Shhh, it's fine," Pete said, but his knuckles started to turn white as he gripped the steering wheel. He eased the truck into drive and put the gas pedal down gently.

The truck's growl rose to a roar. It inched forward—and stopped.

Pete took his foot off the pedal. "Okay," he said.

"Okay? Okay what?"

"Okay, we're going to be stuck," he said. "If I put the pedal down again, we're going to end up with our rear tires buried, just like the Martins are."

"So, now what?"

He bit his lip. "I'm not sure. But I have a feeling we're about to see a lot of trucks in the same situation, so this might be up to the show officials."

"What can they do? Order every tow truck in Maryland? There are hundreds of trucks!" I watched mud fly from the rear wheels of another truck a few dozen feet away. Its driver stopped before it got fully stuck, but the consequences of all this rain were clear.

None of us were getting out of here anytime soon.

I turned in my seat to look back at the showgrounds behind us. "I wonder if that food truck is still there."

"You want food now?"

"Not now, but I might in an hour or two."

I was right; we did end up hungry. But the food truck, parked on higher ground and with a driver who clearly sensed the danger of being mobbed by several hundred starving equestrians, hit the road a few minutes later. We saw him drive past on the main road, leaving all of us behind to fend for ourselves.

The show office didn't call in every tow truck in Maryland. Instead, they sent out a tractor, and that lone tractor hauled out every single truck and horse van in the parking field, one by one. Personally, I thought it would have been nice if the show manager had instituted a first-stuck, first-hauled-out system, but they went with the more expedient and less confrontational approach of starting with the trucks closest to the road and moving slowly back.

Since we'd arrived very early on Thursday, we were one of the closest to the stabling, and farthest from the road.

The rain hammered on the truck with unending enthusiasm while we waited our turn. Every single truck and trailer combination at the event had to be hauled out. There were no exceptions. No one could free themselves. The mud was growing deeper. There was only one tractor. I thought the day would never end.

When our turn finally came, we watched through exhausted eyes as the tractor driver hopped down, attached his winch to the truck's front, then gave Pete the thumbs-up. Slowly, the tractor lurched forward and took us with it. The horses, who had long since given up hope we'd ever leave, startled and kicked. I rubbed my face wearily and hoped no one hurt themselves. Or each other.

And then we were on the road, the tires grinding on the gravel, and as the tractor driver waved us away, I looked at Pete. "Can we please just go back to Florida?"

For a moment, I really thought he might agree. Things had gone so badly with India, and then this ridiculous rain and mud situation calling off the whole event while stranding us for hours . . . it just didn't bode well for the three-day event in a few days. I thought the eventing gods were trying to tell us something.

But Pete was determined. We'd come for Chesapeake Three-Day

Event, he said, and we were staying through Chesapeake Three-Day Event. Bad luck was just bad luck.

I snorted, but I let it go. We drove back to Joan's farm in silence, the radio chattering softly to itself about flooded roads, downed trees, and traffic.

"Two more weeks," Pete said that evening as we sat at the Blue Plate Diner waiting for our fried chicken—the only thing hot and greasy enough to overcome the cold and wet of this day. "Two more weeks, Jules, and then we can pack up and go home."

Gemma made Jack clap his little hands. "Home! Home!" she said. "Jackie-boy is excited to go home."

"Two more weeks is forever," I said, determined to be a mope about it—if only because earlier I'd been willing to give Maryland a pass, and then it had gone and done something completely rude.

"You would never forgive yourself if you skipped this event with Mickey," Pete reminded me. "So don't even act like going home before the event is an option. We both know it's not."

And I had to admit, the man made an excellent point. Mickey deserved a shot at this three-star course, and my career needed the jolt of finishing a three-day event.

Our plates arrived, making satisfying *plunk*s on the table as the high-school-aged server set them before us. Iced teas were refilled. Napkins were passed out.

We fell into our meals like we hadn't eaten in a hundred years. I did remember to set aside a few pieces of chicken for Marcus, who was snoozing in the middle of our bed back in the RV.

A curly-haired woman breezed through the restaurant, stopping at tables to talk with guests. She seemed to know everyone by name. "That's Nikki, from the bakery," Gemma said. "I talked to her the other morning when I went to get us breakfast."

Gemma had taken to popping out early for morning pastry runs. No one was complaining about the girl's initiative. I was developing a new appreciation for chocolate croissants, and of course that ham-and-cheese croissant was so good I should probably consider abducting Nikki and taking her back to Florida with us.

"She really knows everyone," Pete said appreciatively. "Including you, Gemma. Here she comes."

"Hello," Nikki said, smiling warmly. "You must be our eventing family!"

"That's right," Gemma said. "This is Jules, and Pete. And, of course, you know Jack."

"I know him," Nikki agreed, tickling Jack under the chin. "Such a cutie! Well, I hear your event down at Pin Oak got called off today. Shame. I don't know where this rain came from."

"Where'd you hear about that?" I asked, surprised. Eventing news was typically only for eventers. It wasn't exactly a newspaper-ready sport.

"Kevin, my husband. He's a farrier. He said you rode into Long Pond not too long ago, got lost in the woods? You'd be surprised at how often that happens."

"Red hair?" Pete asked.

"That's him," Nikki said fondly. "He was there today to tack on some pulled shoes before afternoon lessons, and Nadine told him about the event getting flooded out."

"Oh, was she there?" I wondered if she'd seen Pete's crash and burn in the warm-up area.

"No, she just heard through the grapevine," Nikki said. "You know how it is. Oh, speak of the devil. Hey, Nadine, Sean!" Nikki waved to the couple, who had just come in the front door and were shaking out their wet jackets.

Nadine and Sean came over, looking freshly showered and in their comfy clothes, the way a pair of barn employees often do in the evening. "Hello, eventers," Sean called. "Glad to see you didn't sit in the mud for the rest of the day."

"It felt like it," I told him. "Took two hours to get out of there."

"Craziness." Nadine shook her head. "I bet that doesn't happen in Florida!"

I gave Pete a beady-eyed look. He ignored me, saying, "It was definitely an experience for the diary."

If that man really kept a diary, I was going to move heaven and earth to find it and read it.

He glanced at me and correctly read the dangerous light in my eyes. "I don't actually keep a diary, Jules."

Damn.

24

THE RAIN STOPPED late Sunday night, and the weather forecasters promised us a mostly dry week with a fabulous weekend to come. We needed both. With the move to Chesapeake on the Eastern Shore next Tuesday, we had to handle any last-minute schooling concerns with the horses who would be competing, set up our feed and supplement routines for the horses who were staying behind at Joan's, and try to spend some time with Jack and Gemma as well. They were staying back at Rosemary's farm while we went to Chesapeake, since Pete and I would be camping in the horse trailer for the weekend. If I drew a line in this traveling eventing family game, it was at having Jack sleep in the cramped living quarters of our trailer.

And, of course, we were fitting in the final prep on the competing horses.

Pete and I managed to squeeze in a cross-country school at Catoctin Green, Mickey and Barsuk trotting out together happily.

"We make a funny picture together," Pete observed. "My little gray with his faded dapples and your big gray with his plain coat."

"You could just call him a white horse, Pete. You don't have to say he's plain."

"A white horse," Pete scoffed. "What are you, five years old?"

"Yes," I said. "I'm five years old and riding my princess dream unicorn, and you're the mean, jealous boy who wants to take him away from me." I nudged Mickey into a canter and laughed as Barsuk bounced after us, unwilling to be left behind.

We let the horses step out in a hand gallop along a well-worn horse path, heading vaguely in the direction of Catoctin Green's water complex. As they settled into their strides, I let my thoughts drift toward the coming week. Drive to Chesapeake on Tuesday, first horse inspections Wednesday, dressage for Pete and Barsuk on Thursday, the rest of us on Friday, and then cross-country on Saturday—that big, salty Chesapeake course loomed large in my brain. I'd been having dreams about the event's signature jump, a huge carved octopus whose body formed the first fence into the water, with tentacles that rose out of the water to form subsequent fences in the complex.

It was terrifying, and I didn't scare easy.

But hey, we'd practice the water right now, just to remind Mickey that the hard part was bouncing up and out of the water, not the way the fence looked. It was probably more about my nerves than his, actually. Who knew I harbored a deep and inexplicable fear of giant octopi?

"We destroy the octopus, finish in the time, then show Sunday, quick victory gallop, and we're packing for home," I murmured as the horses dropped down to a forward, head-swinging walk to maneuver through a gate between pastures.

"What's that?" Pete asked. "Something about a victory gallop?"

"Well, I'm not planning on losing," I told him. Mickey tucked his tail as we went through the half-open gate and bounced in a tight circle.

"I thought it was all about finishing?" Pete held Barsuk with a firm rein and made him go through the gate nicely. "Didn't you say to me, several times, this was all about a completion for you?"

"Pete, get a grip. I'm never going to *not* try to win."

He shook his head, grinning, and rode Barsuk so close that our knees bumped. "You're a danger to yourself and others, Jules Thornton," he said. "Still somehow ambitious to a fault."

"Thornton-Morrison," I corrected him, taking his usual line. "Don't try to disavow me now. You're stuck."

We reached the water complex and took turns splashing the horses through the drops and cantering out. The sunlight was cool, and the water was cold, making the horses jumpy, their ears flicking back to us for reassurance every time they landed in the pool. "Kind of like the spring at home," I told Mickey. "Always seventy-two degrees, right, boy?"

When we decided to get serious about trying the lines in the complex, Pete gathered Barsuk's reins and took the horse to the shelter of a tree a couple dozen feet away, while I circled Mickey carefully, measuring where we would want to approach from if this were the octopus fence and we were already at Chesapeake. It wasn't a perfect approximation, but I thought I could re-create the angles using the diagrams and course walks from the previous year I'd studied over the past few months.

Down a hill, up a slight rise, over the first fence into the water—not an octopus, but just a nice solid log—and the cold water rose up with Mickey's landing, splashing my breeches and boots. Mickey plunged forward, lifting his forehand to let his hindquarters do the hard work of pushing against the water's drag, and took on the skinny log in the water with a hard exhale on landing. I gave him plenty of rein and he bounced out of the pool, then hopped neatly over the skinny hedge a few strides beyond, his gaze never wavering from the horizon as he looked for the next jump.

"We're not on course yet," I told him, circling him and letting his long stride steady and fall into a trot. We pulled up as Pete took Barsuk through the same pattern.

"He's a textbook ride today," Pete said as Barsuk joined us on the other side. "I'm going to go out on a limb and say we're ready."

"You should be." I sighed. "This event is ten years in the making."

"It's not an overnight sport," Pete said stoically.

"For some people, it is."

"Not for us." Pete started Barsuk along the path toward the next complex of fences. "We do things the right way. The slow way."

Mickey bounced after him happily.

We rode side by side for a while, squinting into the late-afternoon sun. I glanced at Pete after a few minutes of silence, noting the thoughtful look on his face. "What's on your mind?" I ventured.

"India," he said. "Wondering what broke his brain at Pin Oak."

"I told you, it's the rain."

"But he can't be scared of the *rain*," Pete insisted, exasperated. With every day that had passed since the cross-country warm-up debacle, he'd grown more dissatisfied with my story that Mimi had never been able to get this horse to work in the rain. Even though it had come from two people—Sandy and Rose Martin. I was very close to suggesting he just ask Mimi, herself. But we hadn't heard a peep out of Mimi since the clinic at Long Pond, and I was enjoying the peace. Hopefully, Mimi was figuring out the next phase of her life on her own, and didn't need my help after all. I really had enough to worry about. This morning Lacey had texted me to share that the kids were spending this weekend painting the jumps in the arena, and refused to send any pictures, saying only, *You'll see them when you get home!* Needless to say, I had some concerns.

I'd let myself get lost in thought, and Mickey took advantage of my inattention to dart to the left, pulling me toward another series of jumps. This horse was really unbelievable, I thought, tugging him into a circle. He'd jump a course alone if I let him.

More fun with me on his back, though.

Joan was in the barn aisle when we got back, and she waved as we led our horses to their stalls. "Nice time schooling? I can't believe that was your last ride over there already. Where did this month go?"

I forced a laugh. "I know, right? Went so fast."

More like molasses on a cold day, but whatever. Joan was nice. She didn't deserve my smart mouth.

"I hope you'll come back next year," she was saying. "If you want to put a deposit down on the barn, I'll rent it to you for the same rate as this year. Otherwise, well, I've already had some inquiries for next season . . ."

Pete and I exchanged looks. The hard sell, a year out? Jeez, Joan.

"I don't know yet," I said, slipping Mickey's halter off. He went right for his hay. "I mean, obviously a lot could change in twelve months with horses, which horse is ready for what . . . and we haven't even run the main event yet, to see if it's something that we'll be planning for every year. We might hate it."

Pete bit back a grin. As if hating it was an option. There were only so many three-day events in the United States. We didn't have the luxury of hating any. And if one of us should happen to have a five-star horse next year—which wasn't entirely impossible—then we'd absolutely have to use the Maryland Five-Star up at Fair Hill International as our end-of-year goal. So, we'd be up here either way.

"Well, I'll give you until after the event," Joan said breezily. "I'm sure you'll be ready to decide after that."

"Sure," I said. "We'll tell you Sunday afternoon, right after I come off the show jumping course."

She laughed like she knew I was being a bitch on purpose, which made me like her more, and headed off to mess with her own horses.

Pete gave me a serious look as I went past him to cart in our tack from the trailer. "You know, we could make worse decisions than locking in this year's rate. People will want to stay here because we did."

"Ah, the price of fame."

"I'm serious." He followed me into the trailer's tack room. "All she has to do is tell a few people that we stayed here for our Maryland run and that it's centrally located, and someone will snap it up—"

"Pete, I hate to say this, but we aren't that important yet."

His eyes widened. "That doesn't sound like you at all. Do you have a fever? Let me feel your forehead."

"Stop it! No." I swiped his hand away. "When we're a little farther along, I can see our names being a draw, but right now? We're still splashing around in the shallow end."

"What happened to you being the best rider ever, something I think you remind me of at least twice a day?" He tried to feel my head again, and I jumped out of the trailer, stirrup leathers and girths flapping around me.

"I still believe that, trust me," I told him. "But I'm only running three-star this weekend. People aren't even going to show up to watch our cross-country rounds. We're just padding out the weekend to pay for the big boys in the four-star."

"Is that what you think? Jules, most people on this planet will never get to the point where you and I are right now. Try to remember that. I know it was hard losing the World Equestrian Games spot and retiring Dynamo early and all, but—"

"It's not about that," I snapped, starting back to the barn. "It's not about that at all."

I had to say it twice because of course it was, a little bit. And I wasn't usually reminded of how close I'd come until right before an event, when I remembered how far I had to climb to reach that point again.

25

CHESAPEAKE DOWNS HORSE Park, on the Eastern Shore of Maryland—
a fairly flat and swampy place, where the most serious of the cross-
country course hills were carted in by truck and shaped by tractor.
It was a Wednesday morning in late autumn, and the weather was
hot and humid, with a threat of thunder in the air. Seagulls shrilled
in whirling flocks high above the showgrounds.

Except for the lack of palm trees, I felt quite at home.

Okay, maybe there should have been an alligator or two in the
ponds around the property, just to make things extra Floridian.
But the steamy weather, which made the northeastern types sweat
and complain, along with the beach-day ambiance of the seagulls,
would have to be enough.

Heading for home in just six days, I reminded myself, setting
up the tack trunks in the open tack stall. We didn't have a fancy
setup, just rubber mats on the floor, a power strip for phone char-
gers and a box fan, and two coolers—one for bottled water for us,
one for ice for the horses' legs after jumping.

Kit and Vane had Big Dan next to our row of stalls, and they were sharing our tack room, which made the event feel even more like we were back home. At Florida events, they always stabled with us and the kids from Alachua, to make things convenient given all the students Kit and I shared.

I made sure they had a corner for their tack trunks and installed the third row of portable saddle racks against the back wall, so that Kit didn't have to stack her saddles, girths, and pads on top of each other. In return, Kit slipped a massive box of donuts into the tack room when no one was looking, and Vane brought in a couple gallons of Turkey Hill iced tea and lemonade, putting them into yet a third cooler.

"It's not Publix," she said, "but it's what the folks up here like, so."

"When in Maryland," Pete said, and took a swig from an iced tea jug. His eyes went round immediately. "Phew, that's *sweet*. And they said southerners like their sugar with a side of tea."

"No one has ever said that," I told him, "but I like it."

"Need I remind you, yet again, that you are not southern?"

"Southwest Florida can be southern," I argued.

"About as southern as corned beef on rye," Pete said.

We had a course walk to get through, so I traded out my breeches for shorts and threw some rubber boots into a backpack. No way was I going to sweat around several miles of rolling hill country with tall waterproof boots on just to traipse through two water hazards. I saw a few other women dressed in breeches and their Wellington boots and shook my head.

Florida girls know how to handle swamp weather.

"Are we good to go? Anyone got a map?" Kit asked.

"On my phone," Pete said. "But paper would be good."

I dug around in our show packets and came out with the course maps. "A few lowly three-stars for us, and a four-star for our queen," I said, passing the third map to Kit. She took it with a little grimace.

"Nervous about the four-star course?" Pete asked her. "Don't be. We're literally just walking."

Kit laughed, and we headed out of the barn. I trailed behind them, looking at my map, at the letters *CCI3*-L* across the top. It stood for *Concours Complet International Three Star Long,* and the official description of the level was "Intermediate level, for horses and riders with some experience riding in a three-day event, who are just starting to begin international competition."

I couldn't help but feel a little thrill. There was such a promise in those words: *just starting to begin international competition.* Just starting, just starting! As in, this weekend was only the beginning for Mickey. After all these years, a new chapter was opening. And yes, I was "only" going Intermediate . . . but, like Pete said a few days ago, hardly anyone else in the world would ever do it.

"These are some serious hills," I said half an hour later. "I was told this place wouldn't be quite as hilly as Pin Oak, but . . . I'm impressed."

Pete was standing in the shadow of a massive log complex. "This jump is almost bigger than our house in Florida, and you're talking about the hills?" He leaned against the central log, which was situated over a deep ditch.

"Don't act like that jump is scary, Pony Club Pete." I snorted. "It's going to ride like a dream."

This jump's ditch was just there to scare the rider—the horse would never even see it. Especially a horse at this level, who had been jumping ditches since Novice. It was the big, airy log suspended above the ditch that counted. And Pete was right about the size. If anyone got a bad stride to this jump, they were going to know about it.

Luckily, the back side of the log had frangible pins connecting it to its base.

If a horse hit the log with legs or body, the log would come down, and the horse wouldn't be forced into a rotational fall—the big killer of eventing, when the fence didn't move and the horse was spun into the ground by its own momentum.

Things like heels-over-head falls were not considered an acceptable risk in this day and age. I wasn't much of a modernist, but I could appreciate *that*.

"Jumps we can school, we can build, we can figure out at home," I explained to Pete, feeling out the slope with my sneakers. "The hills are tougher. We have rolling hills here and there at home, but there are only a couple of places around Ocala where we get in some serious up-and-down action."

"True." Pete looked at the ground on the far side of the jump, then walked around and looked at the approach again. "Honestly, this isn't the worst thing on the course. Pretty straightforward."

"The ditch got you," I guessed with a smirk, and Pete shrugged and nodded.

We walked down the slope on the opposite side and took in the water complex up ahead. The famous octopus jump, which looked like a horrifying sea monster at this distance—and probably up close, too—spread its tentacles wide. "That's the most terrifying jump I've ever seen in my life," I said. "We probably should have boycotted this event just because of it."

"Look at the eyes," Pete said, giving a little shudder. "What's that horror writer's spooky squid god?"

"Pete, do you think I've ever read a horror novel?"

"Not a fan of krakens?" a familiar voice called.

We looked along the gallop path and saw Sandy Sullivan ambling along, two corgis bouncing through the tall grass on either side. He had a walking stick that he leaned on with every step. I admired him for continuing to ride at the upper levels when he wasn't sound on the ground anymore, but that was one of the great things about riding. You really didn't have to quit until you were dead, with very few exceptions.

That was surely the thing that was bugging Mimi. She was an exception.

"I'm more of a shrimp person," I said when Sandy caught up with us. "You know, once their heads and tails are gone and they're deep-fried."

"That would make an interesting jump," Sandy mused. "Just a large hunk of breaded shrimp. Maybe with a side of cocktail sauce?"

"I'd prefer just about anything to that creature."

Sandy looked at the octopus. "It really is disgusting, isn't it? A work of art, but would you want to look at it every day? I wouldn't put it in my pasture."

We walked down to the water complex together and examined the octopus from every angle. Like the ditch under the log we'd just left behind, the gruesome sea monster wasn't designed to scare the horses; it was to psych out the riders. All it took was a little tension on the rider's part to tell the horse that this was something out of the ordinary; otherwise, their brains would just say, *Another jump!* and they'd leap over it as if it was a plain old log.

No one would ever want to scare a horse on purpose, but a lot of course designers clearly found it hilarious to frighten the riders, since we prided ourselves on being the toughest equestrians this side of jump jockeys and bronc riders.

"This spot right here will be the takeoff point if you want a direct line through the water to the exit fence," Sandy said, pointing at the ground with his walking stick. "If you mark this place in your head, just left of center—"

"Sandy, why didn't you tell us India had never finished a course in the rain?" I interrupted, unable to let it go for another minute.

The gray-haired man looked at me from the other side of the giant octopus. Beside him, one of his corgis dove into the water and went gliding through the hazard like a swan. The splashing seemed to shake him out of his silence. "Mimi was embarrassed about that," he said finally. "And I was embarrassed that I insisted she take him out on that rainy day to gallop the point-to-point. I said the horse needed a trial by fire." He shook his head. "I ended her career."

I exhaled, suddenly regretting asking him anything. It was all done now. There was no use asking him to relive his mistakes. I knew what it was like.

26

IN THE END, the octopus was almost my undoing.

The hot, humid week continued through the first horse inspections and our mostly quiet dressage days, and the forecast said it would carry into Saturday and the cross-country. It was unseasonable weather, made worse by some kind of a tropical storm out in the Atlantic well past its due date and some fires inland that were sending smoke our way. Even Pete and I were starting to feel the weight of all that unhealthy air, and the tropical storm was close enough to give me a barometric headache that arrived each morning when I opened my eyes and stuck around way past closing time.

"I get those every time it rains," a woman at one of the mobile tack stores told me when she saw me rubbing my forehead instead of admiring her rainbow of saddle pads.

"I live in Florida," I told her. "I only get them when there are hurricanes around."

Her eyebrows disappeared into her fluffy bangs. "You think that big storm in the Atlantic is coming here?"

I leaned on the counter, sensing an opportunity to cause some mayhem. "Well, I'm not a meteorologist," I began, "but when I see a storm like that, my first thought is—"

"Jules," Kit interrupted, tugging at my elbow. "Come see these browbands. Sorry," she said to the clerk. "Obsessed with these bridles, though." She dragged me away, whispering in my ear, "Do *not* frighten the natives!"

"Kit," I said rebukingly, "they prefer to be called Eastern Shore-ians."

"Well, I think you made that up."

We looked at the browbands long enough to satisfy the owner of the shop, and then Kit hustled me out. "I can't take you anywhere," she said.

"That's Pete's line."

"I'm practically your sister-wife at this point, aren't I? We basically all live together."

"Well, except you still live in Ocala," I reminded her. "And I don't think Vane would agree to adding me to your marriage."

"About Ocala . . ." Kit looked up and down the vendor row. With the dressage over for the day and no one competing until tomorrow's cross-country began, there were plenty of people milling around the mobile tack shops, artist tents, and food trucks set up near the main jumping arena. Her eyes roved the crowd like she was making sure she didn't know anyone in the pack, and then she said, "I wanted to ask you if you'd consider letting us put a tiny house up at Briar Hill."

I felt my mouth fall open. "Oh," I said blankly, and then I thought about it.

We had plenty of land, most of it still wooded. The farm had been home to cattle and horses decades ago, with a few acres committed to crops like citrus, but the surrounding forest had taken over and we only had five acres or so of open land.

Everything else was waiting till we had the money and the time to begin clearing it and putting it to use. It was too much work for Pete and me to even attempt ourselves while we were trying to build up the eventing business.

We'd known for a while that we should be earning more money with the place, but when we'd rented RV spaces to Grace Carter and her friend over the summer, it had been exhausting. We'd eventually figured it out, but I felt like we had to be extremely picky about who we wanted living with us on the farm. In fact, I really thought it needed to be someone who was part of the business—people who were helping, instead of just paying money and causing us more work.

It would be really nice having someone else around to mow paddocks, nail up fence boards, and enjoy the fireflies in the evening.

Especially someones like Kit and Vane.

"Kit," I said, "I would love for you guys to put a tiny house up at the farm. Yes. Please do."

Kit's smile lit up her face. "Oh, wow," she breathed. "Thank you!"

"Don't thank me yet," I warned her, grinning. "You haven't seen where I want you to put it."

"In the middle of an actual briar patch on a hill, I'm sure."

"Well, no one said life with me was easy! But don't worry— I'll lend you a mower so you can cut a path through the briars. Wouldn't want you getting scratched up every day on your way to the barn."

"You're a pal, Jules," Kit said, squeezing my hand. "I mean it."

"I try," I said, and, in her case, it was true.

It's just an octopus, just an octopus, just an octopus," I chanted to myself, making Mickey's trot match the cadence of my words. Using one-two, one-two, one-two as a metronome to find a balanced trot was tired; making up songs about scary cross-country jumps was wired. I'd had a dream about the octopus coming to life and slapping at the water with its wooden tentacles, trying to smash Mickey and me like a giant kraken Whac-a-Mole.

I'd woken up in the horse trailer's hot gooseneck sleeping area in a cold sweat, confused about why I'd developed a paralyzing fear of octopi so late in life. But maybe I'd always been afraid of them and it had simply never come up before. I'd never been big on beach days.

Mickey nodded his head and snorted, seeming to enjoy the sticky morning.

He was the only horse in the warm-up who looked comfortable. The day wasn't too hot by Floridian standards, only in the mid-seventies, but with humidity to match. It was about thirty degrees too warm to be seasonable, I'd been told by a grumpy ring steward this morning, and the medics on the cross-country course were on high alert for heat exhaustion in both horses and riders.

I looked across the wide plains of the Eastern Shore, dotted with the woods and dark hills that the course designers had planted and mounded out here in an attempt to make this event as taxing as anything the inland farms could manage, and I felt like I could see all the way to the Atlantic, hidden behind a film of haze and dirty yellow-gray clouds that rested against the horizon like a forgotten beach blanket. The ocean was more of a sense than a reality to a Floridian like me, raised along the coast but rarely making the effort to visit. When all the long roads run north–south and all the short ones run east–west, you develop a certain sense of direction that only works along the ocean-side.

Lucky for me, I lived on a peninsula.

Pete trotted up on Barsuk. He didn't look too fussed about the weather, either, but his neck was dark with sweat where the reins were rubbing, and I spotted a dash of lather above each eyelid. "I'm heading down to the start box," Pete said. "Two ahead of me."

"This is it, then," I said, feeling a rush of excitement. I was really enjoying competing against Pete in the same division, my drive to win somehow all mixed up with how much I loved him and enjoyed watching him succeed, too. It felt like a win for Pete was a win for me, a win for *us*, and I loved that, like we were the ultimate team. "I wish you the very best ride you've ever had," I told Pete, and I meant every word.

"Thank you, my love," he said, leaning in his stirrups to give me a kiss. I turned my head slightly so our hat brims wouldn't bang into each other and we exchanged a brief horseback kiss that was still enough to elicit some whoops from other riders.

"Cross-country types," I drawled, rolling my eyes, and Pete laughed.

"Get a room!" Olympian Howard Tanner called, and several other riders roared their approval.

"We need to beat them," Pete said.

"Both of us," I agreed.

"Okay, dear, sweet, not-at-all ambitious wife," he told me, smile glinting. "Away we go."

I watched him trot Barsuk across the field toward the tents marking the starting box, and felt the slightest tremor of nerves. They were normal nerves, not a portent or a premonition, but they sizzled through my system like a flash of lightning anyway, making Mickey shy sideways.

"Safe home," I whispered.

We had to finish our own warm-up while Pete was still on course, which made it tough to concentrate. I did all my usual moves on Mickey with automated gestures, working him through canter lengthening and shortening, bending him around my leg, even doing a few quick halts to test the old brakes. I needed maximum flexibility and discipline from him on this course. There were bounces, skinnies, corners, difficult approaches and blind leaps—and that was just one complex.

I jest, I jest. It took three complexes to add up to all of those hazards. But it was definitely a course that didn't let up on a horse and rider for more than fifteen or twenty strides of gallop. When the jumps came up, they came up bundled, mean, and ready to do battle.

The jumps that were holding everyone's imagination hostage this weekend were, of course, the octopus and its tentacles. Blogs were covering the creation of this jump in detail; Instagram was full of course walkers taking selfies with its malevolent face or hanging over its tentacles. When we'd been shopping yesterday, I'd noticed several girls dressed all in purple with purple extensions in their hair, cosplaying as the octopus. It was becoming the symbol of Chesapeake Three-Day Event and, if things kept escalating, it would be the symbol of all of eventing by the end of the weekend.

Our division was the first one to take it on; the four-star riders wouldn't go until later, to make it easier for the VIP ticket holders and tailgaters to get out here and get their cocktails on. It hadn't been lost on any of us when we'd walked the course that the lion's share of the tents and tailgate sites faced the water complex and that smirking, swirling octopus.

"And now it's in your head," I muttered, bringing Mickey down to a trot.

There was a TV set up in the starting box tent and suddenly, I knew I had to get over there and see Pete gallop through the water complex. I let Mickey stretch out on a loose rein, heading for the starting box a full ten minutes before our start time. He thought we were going right in, and was annoyed when I pulled him up and walked him to the tent.

"Sorry, buddy, not time to gallop yet," I said, circling him. He jerked his head up and down, feeling betrayed.

A teenage girl poked her head out of the tent. "Do you want to see Pete?"

I smiled gratefully. "I'd like to, but this guy might take your tent down."

"Hang on," she said. "I've got a laptop here. I'll pull up the feed and bring it out."

In a few moments, the kid had effortlessly brought up the cross-country livestream and walked it over to Mickey and me. The sun made it hard to see, but she held her hand over the screen to block some of the light, and I was just able to see Barsuk's ghostly gray on the dim feed. "One jump out from the water," she said, turning her head to catch the TV feed inside the tent.

I leaned down. Mickey sidestepped and the girl fluidly moved with him, accustomed enough to horses to read their body language without even thinking about it.

Barsuk bounced up to the octopus and hopped over it without a moment's hesitation. I saw Pete hang back over the drop, and the water splash as they landed. Stride—stride—up and over the tentacle reaching up from the water, and then flying on toward the next one.

I sighed—relief for Pete, relief for me. That was one bogeyman I didn't have to worry about.

"Nice of him to clear the way for me, show me how it rides," I told the girl, and she grinned.

"You good?"

"I'm good," I said. "One more warm-up fence for this guy, and we're ready to hit the links."

Mickey bounded over the course like a cork shot from a pop-gun. From skinny hedges to crooked corners, he never tipped his head away, never offered to runout or find an easier way around.

The jumps, Mickey was certain, were put there for his amusement. And he didn't want to miss a single one.

We went charging down to the water complex and, as the tents drew into view, he took his first stuttering step of the morning.

That was when I realized what that octopus meant. It wasn't really about intimidating riders any more than it was about horses. It was about getting attention, about every person who attended the event wanting to get pictures of horses going over it, the best free advertising an event could ask for. And so all those spectators, all those tents and tailgates, all those day-drinking screamers who would show up for the four-star riders later today—well, some of them were ready to get started.

Mickey had been to some decent-sized events, but nothing with a spectator section on the course like this one. He stared at the curving row of white tents, his ears flicking uncertainly as music blared from a tailgate party. His gallop lost a little steam, and he lifted his head, his entire posture asking, *What in God's name is that?*

"It's fine," I told him, putting my leg on and pushing him forward. "We didn't come all this way to get slowed down by a party!"

For a moment, he continued to stall, conflicted.

"Mickey, come *on!*" I shook the right rein, drawing his attention toward the water complex. Ten strides out, he realized the octopus awaited and his attention locked in.

We were back in business.

Soaring over that smirking sea creature's purple face, all I could think was, *Suck it, Maryland.*

As a black-tied waiter poured me a glass of wine, I folded my menu on the white tablecloth and smiled at Pete. "Calamari," I told the waiter. "Please."

240 | Natalie Keller Reinert

"Excellent starter," she agreed, and left us to our drinks.

Pete's smile turned into a smirk. "Were you planning all day to devour an octopus in triumph? And if so, should I remind you calamari is actually squid?"

"No, it didn't occur to me until we were through the finish flags," I said. "Close enough, by the way. I didn't expect you to go all out with a restaurant like this when I suggested it, though. This is the fanciest dinner we've ever had at any event. Or ever, really."

"I think we deserve it," Pete said, picking up his wine. He tipped the glass in my direction. "A major milestone was met today, Jules. For you, especially."

He wasn't kidding. I still couldn't believe it. First after the cross-country in my first three-star.

No matter what happened tomorrow on show jumping, we'd take this winning feeling home to Florida with us.

"You're going to pin at your first three-star with Barsuk," I told Pete.

"Right below you?"

I smiled and reached across the table, taking his hand. "Yes. Right below me."

27

SUNDAY MORNING'S HORSE inspection was a little more challenging than Saturday's—the wine at our fancy celebration dinner gave me a muzzy head to start the day, and when I couldn't find the good tasseled boots I'd brought along for the jog, I just pulled on my paddock boots and gave up on the fashion show.

It had been a half-hearted attempt at looking cute, anyway. I wasn't big on the whole preppy dress-up game, and without a groom of our own to handle the horses, there was little point in trying to keep civilian clothes clean.

A few horses were kept back for a second inspection, but ultimately it looked like most, if not all, of the competitors in our division would go on to show jumping. With a 10 A.M. start time in the arena, we didn't dally. Pete and I took our gray horses straight back to the barns, threw sheets over them to keep them from rolling and staining their coats, and then went over our course, making sure we knew every fence and distance we'd be riding over in two hours' time.

I shouldn't have been nervous, but there was a balloon in my chest that inflated every time I thought *You're in first place*, which was approximately every forty-five seconds, and when that happened I did find it a little hard to breathe.

Mickey, happily, had no trouble breathing. The horse had been competing since he was a racehorse at the tender age of three, and he absorbed my nerves like a giant sponge.

We stepped out for the show ring alongside Pete and Barsuk, ready to keep things in first place until the very last rail was jumped.

"Why are we doing this?" I asked Pete as we watched the horses lower in the division swing around the course. *Thunk*—a pole went down. Another hope dashed for someone just like me.

"What else would we do?" Pete asked in reply.

It was a very good point.

Pete went into the ring two horses before me, Barsuk flicking his tail in such a sassy fashion that I knew they'd go clear. There was no need to hold my breath, no need to gasp, no need to bite my fingernails with nerves—the little gray did his job and finished with his ears pricked. Pete clapped him on the neck and gave a wave to the crowd.

"Peter Morrison finishes the three-star division with a final score of thirty point two, for third place," the announcer said.

Unless the next rider or I dropped a rail, had a stop, or took a tumble, I thought.

A smiling amateur went into the ring next, riding a gleaming schoolmaster who could have done the course blindfolded and without a rider. I picked up the reins and walked Mickey around the warm-up arena adjacent to the ring, then gave him a little jog and a short canter.

The smiling amateur came out still smiling.

Third place for Pete.

Unless I screwed up out there.

"Finally, we have our first-place finisher after cross-country, Danger Mouse, ridden by Jules Thornton-Morrison!"

I looked around, wondering how I'd gotten into the arena. Spectators dotted a half-full grandstand, clapping for Mickey and me. There were some whistles, a few shouts of "*Woooo Jules!*"

And suddenly I understood it all again, where I was and who I was and why I was. It was for this, the horse and the glory and the impossible chase to be the best, a reason that was nothing and everything all at once.

"Let's fly, Mickey boy," I whispered, and the horse I had pinned so many dreams on cocked an ear back to me and bounced into a canter.

The bell rang, and we were off, taking flight for the last time in the great, insane, insatiable state of Maryland. Everything welled up in me, the worry and work of the past year, and then it was gone, no space in my brain for anything but getting Mickey around that course clean and clear. With his ears pricked ahead of me and my hands close to his muscled neck, we went to work.

A cheer went up from the crowd as we closed out the final jump with one last victorious kick, and I slapped Mickey on the neck in triumph. He switched his tail and bolted through the timers, but we didn't need his afterburn to kick in—we were ahead of the time and not a single rail in that blessed arena had hit the ground.

"Jules Thornton-Morrison and Danger Mouse complete a remarkable weekend to win the three-star division at Chesapeake Three-Day Event," the announcer exclaimed. "Let's congratulate the winning team!"

Cheers. Applause. For *us*—for Mickey and me! I closed my eyes against the tears threatening to spill over. Against my eyelids I saw all of it, everyone and everything that led to this day: Pete and Jack and the co-op kids, the old barn where I'd first welcomed Mickey to Florida, the fights and the triumphs and the sleepless nights wondering what I'd do without him, what I'd do *with* him, and if I'd ever feel like I could ride this horse the way he deserved again.

I opened my eyes, brushing at my cheeks before anyone could see my tears, because Pete and the girl who had come in second on her quiet, confident schoolmaster were entering the ring, while a volunteer brought out the rosettes. She clipped the blue rosette to Mickey's bridle for me and he shied at the fluttering ribbon. "Lead the gallop," she said, patting Mickey's neck.

When it was all over, the victory gallop complete and the crowd dispersed and the jump crew waiting for us to leave so they could set the rails up for the two-star competition, I looked at Pete and sighed for such a long time it felt like every last molecule of air had left my body. I sucked in fresh oxygen and shook my head, laughing at my own light-headedness. "Can you believe it?"

Pete dismounted from Barsuk and straightened the yellow rosette on his bridle. The horse nipped at the ribbons hanging near his mouth, ready to devour the silly prize. "Can I believe what, Jules? That you beat me? Not really."

I swung out of the saddle and hugged Mickey, then reached out and hugged Pete one-armed, the other hand holding Mickey at bay as he tried to lean in to bother Barsuk. "Admit it, Pete. I'm just better than you."

He shook his head, pressing his lips together—although he was smiling, barely holding back laughter. "Mm-mmm."

"Fine," I told him. "I'll just have to trust the judges and the results." And I pinched him on the behind.

A few girls nearby saw me getting sassy and shouted their appreciation for Sweet Pete. "So, apparently *that* nickname is still around," I said, letting him loose.

"To my fans, I will always be Sweet Pete," he declared, and spinning around, he blew a few kisses to the girls.

Not to be outdone, Mickey nipped at Barsuk, squealed, and tried to spin and run away.

"The stewards are giving us the stink-eye," Pete stage-whispered, pointing to a pair of annoyed officials standing near the in-gate, where the jump crew were busily hauling in new standards for the course they were erecting.

"Let's get out of here before they change their minds about this giant ribbon," I told him, and we hustled our horses back to the barn.

28

"I had no idea you'd be leaving so soon," Rosemary said.

I paused midway down the RV steps, suitcase in hand. "We've finished Chesapeake and the season here is over," I reminded her. "There aren't any more events in Area Two until . . . gosh, next year."

"Right," Rosemary agreed. "You rented through the end of the month, so I just assumed you'd be here a few more days . . ." She seemed worried about something. I couldn't imagine what. We'd paid her in full. Shouldn't she be pleased about getting something for nothing?

"Have to hurry back to Florida," I told her. "The season there is just getting rolling. Our students are waiting, we have to get our younger horses out and competing, all that kind of thing. Plus," I added, casting a smile to Pete, "the longer we stay, the better chance we have of acquiring another horse, and the trailer is officially full now that we're taking Fling with us."

"There's just one thing . . ." Rosemary was rubbing her hands together and looking distressed.

I didn't like where this seemed to be going.

Pete had been pushing an overpacked suitcase into the truck bed, but now he stopped and looked at Rosemary, one eyebrow raised quizzically. "One thing about what?" he asked her.

I felt sick.

"Fling," Rosemary said miserably. "There's a problem with the contract."

"But you said—" I began, and then ran out of words. She said, what? She said go on, take the horse. I sent two grand as a donation to the rescue, crossing my fingers there wouldn't be a scary expense between Maryland and Florida that would make me regret the expenditure. It had been an informal exchange.

I should have known better than to let things be so casual.

"I said that we'd finalize the paperwork for you," Rosemary said. "What I didn't know was that there was already paperwork *done* on her."

"But she's your horse. Isn't she?" I'd sent the money to Notch Gap Farm. That was Rosemary's rescue. Should it have gone somewhere else? Rosemary Beckett did not look like the kind of woman who could scam anyone, though.

"Technically, no," Rosemary explained, while I gaped at her in disbelief. "She belongs to the county humane society. They send me their horses, though, because they don't have the facilities to rehab and adopt out horses. I just didn't realize they had processed an application for her already."

"When? I took the mare over two weeks ago!"

"I know, and I feel terrible. The county just told me. They were closed for Columbus Day and then it took time for them to get through their backlog. The woman there called me this morning and told me that someone was approved for Fling and was coming to pick her up today. I'm supposed to have her here, waiting—"

"Who?" I snapped, suspicion making me utterly furious.

Rosemary quaked in her boots—literally. The poor woman was shaking. I'd have felt bad, but I was too angry to bother letting up on her. And too certain of what she was going to say next.

"Mimi Pulaski," Rosemary said.

"Dammit!" I threw the bag I was holding across the farm lane; it smashed against a fence post and a tinkling of glass told me I'd broken something I'd probably miss later. I didn't care. "I am *sick* to *death* of *Maryland* and *Mimi Pulaski*!"

"I'm sure we can work things out with her," Rosemary quavered. "She's a reasonable woman, and she's respected in this community. She wouldn't want to start some kind of trouble with you when you've been such a help to us—"

I took a breath. "It's fine. It's okay. Don't—don't worry."

Pete looked at me warily. "Jules, what are you planning?"

"I'm going to sit here and wait for her," I said. "And then I'm going to tell her to stick another horse in her empty trailer, because Fling isn't here, and she isn't coming back."

Rosemary glanced around as if Mimi was already approaching, an empty trailer rattling behind her truck. "Not that I'm on her side, Jules, but . . . technically, if you take Fling with her adoption paperwork approved for someone else, that's stealing from the county. I think there'd be some heavy fines, maybe worse . . ."

"You're not going to jail for this mare," Pete told me. "Do not get any ideas about martyrdom."

I sighed. They were right, of course. I couldn't just take Fling— even if the phrase "possession is nine-tenths of the law" did get thrown around pretty frequently in the horse business. It hadn't helped me when Mickey's former owners took him away before the co-op purchased him for me, and it wouldn't help me today.

But I wasn't willing to hand Fling over to Mimi, either. She was part of my string now, alongside Flyer and Rogue and Mickey, and I was going to hang on to her just as hard as I would any one of them.

Mimi had tried to hang on to India and Prince, and I got that, I really did. So now I was going to show her that I understood the predicament she was in, the precipice she felt she was standing over, and I was going to *help* her.

Whether she wanted my help or not.

"Fine. You want to know what I'm going to do?" I asked Pete and Rosemary.

They looked at me with real apprehension on their faces.

"I'm going to drive over to her place and talk to her."

"Jules, that's crazy," Pete said, as if I'd announced I was going to drive over to her house and set it on fire. "The two of you can't talk. You've proven that before. You're like oil and water—"

"No," I insisted. "I'm going to talk to her. You know why? Because I'm a grown-ass woman who just won at Chesapeake Three-Day Event, and I'm too old to have archenemies anymore. This is getting ridiculous. Mimi is just going to have to sit down and have a conversation with me."

And with that, I took the keys from Pete, hopped into the truck, and drove off before anyone could try to change my mind.

Mimi was hooking up her trailer, but she abandoned the task when I arrived and marched right up to me, a fierce expression on her face.

"What are you doing here?" she demanded. "I don't have time for social calls. I have a new horse to pick up. Yes," she added, "I am getting back into the game. I changed my mind. I'll retire when I'm dead and the doctors can all go to hell."

"And Diane?"

A muscle twitched in Mimi's firmly held jaw. "Diane will understand."

"What happens when you get really, truly hurt, Mimi? Will Diane understand then? Or will she realize that you love eventing more than her?"

"Go to hell."

She hadn't figured out how to cross that bridge yet. It was like I figured—Mimi didn't know *what* to do with herself. She had a duty to her partner, but she didn't feel capable of living up to it. I'd had moments like that, too, feeling I had a duty to my family, to stay out of the saddle and stay safe for Jack's sake. I knew how bleak and terrifying that was. And while I'd gotten back into the tack eventually, Mimi had to find a new purpose or she really would break her wife's heart.

"Mimi, why aren't you teaching more at Long Pond?"

She raised an eyebrow. "What? What does that have to do with anything?"

"Those kids love you. And you have a lot to offer them. Why don't you ask Sean and Nadine to hire you on? The school clearly has tons of funding. I'm sure they can handle another trainer."

"Did you come over with that idea, all bright and shiny, thinking you could fix my life?" Mimi jeered. "Do you think I never thought about teaching more?"

"I just thought it would be perfect for you—" I stopped short, caught on the wrong foot. *Idiot, that's exactly what you thought. All bright and shiny, thinking you could fix her life.*

"I think you should leave," Mimi said, folding her arms across her chest. "I have a horse to pick up."

"Mimi, you're not taking Fling. Diane would back me up on this. She's too young and green for you to ride safely."

"Diane will understand," she said, but her voice lacked conviction.

"No, she won't. She'll say you went back on your promise. And she'll be right."

Mimi stared at me, but I thought she didn't really see me. Her gaze was somewhere else, seeing Diane—maybe imagining her life without her partner. I knew eventing, as important as it was to us, couldn't be worth that much. Not now, not when she had alternatives. As stupid as she'd made me feel, rushing over here with my chipper, foolproof plan to get her a job at Long Pond, I still wanted to convince her that teaching could be fulfilling.

I just didn't know how.

And then Mimi did something that surprised me. She turned around and shouted, "Chrissy! Tack up Moe and Windy!"

Chrissy? Moe and Windy? Who was she talking to—and about?

I must have had a dumb look on my face, because Mimi glanced back and smirked. "Did you think I had no plan except to adopt that mare out from under you? It's not all about you, miss. I already have two horses and a working student in the barn."

I was speechless.

A curly-haired teenager waved from around the corner of the barn, and then I heard hooves on pavement. "What kind of horses are they?" I asked, tasting defeat. If she already had youngsters on the property, nothing I said was going to convince her to accept retirement.

"Old horses that need a second chance," Mimi said. "Like me."

That was an interesting reply. I felt like I could work with that. "And why is Chrissy tacking them up?"

"I think they could use a hack," Mimi said, shrugging like it was no big deal. "And I think we should have a chat while they're getting it."

I was utterly confused at this point, but at least she wasn't trying to rush past me with her horse trailer. Maybe once we were riding, we could work things out. Life tended to make more sense on horseback.

Mimi put me on Windy, an older mare with three white socks

on dark, full-boned legs and a barrel-shaped body. "I bred this horse," she said, handing me the reins.

"You're kidding."

"Nope. Fifteen years ago. Sold her to a friend, but I felt like my life was going to hell, and I just had to go and get her back. The friend understood. I'd do anything for this mare," Mimi reflected. "I'd probably kill anyone who tried to hurt her."

I hoped it was hyperbole, but even if Mimi was absolutely serious, her devotion to a horse she'd bred just sharpened my feeling of kinship with her. We could have been friends once, if I'd met her before the horse world chewed her up and spat her out. Surely she'd been like me, ambitious beyond belief and desperate for a chance, and she just hadn't gotten it. The right horse hadn't come along. The right client hadn't paid her way. She'd scraped out a living in the business, and even that was more than many would-be equestrians would ever get, but I was sure Mimi had always wanted more.

She used a three-step mounting block to get onto Moe, an old bay gelding with gray hairs on his nose—she said he came with Windy—then pointed his nose toward a gate at the back of the property. Chrissy ran ahead of us to open it and close it behind us. "Back in an hour, Chrissy," Mimi told her, and the girl nodded appreciatively, like she was looking forward to the break. I wondered what Chrissy would use that free hour for: maybe she'd take a nap, or go through all Mimi's filing cabinets, or eat a pint of ice cream. Probably she'd just clean stalls.

"She's a good girl," Mimi said. "Ride on up here next to me. The trail's wide enough and the horses like it better that way."

I gave Windy a nudge, and she plowed her way forward, taking bites from the long, seeding grass along the side of the trail. We were going directly into the woods along the base of the Catoctin Mountains, and I wondered how far away Long Pond was by trail.

The trees closed in around us, the last of their orange leaves giving our skin a golden tint. I felt like I was riding directly into the sun. Mimi turned her face up to the leaves overhead and sighed. "I love this time of year."

I said nothing; she was suddenly being very human, and that made her seem dangerous. I wondered what she had planned for me out here in the woods. I should have told someone where I was going.

"I guess you don't get much of a fall in Florida," she continued. "Just more hot weather."

I shrugged. "It's fine. We don't get much of a winter, either, and that's the way we like it."

"I like seasons," Mimi said.

I'd heard this argument a hundred times before and I didn't feel like getting into it again. "Why are we out here, Mimi?" I asked instead.

She sighed. "I know you took that mare," she said, "and I was going to kick up a fuss about it, because I do like her. But dammit, you're right about Diane. She'd be furious if I brought home a green bean like that. So take the mare to Florida and good luck to you."

My sigh was one of relief. "Thank you," I replied. "I hope you understand—"

"I'm letting you take her, but I don't want you to think I'm doing you a favor," Mimi interrupted. "I still don't like you."

"Okay, and that's what I can't figure out," I told her honestly. "A lot of people don't like me and that's normal because I have a terrible personality. But you didn't like me before you met me. At least give me a chance to wow you with my shitty personality before you take a stand against me. That's what I say."

She laughed rustily. "Now, see, *that* makes me kinda like you."

I shook my head. She was impossible.

"I look at you and see someone who got it all handed to her. Even that horse of yours. Mickey."

"Now, I think you've got it wrong," I started, but Mimi kept going.

"I've seen the blogs. I know all about you. Little Miss Can Do Nothing Wrong comes up to Ocala, starts her own farm, gets that good horse right off the bat, over several *much* more qualified applicants, moves on to Briar Hill Farm of all places! Marries the grandson! Then buys her own farm! What hasn't gone well for you, Jules Thornton-*Morrison*? I mean, marrying the Morrison boy alone shoulda been enough, but you had to be a teen prodigy and a gifted coach at the same time. And Danger Mouse . . ." She trailed off.

"What about him?" I asked cautiously. There was a lot I wanted to correct about her version of my life, but that could wait.

Mimi turned steely eyes on me. "Don't you know you got him instead of me? All those years ago. I was in Florida trying horses, and I wanted to get on him. Contacted that half owner who was handling everything, whatever-her-name-was. I would have done anything for a Donnelly horse. But he never left your farm. I got told he was staying with the girl who had him for short-term boarding. That she was young and talented and good with him, and they wanted to give *her* a shot. Not me, even though I'd been working my whole damn life for a horse like that. No, they were betting on you. Young and fresh."

I stared at her. I didn't know what to say. Never, not in a million years, would I have suspected Mimi Pulaski had put her name in the ring for Mickey. No one else had ever made a confession like that, and now I wondered who else in the eventing community had been hoping to turn the gray gelding half owned by Carrie Donnelly into their next big horse.

For whatever reason, she truly thought she'd had a shot with

Mickey, and now she was watching me turn him into a star, while my husband took over her horses. And now that I knew, everything else started to make sense. I'd hate me, too.

"Mimi," I said slowly, "I didn't know that, and I appreciate you telling me. If it helps any, Mickey and I were meant to be. He's not just a horse I was riding for an owner. He's my horse, all the way through. I went through a lot to keep him—sales, syndicates. It has been a rocky road."

She shrugged. "I guess it does help me a little to know you've been together for such a long time. You sure took your time with him, though. You should have been up here doing the three-day event years ago."

"Like I said, I had some roadblocks along the way. You want the real story, or you want to believe I've been lucky all this time?"

"I want you to admit you've been lucky, first. Then I'll consider listening to what you've got to say."

I looked down at Windy's fuzzy neck. She was growing a thick fur coat, prepping for the cold northern winter. So many riders spent their whole careers hoping they could earn themselves just one winter in Florida, and I'd been born there. So many riders wished their whole lives to win the lottery so they could buy a farm, and my grandfather had left me just enough to realize that dream. And everything had snowballed from there.

"Luck doesn't even begin to describe it," I said.

Mimi was quiet for a few strides, considering. Then she said, "Okay, hotshot. I'll take it. Now, you tell me how hard your life has been."

I grinned. "I have some stories for you."

And then she said, 'Jesus, girl, you were born cursed, weren't you?'" I laughed, and Pete shook his head. He'd fed the horses before I got back, and now we were standing just outside the barn, enjoying one last sunset over the Catoctin Mountains, as we waited for them to finish their dinners.

"So, it's over?" he asked.

"Sorted out. Fling gets on the trailer for Florida in the morning. And Mimi agreed to work out a deal to teach more at Long Pond. I really think it's going to be the thing that saves her, Pete. She won't improve their dressage scores, but those kids will be good for her and she'll scare them all into working way harder than they would have otherwise. Everyone will win. And she can keep those two old horses of hers. Diane came out while we were untacking them and said she wasn't surprised to see them, just surprised it took Mimi so long to bring them back to the farm."

"She's not upset about Mimi having horses?"

"As long as she doesn't event, she's fine." But I wondered how long it would be before Mimi managed to get permission to ride one of her schoolmasters over a little Starter-level course. How much trouble could she get into jumping a few little logs? It would be fine.

It was all going to work out.

"I don't suppose you figured out India's thing, did you? Probably forgot to ask, since you were so busy telling her your life story."

I made a face at Pete. "Oh, I asked her. Here's the thing: she doesn't know *why* he's afraid of the rain. In fact, she said, she doesn't think he's afraid of rain. She thinks he's just a priss who doesn't like it and decided he doesn't have to do work when it's raining." It was kind of a backward way of looking at horse psychology, but I wasn't surprised. Mimi was old-fashioned. "Sorry we don't have a definitive answer."

"He's going to learn to pray for rain in Florida," Pete said grimly. "It's rain or a million degrees in the sun. Those are the choices."

I smiled happily. "Home soon, Pete!"

"You'd pick the rain, wouldn't you?"

"Of course I would. But I'll take the sun, if that's what's offered to me. I just want to be back in Florida."

29

FLORIDA WELCOMED US back with gray skies, scattered palm fronds, and the threat of a late-season tropical storm, ushering in our own particular version of fall. I welcomed it all—hey, at least the temperature was in the low eighties. For a few days, my weather app still had Maryland in the favorites, so I could see they were expecting frost and a windstorm to finally whip away the last autumn leaves from the trees. *Goodbye until next year,* I thought, deleting the location from my app.

Yeah, we'd probably go back next year. I had to defend my title, after all.

Would Rogue be ready for a two-star competition in twelve months? We'd have to see.

I had braced myself to come home to a mess after letting Lindsay and Maddox stay at the house, but found it was immaculate. It turned out the co-op moms kindly sent up a housekeeper to give the place a good cleaning, and they'd left us food in the fridge to see us through until we could make a grocery store run: Publix fried chicken, macaroni salad, a big bag of salad greens, and chocolate-chip cookies.

"Blessed," Gemma breathed when she opened the fridge door. "And look, Jackie-boy, applesauce!"

Jack squealed. Marcus sat beside him, ready and willing to clean up whatever food made its way onto Jack's face and shirt. "Mawk," Jack said affectionately, patting Marcus on his head with a careless hand.

In the barn, Lindsay gave me the rundown on what all the left-behind horses had been up to while Pete started mixing dinner feed, Maddox hovering over him saying that he hoped he'd done things right while we were gone.

"I'm sure you did, or the horses would all be dead," Pete told him.

Maddox nodded gravely, taking everything Pete said extremely seriously.

It was nice to have a barn family, I thought, biting back a grin at Maddox's worshipful gaze as he followed Pete around. For a long time, I'd fought against the conventions of being a riding instructor, of having boarders and students, but I'd been wrong. If I'd come home to a barn full of horses in training with absentee owners, the way I'd always thought I'd wanted, I wouldn't enjoy nearly such a nice homecoming as this one.

Once all the horses were fed, I brought everyone down the shed row to admire Fling, who pinned her ears and glowered at us between huge bites of her grain.

"Quite an attitude on her," Lindsay observed, sounding impressed.

"She's a Jekyll and Hyde," I said. "Walk down the aisle and see what she does." Fling had developed an interesting trick over the past few days in Maryland, and I was hoping she hadn't given it up after the long drive south.

Lindsay and I backed a few stalls away. Fling came to the door, looked out at us, and picked up one foreleg, brushing it against the stall grill while she begged for attention.

"Now go to her," I told Lindsay.

She walked up to Fling, who retreated into her stall with her ears flicked back as soon as Lindsay was within a few feet of her.

"Okay, that's hilarious!" Lindsay declared. "I'm obsessed."

"Just make sure her stall door is slid closed when no one's in the barn," I said. "She's a jumper."

"Aren't all these horses?"

"No, I mean, she's an escape artist. She doesn't stay in when she thinks something more fun is going on without her."

Lindsay looked even happier to learn my new mare had such an impressive flaw. "So, where are you going to turn her out?"

"I think in the back, with the broodmares," I said, considering Fling as she poked her head out again, acting as if she had wanted to be friends all along. "She's got a broodmare attitude, so they should get along okay. I think if she's with buddies, she won't want to run away. It's going to be the opposite problem, keeping her from jumping into paddocks and chasing after friends when we have to split them up for some reason."

"Like when the broodmares all have foals in a few months," Lindsay said.

"Yeah, exactly." The prospect of foals distracted me for a few minutes, and by the time we were back on the subject of Fling, Pete was passing out hay and the horses were whinnying the barn down, demanding their overnight hay be served immediately.

"And how is everyone up at the co-op? Ready for our first event next weekend?"

Lindsay shrugged. "I don't go up there very often."

"Lindsay! I know that's not true. I get all the reports from Lacey, don't forget."

"How much did she tell you? It's all lies. I seriously just texted her every day to make sure she didn't need my help with something. She's really incompetent, Jules. I think you should fire her."

"Oh, stop."

"No, I'll prove it to you. I'll show you the texts. You'll see." And Lindsay, committed to her bit, pulled out her phone. The wallpaper was a close-up photo of her horse, Jim Dear, eating an apple. All of his long yellow teeth were exposed and his eyes were rolling back in his head. It was the least appealing picture of that beautiful Thoroughbred imaginable, so of course that was the one Lindsay went with. I loved her, but the girl was crazy.

"It's fine," I said. "You don't have to show me every conversation with Lacey."

"No, I *want* to," Lindsay insisted, and she followed me down the shed row, waving the phone at me.

I looked at Pete, throwing hay over the stall grills. His eyes met mine, and he grinned, shaking his head at Lindsay's behavior. Behind him, Jack and Gemma sat on the clean-swept ground in front of the feed room, playing with Marcus.

And a few stalls beyond, my chestnut horse Dynamo leaned over his stall door, glanced in our direction, and nickered. Mickey poked his head out of the neighboring stall and joined in, his deep voice joining a growing chorus of chatting horses.

I thought I knew what they were saying—it was what we were all feeling. Eventing was great, travel was exciting, and championships were worth celebrating. But at the end of it all, after the galloping was finished and the leg wraps came off, wasn't it wonderful to come home?

ACKNOWLEDGMENTS

This one is for all the Jules fans.

I never intended to write a sequel, and definitely not a series, when I wrote *Ambition*. But as the years went by and *Ambition* found loyal fans, the messages and requests began to pile up. "When will there be more Jules? What happens next?"

I didn't know what happened next, so I kept on writing other books—also set in Florida, also about equestrians—and tried not to think too much about Jules. But of course, a character that strong-minded never really goes away.

When Grace Carter and Seabreeze Equestrian Center became a part of my fictional world, I had an idea of what might happen next. And that's how Jules went to meet Grace. I think they're a match made in heaven, so thanks to everyone who waited for this one! I needed time to bring a character to life who was tough enough to boss around Jules.

For the setting, I'm thankful for the time I spent as a manager at Grand Cypress Equestrian Center in Orlando, Florida—a beautiful stable that existed in the never-never land between theme parks and a tourist strip. At Grand Cypress, we educated so many riders, whether they were local kids, busy working parents with hardly any time for their horse, or out-of-towners with some spare time to ride. It's no longer part of the central Florida horse scene, but there was a brief period in history when you could sit on your horse in a beautiful dressage arena, and watch the Walt Disney World fireworks light up the sky just a few miles away. Our struggle to keep this stable relevant and operating in such a rapidly changing environment inspired Seabreeze Equestrian Center and my trainer Grace, who was determined to keep her farm running despite the pressure from developers and a changing client base.

The original edition of this work was polished and made better thanks to the thoughtful editing of Caroline Bleeke. Once again, this beautiful new edition has been a team effort by the Flatiron Books crew. Thank you to Megan Lynch and the rest of my stellar team: Jon Yaged, Mary Retta, Maris Tasaka, Nancy Trypuc, Marlena Bittner, Malati Chavali, Emily Walters, Ryan T. Jenkins, Eva Diaz, and Keith Hayes.

Thanks to my fabulous agent, Lacy Lynch, and her wonderful team at House of Story, including Dabney Rice and Ali Kominsky, for helping me take this journey.

About the Author

Natalie Keller Reinert is the award-winning author of more than twenty books, including the Eventing and Briar Hill Farm series. Drawing on her professional experience in three-day eventing, working with Thoroughbred racehorses, mounted patrol horses, therapeutic riding, and many other equine pursuits, Natalie brings her love of equestrian life into each of her titles. She also cohosts the award-winning equestrian humor podcast *Adulting with Horses*. Natalie lives in north Florida with her family, horses, and cat.

www.nataliekreinert.com